DARK HEALING

BLIND TRUST

THE CHILDREN OF THE GODS
BOOK SEVENTY-TWO

I. T. LUCAS

1

KIAN

Kian wasn't looking forward to the conversation he was about to have with Vanessa, and wished someone else could do it for him.

As a female, Bridget was probably a better choice to handle a delicate subject of this nature, but that meant telling the doctor about the therapist's inappropriate conduct. So far, the only ones who knew were the Guardians who monitored the security feed in the dungeon, who had informed Magnus, who had told Kian, and as always, the buck stopped with him.

He had the distinct displeasure of confronting Vanessa about kissing a prisoner.

When the knock came, he rose to his feet and opened the door with his most charming smile plastered on his face. "Good morning, Vanessa."

"Good morning, Kian." She walked in, her high heels clicking on the hardwood floor.

The female was always dressed to the nines, her hair styled, her makeup flawless, and the scent of a luxury perfume following in her wake.

She was the last person he would have expected to get involved with a prisoner accused of murder, no less. Not that one kiss meant involvement, but it was so bizarre and out of character for Vanessa that he suspected there was more to it than a momentary lapse of reason.

Then again, his own sister was mated to a killer.

Kian had been so enraged when Amanda had made it clear that Dalhu was her chosen one-and-only and that she wouldn't give him up no matter what Kian's opinion on the subject was. He was still ashamed of the way he'd treated her, but at the time, he could not even bring himself to talk to his sister.

If not for their mother's intervention, things might have deteriorated even worse than that, but it had all ended well. Kian had accepted Dalhu, at first cautiously and later wholeheartedly.

Despite the guy's dark past in the Brotherhood and the evil deeds he had committed in Navuh's name, he was a good male who had been born in the wrong place at the wrong time and had done the best he could under the circumstances.

He was also perfect for Amanda.

Maybe the same was true of Vanessa's prisoner, and this time, Kian wasn't going to prejudge before learning more.

Pulling out a chair for her, Kian waited until she was seated and then pulled out the chair next to her.

"How is the assessment of the Kra-ell going?" he asked, to start a conversation without jumping right away into the murky waters of the real reason for their meeting.

He would ease into it.

"You didn't say what you wanted to talk to me about, but I suspected you wanted to see my progress, so I prepared an initial report." She sounded nervous, and Kian had a good idea why.

Vanessa was a smart lady, and she must have guessed the reason behind the summons.

"I've browsed through what you sent me this morning, but I didn't have time to read through it. Can you give me the highlights?"

"Of course. My method was to conduct a short introductory meeting with as many Kra-ell as I could fit into my daily schedule and complete an intake form to provide their basic information. How old were they when they boarded the settler ship? Did they want to leave their home world and travel all the way to Earth to establish a new colony? Who were their pod mates, did they have children, and if they did, how many, and so on. I included all that information in the report I emailed you. I also asked them about their experiences in Igor's compound and their interactions with the eight prisoners." She paused her rapid-fire monologue to take a sip of water.

There was a total of ten prisoners, but since Igor was not getting a trial, and his second-in-command was a special case as well, she was right not to include them in the count.

"Did you include what the Kra-ell told you about the prisoners in the report?"

"Only the highlights. I didn't have time to prepare anything elaborate."

"Did you ask them any questions about Igor and Valstar?"

She shook her head. "I didn't bring up specific names. I talked about them as a group, calling them Igor's pod mates. So far, none of the interviewees have singled out Valstar or any of the other prisoners as particularly abusive. The worst offenders were dealt with by Jade and Kagra."

"Good. What is the general sentiment toward the prisoners?"

Kian hoped the Kra-ell he'd accepted into the village weren't vicious and wouldn't demand the execution of the eight males who had done terrible things, not because they were terrible people, but because they had been under the control of a powerful compeller.

Being at Igor's mercy for less than a minute had shaken Kian to his core. After experiencing the power of the guy's compulsion first-hand, he was much more sympathetic toward Igor's former pod members.

He'd never felt as helpless as he had in those brief moments.

Hell, he still wasn't back to himself despite having no physical reminder of the brutal attack. It wasn't about the surprise or being caught off guard or even about the injuries he'd sustained. It was about realizing the guy's immense power and that there were more like him out there.

Hopefully, Igor hadn't lied about the Eternal King's other assassins not being powerful compellers. While the Kra-ell's physical strength was formidable, it was much easier to mitigate and safeguard against than the mental power of Igor's compulsion.

Vanessa sighed. "Those who had the males of their tribes slaughtered are divided. Some are willing to admit that those of Igor's pod members who are still alive are not inherently bad and that they were Igor's victims just as much as everyone else in that compound. Yet others want them dead regardless of the mitigating circumstances." She smiled sadly. "It's the old moral dilemma of whether we should judge people by their deeds or by their intentions. In that respect, our laws are more forgiving than those of the Kra-ell."

Kian nodded. "They want revenge, and I can understand that. Those females saw Igor's men murder their tribesmen while they stood frozen by Igor's command. I suspect the killers' faces will forever represent evil to them."

"Precisely. One of the females from Igor's pod said she wanted them all dead despite not losing any family members.

Her rationale was that they were corrupted by their evil deeds. In her opinion, the only way they could redeem themselves was by dying and getting another chance to do better in their next incarnation."

"Maybe that's an argument we can use in the prisoners' favor." Kian drummed his fingers on the conference table. "Coming to live in the village with us is like a rebirth."

He was no lawyer, and he was talking out of his ass, but he really didn't think that those males deserved the death penalty for what they had done, and no one could accuse him of being a softy or forgiving of crimes.

It wasn't so much about mercy as it was about fairness.

As someone who had been under Igor's control for mere moments, Kian knew that if Igor had commanded him to kill Brundar or Anandur, he would not have been able to resist that command. He would have done it and then wished for a death sentence to end his guilt.

Vanessa crossed her legs and steepled her fingers. "I wanted to talk to you about getting the prisoners a lawyer. I can testify and give my opinion, but I'm not a defense attorney. They need a professional."

"Do we have anyone?"

Kian wasn't aware of the clan having any criminal defense attorneys, but in this respect, he wasn't as well informed as his mother. Annani knew what each member of the clan had studied, and he could ask her for a recommendation.

"Not in the village," Vanessa said. "Besides, I think it should be someone from their community. Edna and I are strangers to them. Our special talents and qualifications make us suitable for assessing and giving recommendations, and we can give the trial direction so it won't become a lynch mob, but a defense attorney should be someone who is more familiar with their culture."

"Is there anyone like that?"

Vanessa nodded. "A human who has studied law. Her name is Lusha, and she's the daughter of a hybrid Kra-ell father and a human mother, therefore fully human, but she's still a better choice than any of us."

2

VANESSA

"Does this Lusha have any trial experience?" Kian asked.

That was the first question Vanessa had asked the girl, and the second had been whether she felt she was up to the task.

"Regrettably, she doesn't, but she's willing to defend Igor's former pod members, so that's great. She's also pretty fluent in English, and naturally, she speaks Finnish and Russian. That will make things so much easier for all of us." She smiled. "Especially me. I felt so uncomfortable about asking Toven to translate every time I interviewed a Kra-ell who didn't speak English or any of the other languages I know."

Kian nodded. "I'm sure he was glad to help."

"He was, but still. I'll be much more comfortable working with Lusha. The only problem is that she's in Safe Haven. We will need to bring her here."

"That's not a problem if she's willing to come."

"She is. In fact, she's excited about the opportunity to be in charge of a murder trial. Her only objection was defending Igor, and when I explained that he was not getting a trial, she was relieved. She's eager to come here and see the village. She also asked how much time she would have to prepare their defense. She will need to conduct her own interviews and probably research Kra-ell laws and talk with Jade."

Kian shrugged. "It's up to the Kra-ell. I'd rather be done with it sooner rather than later because of the resources we are dedicating to keeping their prisoners in the dungeon, but I will not jeopardize these males' lives by forcing their attorney to rush."

"Thank you." Vanessa let out a relieved breath. "I want to give them the best chance they can get, and I think I can convince Jade to allow more time for the trial."

As Kian pinned her with a hard look, Vanessa braced for what was coming. She hadn't been sure the Guardians would bother Kian with news of her inappropriate conduct with Mo-red, but when he had texted her last night and asked her to stop by his office first thing in the morning, she had guessed he'd heard about it and was going to chew her out.

That was why Vanessa had spent most of the night preparing the report. She had hoped he would be so impressed with the work she'd put into it that he would let her misconduct slide.

After all, she hadn't endangered anyone, and Kian couldn't care less about her lack of professional conduct.

"Security informed me that you did something unexpected with Mo-red. Care to explain?"

Vanessa swallowed. "I assume that you're talking about the kiss."

He arched a brow. "Is there more?"

"No."

"Good." He leaned back and crossed his arms over his chest.

Vanessa was about to use the research excuse she'd prepared, but looking at Kian, she realized he would never buy it. If the question had come from Jay or Theo, she could have gotten away with it, but she couldn't lie to Kian.

"I'm waiting," he prompted.

The truth was always better than a lie.

"I'm drawn to Mo-red. I can't explain it, but I've never felt like that about anyone, and it was driving me crazy that I couldn't act on it. We were talking up a storm of sexual innuendos, and then he said that he needed to get at least one kiss from me before he died, and I could hold off no longer. I kissed him." She crossed her arms over her chest. "We are both consenting adults, and technically, I'm not Mo-red's psychologist. I am visiting him in the capacity of an advisor on your behalf."

The last thing she'd expected was for Kian to smile. "As long as you didn't take advantage of a helpless male, I don't mind one way or another, but it is problematic on several levels."

"I know—"

He lifted a hand to stop her. "You are a smart lady, and I doubt Mo-red could have fooled you into giving him a favorable assessment by flirting with you. But when the news comes out, and it will, others might think precisely that. The result might be detrimental to Mo-red. If his accusers think that you are biased, your testimony on his behalf will be worthless. If you care for the male, you should stop interacting with him in such a familiar way and stay professional."

Vanessa briefly closed her eyes. "I tried. But it was no use. The pull between us is undeniable." Kian was very understanding, and maybe she could use the opportunity to ask for what she wanted. "Is there any way you can release him into my custody? He's not a danger to anyone, but for appearance's sake, he can wear a couple of cuffs and be restricted to my house. I can conduct the rest of the interviews there while he's in the other room." She took a deep breath to brace for what she needed to say next. "He might get a death sentence, Kian. Every moment he's locked in that cell is a moment he could be spending with me. It's tormenting me to even think that, and I try to block those morbid thoughts, but they persist, churning in my mind every minute of the day."

Kian's eyes were full of compassion, but he shook his head. "The best I can offer is for you to move in with Mo-red at the dungeon. Some of the cells are still outfitted as guest suites, so you could be reasonably comfortable, but you should consider that you might be compromising his defense."

All Vanessa could hear was Kian's offer for her to move in with Mo-red at the dungeon. She pounced on that and completely disregarded his caution. How come she hadn't thought of that?

It was a brilliant solution, and it might actually help Mo-red's defense. If she, an immortal female—a descendant of the gods—was willing to have a relationship with a male that some of the tough Kra-ell considered a monster, they might change their minds about him.

"I'll take your offer." She extended her hand to Kian. "Thank you."

3

JADE

Jade stood in front of Igor's cell and waited for the Guardian to wave his hand over the lock and open the door.

Next to her, Kian pushed his fingers through his shoulder-length hair. "Are you sure you want to do this alone?" he asked. "I know that it would be more satisfying to you, but I think Igor would find it more believable if I came along. After all, it is supposed to be my decision to put him in stasis, not yours."

He had a point.

On the one hand, she didn't want anyone taking away from her joy of informing Igor of his impending temporary death, but on the other hand, he might think that she was bluffing, and then the entire exercise would fail because he wouldn't panic.

"You might be right."

Besides, there was a risk involved in her doing the informing. What if Igor considered it a breach of their agreement and told Kian about the twins?

Perhaps she shouldn't be there at all when Kian told Igor that he was about to be put in stasis?

Come to think of it, the same was true about the pound of flesh she craved to take out of the monster. All he needed to do to make her stop was to threaten to tell Kian about the royal twins.

The simplest solution was to come clean and tell Kian the big secret she'd been keeping and get it off her chest.

Kian was so concerned about the assassins Igor had told them about, that the news about the twins would probably be little more than a curiosity to him.

She turned to face him. "Before we go in, we should talk. In your office."

Kian arched a brow. "Are you getting cold feet about facing Igor?"

"Cold feet?" She looked down at her combat boots. "My feet are warm."

He laughed. "It's an expression. Your English is so good that I sometimes forget you haven't lived here long and that you haven't been exposed to all the idioms that make up half of this language. Cold feet means having second thoughts."

"I'm not having second thoughts." She glanced behind him at Anandur and Brundar. "I need to talk to you alone."

The smile slid off his face. "I have no secrets from them, but let's go to my office."

"Thank you." She cut a look at Brundar. "It's not personal. If Kian decides to tell you about it later, though, it can't become one of the rumors circulating the village. It needs to stay between us."

As Brundar nodded, Anandur put a hand over his chest. "I only gossip about things that are not deemed a secret, and only if the gossip is juicy."

The guy liked to turn everything into a joke. It had been amusing initially, but it was getting annoying. No wonder his brother didn't talk. If he did, he might provide the redhead with more fuel for his amusement.

Jade let out a breath. "Okay then, but this is as juicy as it gets, and if you breathe a word of it to anyone, and that includes your lovely mate, I will eviscerate you. You might not die from it, but it will hurt worse than hell."

Brundar's lips twitched with a smile. "I like you."

"Thanks. I like you too."

"Weirdos," Anandur murmured under his breath. "No sense of humor."

When they reached Kian's office, he closed the door behind them and walked over to the refrigerator. "Do I need a beer for this?"

"You might not, but I do." She sat down on the chair that Brundar pulled out for her.

"Sounds ominous," Anandur said.

"It's not." She took the bottle Kian handed her and twisted the cap off. "I've been keeping a piece of information from you, but I've decided that I trust you enough to share it." She took a long sip from the beer and then wiped her mouth with the back of her hand. "The reason I kept it from you was a previous vow, which obligated me to protect the secret. I had to be sure they were in no danger from you before I could tell you."

Kian shook his head. "I'm more confused after that preamble than I was before. Who are they, and what are you trying to say?"

She let out an exasperated breath. "I'm apologizing for keeping this information from you, and I'm trying to explain why I felt it was necessary for me to do so."

"Okay, now I get it. Please, continue."

She hesitated. "Just one more small preamble. Until Igor confirmed it for me, I wasn't even sure there was anything to tell. It was just a suspicion I had."

Kian groaned. "Just get on with it, please. I don't have all day."

4

KIAN

Jade picked up the bottle and took another long swig before putting it down.

"I know that you want me to get straight to the point, but some background information is still needed for you to understand the big picture."

Leaning back, Kian crossed his arms over his chest. "I'm a big picture kind of guy."

The secret Jade had been keeping must be of monumental importance. She wasn't the type to make a fuss over trivial matters, and since she'd trusted him with the lives of her people, he couldn't imagine what it could be.

"Before getting drafted by the lottery to join the settler's ship, I served in the queen's guard. I joined as soon as I was eligible, and I advanced through the ranks fast. The last position I held was as a shift commander of the queen's personal quarters." Jade lifted the beer bottle for another sip. "Everyone in the queen's personal guard had to vow to protect the queen and her family with their lives. That included her consorts and children."

Kian nodded. "Given how sacred vows are to the Kra-ell, that makes sense. By demanding the vow, the queen assured herself of her guards' loyalty. It's a very useful tool to control people, which once again shows me the power of religion." He smiled at the brothers. "That being said, I'm glad that I don't need my personal guards to vow anything to be absolutely certain that they will protect me and my family with their lives. I earned their loyalty instead of demanding it or forcing them to give it."

Anandur tapped his chest, and Brundar nodded, but his lips twisted in a wince.

Despite everyone's reassurances that he hadn't failed Kian by not preventing Igor's attack, he still couldn't forgive himself for that.

Jade crossed her arms over her chest. "Yes, well, our entire society is ruled by vows, and they don't have an expiration date. Once a vow is given, it's good for the life of the giver."

Evidently he'd managed to offend her, and in retrospect he should have realized that he would. Syssi would have never made such a mistake.

"I'm not trying to belittle your beliefs, and I apologize if I offended you. I was just stating a fact and trying to compliment Anandur and Brundar at the same time."

She nodded. "I understand, and I'm not offended. When I served the queen, she had five children. One daughter and four sons, which is a common gender distribution for us. What was very uncommon was that her two eldest children were twins. A sister and a brother. In fact, it was so rare that they had been dedicated to priesthood from birth. Usually, no males served as priests, but since twins were believed to share one soul, both siblings were accepted into the service of the Mother of All Life by the high priestess."

Kian frowned. "Why would the queen dedicate her only daughter to the priesthood? Wasn't she the heir?"

"Many have wondered the same thing, and rumors circulated that the twins had been born with defects. Since they were sequestered and no one got to see their faces, those rumors were reinforced."

Anandur lifted his hand. "Was it common to sequester acolytes?"

"It was not. Priestesses are veiled when they deliver sermons or provide consultations, but they are not required to be so every moment of the day. The same goes for acolytes, hence the rumors. The twins were veiled from head to toe at all times, even when they strolled in the queen's private gardens."

"What about their servants?" Kian asked. "The cleaning people, whoever made their clothes? Someone had to see what they looked like."

Jade shrugged. "As I said before, everyone in the queen's service had to vow to protect her and her family, so even if someone had seen what the twins looked like, no one talked. Anyway, as a member of the queen's personal guard, I've seen the twins stroll through the gardens many times, and my curiosity getting the better of me, I paid attention to the way they held themselves, their gait, and the sound of their voices. I was trying to figure out what was wrong with them, but if anything was, it hadn't affected their health. Their postures were regal, and their gait was smooth and energetic."

"Did you ever find out?" Anandur asked.

"I'm getting there." Jade took another sip from her bottle.

"Perhaps their deformity was mild," Kian said. "It could have been as simple as a problem with pigmentation." He leaned forward. "Or as complicated as them being hybrids."

Jade smiled. "I suspected that, and I wasn't the only one, but when I finally got to see the twins, they not only looked perfect in every way but perfectly Kra-ell as well. They weren't hybrids."

"Are you sure?" Anandur asked. "And how did you get to see them?"

5

JADE

Anandur's question had brought Jade to the difficult part, the one she was still not a hundred percent sure about.

"When I was settling down in my pod, the members of the pod next to ours were brought in, and I thought that the postures and body language of two of its members seemed familiar. I tried to figure out where I had seen them before when it hit me—they had the same bearing as the royal twins. I would have dismissed my suspicions as my imagination getting the better of me or an eerie coincidence, but there were other oddities about that pod. The number of males and females in theirs was equal, while ours and the one on our other side had the normal Kra-ell distribution of about four males to every female. Also, the technician in charge of their pod seemed nervous."

"Was he or she a god or a Kra-ell?" Kian asked.

"All the techs were gods, and everyone I saw was male." She huffed. "I told you that their society had a weird attitude toward females. They were revered and cherished and kept on a pedestal. If a female god had a job, it was at the top of the ladder, not at the bottom." She chuckled. "I guess they were not as different from the Kra-ell as they thought they were. Still, the gods were ruled by a male, and their females didn't fight in wars, so there was that. I have to admit that their society was more egalitarian than ours, but I still think that it was leaning slightly toward patriarchy, while ours was firmly matriarchal."

Kian leaned back in his chair. "If we assume that both societies started from the same root species that held females in higher regard than males, then it makes sense."

"It kind of does," Jade admitted. "I've never thought about it that way, but you might be right. Anyway, the two I suspected of being the queen's children looked fully Kra-ell, and I couldn't see anything wrong with them, so I wasn't sure it was them until Igor confirmed it for me. He knew that they were on the ship."

"Did he know why?" Kian asked.

"No. Once he confirmed it for me, I asked him if he was sent to kill them, but he evaded the answer, then I asked him in front of you if he had any directives other than killing the Eternal King's children, and you heard his answer. He said that they were the only ones he was sent to kill."

Kian's brows dipped low. "That doesn't make sense. If Igor was sent by the gods to eliminate Ahn and his siblings, how would he even know about the Kra-ell queen's children being on board? Who would have told him and why?"

"I wondered the same thing, and then it occurred to me that it might have been part of their peace treaty. An eye for an eye kind of thing, but now that I actually say it out loud, it sounds absurd. The queen would have never agreed to that."

"Why would she even put them on the ship?" Kian pushed to his feet and opened the refrigerator. "I need a drink."

"Maybe their lives were in danger?" Anandur suggested. "Was it common for royal siblings to eliminate each other?"

Jade shook her head. "Only a female could be the next queen, and the female twin was to become the next head priestess. The queen must have hoped to give birth to another daughter."

Kian pulled more bottles of Snake Venom from the refrigerator and brought them to the table. "So, your suspicion about the twins is the secret you've been keeping?"

Jade nodded. "I didn't know what you would do once you found out. Would you consider the royal children a threat? Would you want to eliminate them?"

"Why would I?" He popped the lid and took a sip. "Are they dangerous to my clan?"

"Frankly, I don't know." Jade reached for the fresh bottle of beer. "I don't know anything about them or why they were sent to Earth. The queen was a powerful compeller, so her children might be powerful as well, and we all know what compellers can do."

"It all depends on their intent," Kian said. "Toven is a powerful compeller, and I don't fear him. In fact, I consider him a great asset to my clan. We couldn't have saved your people without his help."

"I know, and I'm forever in his debt. He's also a nice male, and he has family in the clan that he wants to protect. The twins do not." She smiled. "Well, now that we are part of the clan, they might be in the same situation as Toven." Jade spread her arms. "We are all the children of the Mother."

She hoped that was how Kian would one day see her and her people. For now, they were still wearing locator cuffs and were not allowed to leave the village unescorted, so they weren't full-fledged members yet.

Kian arched a brow. "Do the twins have any royal blood relatives among the people here?"

"Very distant," she admitted. "But don't forget that they were raised as acolytes. They are supposed to regard all Kra-ell as their children. The priestesses are considered to be the embodiments of the Mother of All Life, and since the male twin was also an acolyte, he is her embodiment as well."

It was a slight exaggeration meant to portray the twins as peaceful clerics, but given Kian's stern expression, he wasn't buying it.

"The fact that they were raised for priesthood doesn't mean that was the only thing they were taught. Their mother might have been preparing them for ruling the new colony on Earth. Otherwise, why send them with the settlers?"

Jade let out a breath. "I wish I had answers for you, but your guess is as good as mine. I got Igor to vow that he wouldn't tell you about the twins in exchange for sparing his life, so I couldn't ask him what he knew about them in front of you. He might not have a lot of information about them, but perhaps we should find out what he knows before we put him in stasis."

6

KIAN

So that was why Jade was revealing the big secret she'd been guarding up until now.

She wanted to ask Igor about the royals but was afraid that he would spill the beans now that her vow to him was about to become less relevant, and once he was in stasis, the information she wanted would be lost.

Jade had vowed not to kill him or sanction his killing by any of her people, but her vow hadn't included protection from the clan because she couldn't have promised that even if she wanted to. It wasn't her promise to make.

Igor had probably assumed that he was safe because the gods did not approve of capital punishment, and therefore their descendants didn't either, but being put in indefinite stasis was as close to a death sentence as it got.

As far as Igor was concerned, it would be a deal breaker, and he would talk just to get back at Jade.

Then again, the guy was so unpredictable that it was foolish to assume anything about him.

Kian still wasn't sure what game Igor was playing, and he had a feeling that the guy was several steps ahead of him.

Jade was still looking at him with an anxious expression on her face, awaiting his response.

He nodded to put her at ease. "If you want to question Igor about the twins, we need to get Andrew here. Otherwise, Igor can make up any story he thinks will benefit his agenda, and you will not know whether he's telling you the truth or not. Naturally, we can't tell him that we are putting him in stasis, either. He will use the information as a bargaining chip to make a deal that will leave him awake."

Jade grimaced. "I hadn't thought of that angle. I was afraid that once Igor learned we no longer needed him because the Odus could do the same thing his brain did, he wouldn't feel obligated by the deal he'd made with me and would tell you about them. I figured it was better if you heard it from me."

Kian smiled. "You also assumed that after learning about the assassins, the twins would no longer seem like such a big threat to me."

"Yeah. That was part of it too. Also, since it's possible that those assassins got more than one job, and they might be after the twins as well, I need your help to find them to uphold my vow to the queen."

"A loophole," Anandur said. "Smart."

"I'm not sure it is." Jade pressed the heels of her palms to her temples. "I'm trying to navigate my different responsibilities and obligations as best I can, but it's getting more complicated by the hour. The Mother expects too much of me."

Kian could empathize with that. "I feel like that every other day. The challenges just keep mounting." He pulled out his phone. "I'll check with Andrew on when he can get here."

It was still early in the day, and Andrew didn't get off work until five-thirty, but maybe he could hop over on his lunch break.

"It will take some time before he answers." Kian put the

phone on the table. "Andrew is super careful, and he never answers my texts from his office. There is surveillance everywhere in that building."

"Why is he still working for the government?" Jade asked.

"He wants to be where he can obtain classified information that is pertinent to the clan."

Jade pursed her lips. "Since your hackers managed to grab our money from Igor, I'm sure they can hack into whatever government information you might need."

"They can't get into everything, and Andrew enjoys having his ear to the grapevine. Besides, I think he likes working there." Kian let out a breath. "The truth is that I don't have a full-time job for him, and a guy like Andrew needs to keep busy."

"Speaking of jobs." Jade squared her shoulders. "Once my people get settled, they will need to fill their time with more than training. Can you provide me with a list of possible occupations they can choose from?"

Kian had been planning to approach her about that, but he'd wanted to give her more time to acclimate. "What do you think they would be interested in?"

"I can't speak for everyone, but personally, I would like to help you combat trafficking. We were not trained in the latest firearms, but with our physical strength and speed, we don't need weapons to fight humans." She bared her fangs. "These will suffice."

"Those humans are often armed to the teeth," Anandur said. "But in most cases, we can immobilize them with a thrall."

Jade grinned. "What we can do is very similar to what you call thralling. I can get humans to put down their weapons, and several of the others can do that as well." She leaned back in her chair and crossed her arms over her chest. "I think those poor women would prefer to be rescued by females."

Kian stifled a chuckle. "Well, only provided that you wear dark sunglasses and don't bare your fangs. Otherwise, they would run into the arms of their captors to escape the scary aliens."

He was being polite. The girls would probably think that they were being attacked by a bunch of female demons.

"Right." Jade uncrossed her arms and reached for her beer bottle. "I spoke to Aliya, and she says that the village could use gardeners, babysitters, cooks, cleaners, and food servers. She says that clan members don't want to do those types of things, and neither do Kalugal's men."

The sneer in her tone hadn't gone unnoticed.

Kian arched a brow. "Correct me if I'm wrong, but in Igor's compound as well as in your old one, you used humans for those kinds of jobs. Your people are just as spoiled as mine."

"True, but this is a fresh start, and I think that it wouldn't hurt them to get their hands a little dirty. If they are willing to do it, will you allow them?"

He wasn't sure about babysitting, but he had no problem with the other jobs.

"Check with your people first, and then we will talk."

Anandur cleared his throat. "With the help of the Kra-ell, we can double our efforts in the war against trafficking. I think that's the best way to utilize their special gifts."

"I agree." Kian reached for his phone to read the incoming message. "Andrew can be here at twelve-thirty, and he can stay for an hour and a half max." He lifted his gaze to Jade. "I suggest that we make a list of questions for Igor so we don't waste Andrew's time."

7

MO-RED

"This game is awesome." Madbar moved his whole body along with the controller. "It's a great way to train with modern weaponry." He kept shooting at the spaceships on the screen. "There are so many options. You need to try this."

"No, thank you." Mo-red went back to reading the tattered book that someone had left in their cell.

He was scanning the words, but if asked what he was reading, he wasn't sure he could answer. The lack of concentration might be the result of him getting weak from the lack of sunshine and fresh air, or maybe it was the worry for Vanessa that was making him so lethargic.

With her around, he didn't even remember that he was underground and that he hadn't seen the sun in days. She was his sunshine, and the warmth she left behind lingered for many hours after she was gone.

Except, he hadn't seen Vanessa yesterday, and he was worried that the stunt they had pulled had gotten her in trouble. The Guardian in the control room had most likely seen them kissing through the surveillance feed, but even if they got lucky and no one had been watching at that moment, the combined scents of their arousal had been hard to miss. When Jay had opened the door to the interview room, the Guardian's response had been immediate. He'd inhaled, and a smirk had appeared on his face for a brief moment before he'd schooled his features back into their impassive expression.

Evidently, the immortals' senses were as keen as the Kraell's, and the Guardian had no trouble guessing what had transpired in the room.

He also might have seen the epic kiss on the monitors in the control room.

What if Vanessa's leader forbade her from ever seeing Mo-red again?

As Theo approached the bars and motioned for him and Madbar to step back, Mo-red's heart started thundering in his chest. Was the Guardian there for him or for Madbar?

Theo unlocked the bars and slid them aside. "Mo-red, come forward."

Were they going to punish him?

As long as they didn't punish Vanessa, he was okay with whatever they did to him. He would never regret that kiss and would do it again if given a chance.

"Where are you taking me?" He offered the Guardian his hands.

"Same place as usual. Vanessa wants to talk to you."

The relief almost knocked him off his feet. "Thank you."

Theo eyed him with a smirk lifting one corner of his mouth. "I don't know how you managed to do that, but congratulations."

Was he congratulating him on winning a kiss from Vanessa?

It was probably a ploy to get him to talk about what had

transpired between them, and Mo-red wasn't going to fall for that.

"On what?"

"I'll let Vanessa explain." The Guardian glanced at the handcuffs he'd just secured to Mo-red's wrists. "I don't know why I even bothered." He stopped in front of the interview room, opened the door, and motioned for Mo-red to go in.

Mo-red frowned. "Aren't you going to tie me to the chair?"

"What would be the point of that? Just go on in." He gave him a slight shove.

Vanessa was where Mo-red expected her to be, sitting behind the desk and looking even lovelier today than she'd looked Sunday night. The gold-colored silk blouse was parted at her throat, revealing the creamy column and dipping low into her cleavage. She wore a bra made of lace underneath, and the edge of one cup was peeking seductively from under her left lapel.

Swallowing the saliva that had gathered in his mouth, he forced a smile. "Hello, Doctor Vanessa." He addressed her formally for the benefit of the Guardians in the control room.

"Hello." She smiled at him. "How have you been?"

He sat on the chair and put his hands on the armrests. "Worried," he admitted. "When you didn't come yesterday, I was afraid that you were forbidden from ever seeing me again."

She winced. "I was called into the boss's office and got a talking-to, but it ended better than I could have ever expected. I'm lucky that Kian is a romantic at heart, and he was sympathetic to our predicament."

Mo-red was greatly relieved that she hadn't gotten in trouble, but he expected the price she'd had to pay was most likely a promise to never do it again. The immortals' leader might have forgiven Vanessa her transgression, but he surely wouldn't sanction more of such behavior.

Mo-red released a breath. "I'm glad, but I guess that there will be no more kisses in our future."

Mirth dancing in her eyes, Vanessa smiled and leaned forward. "Your guess is wrong. There will be many more kisses and hopefully more than that in our future."

His eyes widened. "He allowed it?"

"I asked him to release you into my custody so we can be together. He refused that, but what he offered instead was almost as good. I can be with you down here in the dungeon. We can move into one of the cells that were converted into guest rooms, and I can be with you when I'm done for the day. The only downside is that you'll be alone while I'm interviewing the other prisoners and attending meetings. Also, Madbar will lose a roommate."

"I must be dreaming." He shook his head, and when that didn't wake him up, he slapped his thigh. "How is this possible? I'm a prisoner awaiting trial for murder. How could your boss allow you to be with me without taking precautions?"

Looking a little put out, Vanessa crossed her arms over her chest. "Kian trusts my assessment. If he didn't, why would he ask me to do it? He knows that if I deem you safe, you are."

"Forgive me. I didn't mean to imply that you don't know what you're doing. It's just that if I were in your boss's shoes, I would have been more cautious. What if I was some master manipulator who managed to fool you into trusting me? What if I attacked you the moment we were alone and took you hostage?"

She smiled. "Well, we are alone, you are not bound to the chair, and yet you are not attacking me. So my assessment of you was correct."

"There are surveillance cameras in here. I know that we are watched."

"So? If you had wanted to take me hostage, you also would have wanted someone to know about it, right? What would you have demanded in exchange for my release?"

He swallowed. "The only thing I want is to be with you. I would have demanded that you were allowed to stay with me."

8

VANESSA

"Then you've gotten your wish." Vanessa walked over and crouched in front of Mo-red. "We can be together."

As if he was still bound to the chair, Mo-red didn't move, his hands clutching the armrests with a white-knuckled grip. "For how long?"

And wasn't that the big question. "Until I get you exonerated. I've spoken with Lusha, and she's willing to take on your defense and that of the others. The only one she isn't willing to defend is Igor, but since he's not standing trial, that's not an issue."

"Will there be surveillance cameras in the other cell?"

Vanessa smiled. "Did you listen to anything I just said?"

"Something about Lusha."

"Yes, it was about Lusha. She's willing to defend you."

He nodded. "I'm glad. I think. When can we move into that other cell?"

Vanessa stifled a laugh because Mo-red seemed shell-shocked, and she didn't want to offend him. "Today, if you are ready. I need to go home and pack some things, and the cell probably needs some cleaning because no one has done it in months, but you can move in right now if you wish."

"I would like to see it." He cracked the first smile since she'd told him the news. "It all seems so surreal. Maybe seeing it would make it real for me."

She pushed to her feet and offered him a hand up. "Come with me."

His wrists were secured with handcuffs, and she wondered whether the Guardians would continue chaining him every time he left the cell. With the weaponized cuff on his forearm, the other measures were superfluous. She would have to talk with Magnus about it. He was in charge of the force at the keep, but he probably took orders from Onegus, so maybe she should talk directly to the chief.

Hesitantly, Mo-red pushed to his feet, and even though she was a tall female and was wearing three-inch heels, he towered over her.

She'd seen Mo-red standing next to Theo and dwarfing the Guardian, who wasn't short, but somehow he didn't seem as big when he was sitting down and looking at her with those big eyes of his.

"You're so tall," she murmured as she led him toward the door.

"I'm average height for a Kra-ell male." He stood beside her as the door mechanism activated with a buzzing sound.

As it swung out, Theo was waiting for them on the other side with a big grin on his face and another weaponized cuff.

He lifted it to show it to Mo-red. "The boss demanded additional safety measures."

Vanessa frowned. "Kian?"

"No, it was Onegus. This one is a special order made specifically for your boy toy." He tucked the cuff under his arm and motioned for Mo-red to lift his hands. "You can play kinky games with these." He unlocked the handcuffs, tucked them in his pocket, and put the new cuff on Mo-red's other forearm. "Now you have a matching set."

Vanessa didn't like him calling Mo-red her boy toy, and she didn't know what he meant by kinky games in regard to the new cuff, but the words stirred excitement in her belly. "What does it do?"

"If your boy misbehaves, the cuff will activate a magnetic field and snap together with the other one. But mostly, it's for us so we can use the two cuffs to bind him when we move him from place to place. William is making more for the other prisoners. They will also get ankle cuffs that function similarly."

"First of all, please don't call Mo-red a boy. He is the father of three adult sons, so that's inappropriate. Secondly, how are they supposed to walk if their ankle cuffs stick to each other?"

Theo shrugged. "I'm sure William has thought about it. Maybe it works like a forcefield, so they can't make long strides."

Mo-red nodded. "I imagine it will be like a strong drag that will inhibit the size of the stride."

"Yeah," Theo pulled out his phone and used it to open the door they'd stopped in front of. "I'll program the code into your phone," he told Vanessa.

When the door opened to reveal the room, she was disappointed to see that the bed was only a double, not even a queen. She and Mo-red were both slim, but Mo-red was so tall that his feet were going to hang over the edge of the mattress. There was also a couch, a small coffee table that could be raised to serve as a desk, a console with a television and several books, and a small bar that included a refrigerator, a pod coffee maker, and a toaster.

"Did you stock blood in the fridge?" she asked Theo.

"Not yet. I'll ask Jay to get it."

"Thank you." She turned to Mo-red. "So, what do you think?"

He smiled. "I think it's perfect."

"Do you want to stay here while I go home to pack?"

Mo-red nodded. "I need to collect my things from the other cell, and I need to tell Madbar that I'm moving." His smile wilted. "He's not going to be happy about being left alone in there."

Vanessa turned to Theo. "Can we put Madbar together with Valstar?"

She hadn't evaluated Valstar yet, and it was about time that she got to it, but then maybe it was better if Edna probed him first. The judge had been supposed to do that the day before, but something had come up, and she couldn't get to it either.

Theo rubbed a hand over the back of his neck. "I'll ask Magnus, but I don't think he'll agree to put them together. Valstar is considered a higher security risk than Madbar."

"Well, check with him, just in case."

Mo-red shook his head. "Madbar will not want to room with Valstar. They didn't get along."

"Why's that?" Theo asked.

"Valstar was Igor's right-hand man. Do I need to say anything more?"

Perhaps Mo-red thought that it was self-explanatory, but Vanessa made a mental note to ask him about it later.

9

JADE

While waiting for Andrew, the immortals had decided to get lunch at the coffee shop, which was located in the building's lobby.

Jade stopped next to the green barrier that delineated the café area from the rest of the sprawling open space.

"What's the matter?" Kian asked.

"I didn't bring my sunglasses, and there are too many people there for me to compel them to ignore my alien looks. Can one of you shroud me?"

"I can," Brundar volunteered.

"No need." Kian pulled a pair of sunglasses from the inner pocket of his jacket and handed them to her. "You can use mine."

"Thanks." She put them on.

The fit wasn't bad, and since this was Los Angeles, no one would wonder why she was wearing such dark sunglasses indoors. The city was full of actors and other divas, and Jade could easily pretend to be one of them.

Well, not with what she had on now.

She looked more like a killer for hire than an actress on a

coffee break. But back in the day, when her wardrobe had been full of designer outfits, she could have had fun with a diva act.

Oh, well, she could pretend to be one of Kian's bodyguards. The good thing about hanging around someone who looked like him was that hardly anyone even glanced her way.

Relaxing, she sat at the table and sipped on a cup of dark brew while listening to the males' banter and watching the humans at the other tables. They were sneaking glances at the four of them, but mostly at Kian, probably trying to figure out which movie they had seen him in.

Anandur and Brundar were getting their fair share of looks as well, and she was getting the least.

To be frank, the three males were a sight to behold and less intimidating than her.

The advantage these descendants of the gods had over Kra-ell didn't end with their good looks and the near-reverent admiration those looks earned them. The biggest advantage was that they could pass for humans.

Jade, on the other hand, was too tall for a female, too flat-chested, with strange eyes that were too big, ears that were too pointy, and a tongue that was too long.

Still, she cut an impressive figure, and during her travels a lifetime ago, she'd gotten plenty of attention. But then she'd been dressed to the nines and had been escorted by males that didn't look like fallen angels.

More like straight-up demons.

Had the gods and their descendants introduced that imagery to humanity? Had they implanted those stereotypes in the species' genetic memory?

After all, if they had manipulated the human genome to have herd instincts of blindly following their leaders, they could have done that as well.

Hell, given what they had done with Igor and others like

him, the gods could have done pretty much anything they wanted, and since they had eons to come up with and implement ideas, she couldn't even imagine what they'd created since.

When Andrew walked into the coffee shop, Kian waved him over.

He walked over to their table and put his briefcase on the one vacant chair. "I'll just grab a coffee and a sandwich to go."

Anandur put down his third sandwich and wiped his mouth with a napkin. "I'll get them for you. It will save you a couple of minutes."

"Thanks, I appreciate it. Can you get me a tall black coffee and a tuna melt?"

"I'm on it."

Kian put his coffee cup down. "Since Anandur is getting you lunch, we should head down and start the questioning. You don't have a lot of time."

"True. I don't." Andrew took his briefcase and followed him.

"Are we going in without the redhead?" Jade asked. "Isn't that against the protocol?"

Kian had told her that he was required to take two bodyguards with him every time he left the village.

He smiled and put his hand on her shoulder. "I've got you, don't I? Between you and Brundar, I'm perfectly safe."

"Thanks for the vote of confidence." Jade cast a quick sidelong glance at Brundar.

Ever since Igor's attack on Kian, the guy had been sulking, but then his expressionless face revealed so little that she might have been misinterpreting it, and it was just his usual solemn mood.

When they passed through the door marked as maintenance, she removed Kian's sunglasses and handed them back. "I used to carry a fancy Gucci pair whenever I ventured among humans. I suppose I should get a new pair."

Kian pressed the button for the elevator. "That reminds me that we still need to take care of your finances. First, though, we need to get all of your people counterfeit documentation so we can open bank accounts for you." He motioned for her to enter the elevator. "I assume that most of your people don't know how to drive."

"You assume correctly, and that includes me. When I traveled, I used taxis and hired drivers when needed. I never bothered to learn how to drive."

"There is still so much that needs to be done." Kian let out a breath. "Your people need to learn English, we need to get the kids in school, and we need to get the job situation sorted out."

When Andrew arched a brow, Kian told him her idea about the Kra-ell joining the war on trafficking.

"I think that's a great idea," Andrew said as they exited on the dungeon level. "Perhaps we can expand the effort to other cities or even go after the recruiters."

Kian snorted. "Even with the Kra-ell, we won't be able to clean up all of Los Angeles, let alone venture to other places. It would be helpful if your government got involved, but trafficking victims can't pay lobbyists, so that's never going to happen."

"It's your government, too," Andrew pointed out. "You've been living in the US for over two hundred years, so that makes you a citizen even though you were never naturalized."

"We are not citizens of any country." Kian chuckled. "The term resident alien was never more apt than in our case."

When they stopped in front of Igor's cell, Jade's heart went from a steady beat to a nervous staccato.

Finally, she would get to ask all the questions she couldn't have before and, hopefully, get some answers as well.

10

KIAN

"Well, well." Igor approached the bars. "The truth-teller is back, which means it's time for more questions. I feel so important."

Kian sat down and crossed his legs. It was so tempting to tell Igor that his bargaining chip was no longer relevant and wipe that smirk off his face, but he couldn't do it just yet and risk Igor using information about the twins as his new chip.

Andrew didn't rise to the taunt either and sat down on Kian's right while Jade sat on his left.

Brundar remained standing.

Leaning against the closed door, he pulled out one of his many daggers and a sharpening stone and started methodically working on it.

His excuse was that he was waiting for Anandur to come in with lunch for Andrew, but Kian suspected that he enjoyed intimidating Igor. Not that the guy looked intimidated. His expression was always slightly amused, almost mocking.

"Indeed." Kian wondered how Igor was going to react to what he was about to say next. "Jade told me about the royal twins, and my first thought was that, given the nature of your assignment, you shouldn't have been told about them."

The smirk melted off Igor's face for a fraction of a second and then reappeared as he shifted his gaze to Jade. "After all the trouble you've gone to, vowing to keep me alive in exchange for my silence, you went ahead and told him about them? You disappoint me, Jade. I taught you better."

"You taught me nothing. How did you know about the twins?"

"I know a lot of things."

Kian lifted his hand to stop Jade from getting sucked into Igor's game. "Did the gods tell you about the queen's children being on board the settler ship? Yes or no?"

"It was implied."

The bastard was back to his evasive tricks, but Kian wasn't going to fall for them this time.

"Answer with a yes or no."

Igor cast a quick glance at Andrew before returning his gaze to Kian. "Why should I answer that?"

"Do you want to be fed?"

"Yes."

"Yes, you want to be fed, or yes, you were told that the twins were onboard the ship?"

"I was told that they were on board."

"Why?"

"I don't know why the queen wanted to smuggle them out of Anumati. Perhaps she wanted them to lead the colony. I wasn't privy to her decisions, and neither were my handlers."

"So why were you told about them?" Jade asked. "Were you supposed to eliminate them as well?"

"I told you already. My assignment was to eliminate the Eternal King's offspring. I had no other directives."

Kian glanced at Andrew.

"He's telling the truth," Andrew said. "I think."

Kian had a strong feeling that Igor wasn't telling them the truth. He might have figured out how to circumvent Andrew's lie-detecting even when answering yes-or-no questions.

Uncrossing his legs, Kian leaned his elbow on his knee and leaned his chin on his fist. "Perhaps some of the instructions you were given weren't directives but guidelines. Did you decide on your own to create a new Kra-ell society on Earth?"

Igor's eyes darted to Andrew for a moment. "The decision was mine."

Kian turned to his brother-in-law. "Truth?"

"I'm not sure. He's being manipulative again."

This was going to take patience that Kian didn't have. "Let me rephrase. When you decided to create a male-dominated Kra-ell community, were you following guidelines that were given to you? Or was it entirely your mind's creation?"

Turning around, Igor went back to his cot and sat down. "Why does it matter to you?"

"I'm just curious. Were you the mastermind? Yes or no?"

"Regrettably, I can't take credit for that. The answer is no."

"That's what I thought. Did the gods want to conduct a social experiment on the Kra-ell?"

"Yes."

Jade sucked in a breath. "I'll be damned. He was telling the truth all along. He was just a tool."

Kian shook his head. "Igor was far away from home, in distance and in time, and he had no way of communicating with his superiors or his handlers. He didn't have to do it if he didn't want to." He turned to Igor. "Did you?"

The guy smirked. "I was curious. A male-ruled Kra-ell society was an intriguing hypothesis."

Jade pushed to her feet. "You killed my sons because you were curious if the gods' social experiment would work?"

He shrugged. "Don't be naive, Jade. Far worse things were done to people here on Earth by their fellow humans and for far less compelling reasons. Let me rephrase. Far worse things are still being done. I'm not the embodiment of evil you think I am."

Kian chuckled. "Funny how every evildoer thinks that he isn't the worst. It's not a good defense, Igor."

In this case, Kian didn't need to employ a gender-neutral pronoun. Males were far worse offenders than females, and he often wondered if the cause was nature or nurture, or both. For some reason, most females had a moral line they wouldn't cross, but males could be made to do almost anything. Was the same true for the Kra-ell, though?

Jade was as aggressive and as bloodthirsty as any male warrior, but she was ruled by a code of honor. Was the same true of other Kra-ell female warriors?

"I'm not trying to defend myself," Igor said. "I'm just calling Jade out on her bullshit. She shouldn't pretend to be so naive."

11

JADE

Jade sat down with a huff and crossed her arms over her chest.

She wasn't naive, and she knew precisely what Igor was talking about. Human history was full of terrible atrocities, but one evil didn't excuse another. It only proved that there were many sociopaths like Igor who thought nothing of killing and maiming for their own amusement or curiosity.

What she had to do was stop letting her emotions cloud her mind. There was no point in raging at Igor because he was incapable of feeling remorse.

It also appeared that Igor's lack of emotions was interfering with Andrew's ability to discern whether he was telling the truth or not. Jade was convinced that he knew more about the twins than he was letting on, and that included nefarious plans for the queen's children.

She also doubted that Igor had as much free will as he pretended to have. In fact, she was starting to suspect that he'd been programmed to think that he was making his own choices when, in fact, he'd been following the gods' directives.

From what Phinas had told her about the immortals' special brand of thralling, it could be used to plant false memories, beliefs, and motives in the victims' minds, and perhaps that was what had been done to Igor.

Igor was immune to Toven's thralling and compulsion, but maybe the gods back home had ways to break through his resistance, or what was even more likely, some of them were much more powerful than Toven.

She turned to Kian. "We need to talk."

He frowned. "We are not done here, and Andrew is short on time."

"We can take a five-minute break." She cast a mocking look at Igor. "He's not going anywhere."

"Very well." Kian rose to his feet.

As if on cue, the door to the cell opened, and Anandur walked in with Andrew's lunch. "Sorry it took so long. I waited for the barista to brew a fresh pot of coffee for you."

"Let's go to my office." Kian put his hand on Andrew's shoulder. "You can eat there in peace."

The five of them exited Igor's cell without bothering with a backward glance, and as the door closed behind them, Kian fell in step with Jade.

"What did you want to talk about?" he asked.

"I don't think that Andrew can tell whether Igor's telling the truth or not." She turned to look at Andrew. "I'm guessing that your talent relies on your subconscious picking up slight variations in emotional states, and since Igor either doesn't have any or can manipulate them at will, he can fool you into thinking that you can tell when he's telling the truth even when he's lying."

Andrew swallowed the bite he'd taken off the sandwich Anandur had brought him and put it back in its paper bag. "It's possible. When I tested my talent on you, I couldn't tell whether you were telling the truth or lying unless you had strong feelings about the subject. Igor is a smart cookie, and he was paying attention to my responses. He must have figured that out even before we did and then used it to manipulate me."

"That's not good." Kian opened the door to his office and motioned for her to go ahead. "Now I doubt everything he said except for the things that we could prove or disprove."

"As you should." Jade sat down and looked longingly at the small refrigerator where Kian kept his beverages. "Do you have any more of those vile beers in there?"

He chuckled. "If you find them disgusting, why do you drink them?"

"It's an acquired taste. They are bitter going down, but they are satisfying on some level, and the alcohol takes the edge off."

"Here you go." Anandur handed her a bottle. "There are two more left. Who wants one?"

Kian shook his head.

Andrew lifted his coffee cup. "I'm good."

When neither of the brothers took a beer, Jade shrugged. "I have no problem drinking alone."

"So, what do we do now?" Anandur asked. "Torture or starvation won't work because he can tell us made-up stories, and we would have no way to know whether or not they are true."

"Just put him in stasis," Andrew said. "We can find the other settlers without him, and what he knows about Anumati is most likely irrelevant after seven thousand years."

Kian looked at Jade and lifted a brow. "What's your take on this? What do you think we should do?"

"We need to find a way into his mind. Perhaps a special kind of drug? When Igor mentioned the terrible things humans do to each other, it reminded me of the experiments that have been done on soldiers with hallucinogenic drugs. I know that you are all about ethics, and using drugs might seem unethical to you, but if you are willing to resort to torture or starvation to make him talk, I don't see how drugs are any different."

12

KIAN

Kian chuckled. "You think too highly of me. I have no problem whatsoever with using drugs on that murderer. The problem is that I don't know whether human drugs are going to work on him and in what way. Merlin tells me that the Kra-ell respond to Motrin like humans respond to alcohol, so maybe that's all we need to administer."

He still hadn't asked Igor why he had bitten him and sucked his blood, and he needed him to answer that truthfully.

His mother's safety might depend on it.

Kian would do whatever it took to get the information out of Igor.

Jade took a deep breath. "I'm willing to be your test subject. I just don't know whether Igor's body will respond the same way as mine, given all the alterations the gods did to his body. But since we have reason to suspect that they started with unaltered Kra-ell genes and made modifications to them, there is a good chance that he will respond to drugs the same way as any Kra-ell."

Andrew finished his sandwich, made a small ball from the

plastic wrapper, and put it inside the empty coffee cup. "If my services are no longer needed, I'll head back to work."

Kian nodded. "I'm not a hundred percent convinced that your talent is useless on Igor. I will speak with Bridget and Julian about the truth drug we used on Eleanor."

"The so-called truth serums have limitations," Andrew said. "None of them have been proven to solicit consistent or predictable truth-telling results. Similar to what happens with hypnosis, subjects become more susceptible to influence, and they tend to reconstruct or totally fabricate memories to please the interrogator. Evidence collected with the use of that class of drugs is not admissible in court."

Kian waved a hand in dismissal. "I know all that. Their use is also considered a form of torture and a violation of human rights. But—"

Jade lifted her hand to stop him. "May I make a suggestion?"

He nodded. "Of course."

"I know those drugs are not as effective as they are portrayed in movies, and I wasn't even thinking about them when I suggested that we drug Igor. Anything that will muddle his brain might do the trick. What got me thinking about drugging Igor was that we need a powerful thraller to get inside his mind, but since Toven is the best we have, and he's not good enough even with Mia's enhancement, it occurred to me that he might have better success if Igor puts up less resistance. Hence the idea of drugs."

Kian regarded her with renewed appreciation. The female was as smart as she was fearsome, and that was an impressive combination.

"That's brilliant, Jade."

"It is." Andrew pushed to his feet. "If you need me to come back here after work, send me a text."

"I think we are done with Igor for today." Kian stood up.

"Thank you, Andrew. I appreciate your help." He clapped his brother-in-law on the back.

"Any time."

After escorting Andrew to the door, Kian returned to the conference table and sat down. "It would seem that we are not putting Igor in stasis anytime soon."

"There is no rush," Jade said. "Right? You need the Guardians down here because of the other prisoners, so it's not like you are wasting resources on him." She tilted her head. "With your approval, I can assemble a unit of trusted Kra-ell to assist the Guardians."

"That's actually not a bad idea." Kian gave her a smile. "Your mind seems to be working on overdrive today."

She nodded. "My mind has been clouded by grief and rage for so long that I feel like it's only starting to emerge from the fog and getting in gear."

Kian chuckled. "The fable you wrote to inform Emmett of your existence and location suggests that your mind has been working just fine all along."

She snorted. "Yeah, I have conceded that was inspired. Desperate times and all that."

Anandur made a mock horrified expression and put his hand over his heart. "Oh, my, Jade. You're starting to scare me." He turned to Kian. "Now I know why you invited her to join us. You wanted another mastermind in the village."

"Who's the other one?" Jade asked. "Turner? I would consider it a great compliment to be compared to him."

"I actually meant Kalugal," Anandur said. "But in Kalugal's case, all his formidable smarts are dedicated to making money. So maybe you are right, and I shouldn't bundle you with him. You are more like Turner, except prettier and with more personality. No offense to Turner, but the guy is kind of flat."

Brundar snorted. "You only say that because he doesn't laugh at your jokes."

"He doesn't even get them." Anandur crossed his arms over his chest. "Are we heading home soon? Or are we going back to see Igor?"

"I think we are done with him for today." Kian looked at Jade. "Unless you still want to get in there and threaten him with stasis."

She shook her head. "I want to try the drug idea first, and if that doesn't work, we can use stasis as a threat to get him to tell us what he knows about the twins. I just have a feeling that he knows a lot more than he wants us to believe he does." She let out a breath. "The other thing I hope the drugs would help us to determine is how much of what he has done was indeed his choice and how much he was brainwashed to do. It occurred to me that a powerful god could have thralled Igor into believing that he had free will to act or not to act in certain circumstances, when in fact it was all planted in his head either by thralling or some other means."

"You know what needs to be done." Anandur cast Kian a look that wasn't difficult to decipher.

Annani could probably get into Igor's mind with or without the help of drugs, but Kian had no intention of letting her anywhere near the guy, especially now that they knew that he'd built immunity to tranquilizers.

"Not happening, Anandur."

The Guardian lifted his hands in the air. "It was just a suggestion."

"What was?" Jade asked.

"Never mind." Kian rose to his feet. "Are you done with your beer?"

She lifted the bottle to her lips, gulped whatever was left, and put the empty bottle down. "Now I'm done."

13

VANESSA

Vanessa stood in front of her wardrobe and debated what to pack. Other than a couple of casual outfits for off hours, she needed several professional outfits for interviews and meetings. Then again, since she would have to travel back and forth between the keep and the village, she could always pick up more stuff and didn't need to pack a lot.

In preparation for the trial, the evaluation of the rest of the Kra-ell had taken a back seat to working with the prisoners, which was regrettable.

If she could, she would drag it out forever to give herself more time with Mo-red, but other than her, everyone else was in a rush to get it done. Lusha was scheduled to arrive tomorrow afternoon, and hopefully the girl knew what she was doing.

She was only a couple of years out of law school, and what she'd done after graduating had nothing to do with courtroom drama. She had no experience as a trial lawyer defending anyone, let alone prisoners accused of murder.

Vanessa prayed to the Fates that Lusha was a natural talent and could mount a formidable defense for her clients.

Choosing several versatile outfits, she took them to the bedroom and laid them on her bed. The converted cell didn't have a closet, so she would have to leave them in her suitcase and put it under the bed.

Oh well, wearing wrinkled clothes was a small sacrifice considering the opportunity she'd been given to be with Mo-red—the first male she had ever been interested in for more than casual sex.

Smiling, Vanessa walked over to her lingerie drawer and opened it. Tonight, she was finally going to experience what she'd been fantasizing about for days.

She pulled out several sexy lingerie sets and lovingly put them inside a silk pouch that went into the suitcase.

Had Mo-red ever been with a female who had worn luxury underwear that was meant to entice?

The tough Kra-ell females she'd met didn't strike her as the types who would bother with something as frivolous as that, but maybe his human partners had?

As jealousy washed over her, Vanessa shook her head, picked the outfit on the top of the pile, and folded it carefully in the suitcase.

She'd never been jealous over anyone before, but that was because she hadn't cared who the men she'd been with had sex with before or after her. They had just been fleeting encounters that could have never developed into anything meaningful, even if they were wonderful people, and some of them probably had been. She'd never stayed long enough to find out, but she was a decent judge of character, and she was picky about who she took to her bed.

After all, pleasure wasn't the only reason she'd been engaging with human males.

There was always the hope of conception. She would love

to have another child. Maybe not right now, but sometime in the near future.

The sound of the doorbell ringing put an end to thoughts of babies, and as Vanessa put down the pair of slacks she'd been folding, she wondered who it could be. She hadn't been expecting anyone, and no one came to her house without calling first. Perhaps it was an emergency?

Urgency quickening her steps, she rushed to the front door and threw it open.

The pair standing in her doorway was an unexpected pleasure.

"Jackson, Tessa, what a nice surprise!" She pulled the girl into her arms for a quick hug and then her son for a little longer one. "Please, come in."

It was early afternoon, and Jackson usually didn't come home until evening.

Perhaps they had some news for her?

Maybe all those thoughts about babies were a premonition, and she was about to be a grandma?

Nothing would make her happier, but that wasn't the vibe she was getting from them.

Jackson was simmering, and Tessa was uncomfortable.

Oh. Damn. He'd heard.

Vanessa had called Ruth because she'd needed to talk with someone about what was happening with her and Mo-red. Ruth must have told Sylvia, who must have told Roni, who must have told Jackson.

Vanessa hadn't told Ruth to keep it a secret because she didn't intend to hide her involvement with Mo-red, but she hadn't expected the rumor to spread so fast.

Jackson should have heard it from her, not from Roni or anyone else.

On the other hand, her lovers were none of her son's business. She hadn't shared that kind of information with him before, and she didn't intend to start today.

Except, Mo-red wasn't like any of her casual hookups, and she was moving in with him temporarily. There was nothing yet to tell.

"Can I offer you something to drink?" she asked.

"I would like some tea," Tessa said. "I'll make it while you two chat." She scurried to the kitchen with Jackson scowling after her.

"Tessa avoids conflict, Jackson." Vanessa sat on an armchair across from her son. "You should have left her out of this."

"Out of what?"

She let out a breath. "I know you too well, my son. You didn't come here in the middle of your workday because you missed your mother. Just say what you came to say, and let's get it over with before Tessa returns with the tea."

Jackson huffed. "I don't know how you do that, but it's like you can read my mind. Am I that transparent, or can you do that with everyone?"

"Not everyone, but most. All it takes is being attuned to people. Most wear their emotions on their sleeves."

Vanessa was better at deciphering those emotions than almost everyone else, but she didn't like to boast.

"You're making a mistake," Jackson said. "I came to talk you out of it."

Well, at least he was direct.

"What precisely do you want to talk me out of?"

"Moving into a cell with the Kra-ell prisoner. He's a murderer, Mom. I don't know what he did to charm you, but it's so unlike you to do something so impulsive that I'm sure it's more than just attraction. Besides, it's unprofessional. You're his therapist."

"I'm not. I'm Kian's advisor, and my job was to assess the prisoners, not to offer them psychological help."

He cocked a brow. "Semantics. You didn't meet him in a bar or through a dating app. You met him in a professional capacity."

"Are you worried about me, Jackson?"

"Of course, I am. I want to talk to that Kra-ell and find out what he did to you."

Vanessa chuckled. "Do you really believe that I don't know what I'm doing?"

Letting out an exasperated sigh, he pushed his long bangs back. "I don't know what to think. It's just so unlike you. Why are you doing this?"

"It's simple. I care for Mo-red deeply. He's a good male who's been forced to do terrible things by a powerful compeller, and he regrets them with every fiber of his being. I feel a connection to him that I've never felt with any other male, and I'm afraid that our time together might be running out. I have no control over how a Kra-ell jury will vote, and they might demand his death. Kian promised them complete autonomy in that, and all Edna and I can do is assist and guide. If you are worried about me, think of a way to sway the Kra-ell's opinion about Mo-red and the others who have also been used by Igor against their will to commit terrible crimes."

He chuckled. "Regrettably, I can't bribe them with my pastries. They don't eat normal food."

"We can arrange get-togethers." Tessa walked in with a tray. "Many of them are young, and they seem bored and aimless. Ella and I were thinking about creating a support group for them, but they're so proud and tough that they would never go for it. But perhaps some are into music, and they would like to play in a band."

Jackson shook his head. "We came here to talk my mother

out of shacking up with a pureblood murderer, and you're talking about forming a band?"

Tessa poured tea into the teacups and handed one to Vanessa. "You came to talk your mother out of that. I just tagged along because you wanted me to come with you."

"So, you think that there is nothing wrong with what she's about to do?"

Tessa cast Vanessa an apologetic smile. "I think your mom is a grown, smart woman who knows what she's doing. It's not like she's eloping with the dude. They are in the keep, supervised twenty-four-seven by Guardians."

"I know." Jackson lifted the small teacup and blew on the liquid to cool it. "I just don't want you to get hurt."

Leaning over, Vanessa patted her son's knee. "Part of life is accepting the fact that there is no way to avoid getting hurt. If we do everything we can to shield ourselves from pain, we are not moving forward, which translates into not really living."

14

MO-RED

Since relocating to the new cell, Mo-red had showered twice, not because he needed to get clean, but because he needed to cool down.

At first, he'd tried to read one of the books that someone had left in the room, but it was a romantic story that had quickly gotten too arousing, and given his particular predicament, it was the opposite of what he needed.

That had been shower number one.

Then he'd tried watching some television, but he'd been too distracted to follow even the simplest plot and had turned it off. With nothing else to do, he'd decided to release his pent-up energy by doing push-ups and sit-ups, and after that, he'd needed another shower.

He was nervous like a virgin youth on his way to his first invitation.

Tonight, he was going to have Vanessa for the first time, and he was terrified of doing something wrong. He'd been with Kra-ell and human females, and he knew what was expected of him for both. Pureblooded Kra-ell females wanted a ferocious fight for dominance, and once he established it, the arousal was at such a fever pitch that the ensuing coupling was frantic and intense and quickly over.

With human females, it was the opposite. They wanted to be coaxed and gently teased to get ready, and when they were, he had to be careful not to hurt them.

What did immortal females expect from their males?

Vanessa had only ever been with humans, and he could imitate human-style sex to satisfy her, but she probably expected something different from him.

The question was, what?

She couldn't fight him for dominance even if she wanted to because she wasn't strong enough, and she probably had no wish to engage in such games.

The problem was that most females expected males to know how to please them, and they didn't provide instructions.

Would Vanessa be different and tell him what she wanted?

She was bolder than a human but not as demanding as a Kra-ell, and he was afraid of guessing the wrong thing.

When the door finally opened, and Vanessa walked in with a large rolling suitcase, Mo-red rose to his feet.

"Hello." He relaxed his shoulders and kept his hands behind his back to look as harmless as possible.

Vanessa smiled. "Your eyes are glowing red, but I assume it's not because you want to attack me."

She was so beautiful in her simple outfit of leggings, a long loose blouse, and flats. Without her professional attire, she looked softer, more approachable, and even more delicate and breakable.

Using her phone, she closed the door and walked up to him. "You can relax. No one is watching us, and no one other than the artificial intelligence is listening either." She put her hands on his neck and pulled his head down.

When her lips touched his, the shock to his system was like

an electrical bolt and had a similar effect on him. He was paralyzed, unable to move or return her kiss.

Leaning away, Vanessa looked at him with worry in her expressive blue eyes. "I'm sorry. I should have realized that you would need some time to adjust. Let's start this over." She took his hand and pulled him to sit with her on the couch. "Was Madbar upset because you left him alone in the cell?"

Mo-red cleared his throat to dislodge the lump that had taken residence in there. "He took it better than I expected. He wasn't as upset about my leaving as I thought he would be. In fact, he seemed happy for me. For us. The guy is a better friend than I've given him credit for." He closed his eyes for a moment. "I'm sorry about the awkward greeting. I don't know why I reacted like that. Maybe I've built up too much expectation."

"It's okay." She cupped his cheek. "It's my fault. I should have realized how shocking the move would be for you. One moment you were a prisoner with very restricted freedom, and the next, you are free to do whatever you want to me."

If Mo-red thought he'd been hard before, he was wrong. As her words speared through him, his shaft swelled to uncomfortable proportions, pressing against the zipper of the simple jeans he'd been given.

He swallowed. "It's not about what I want to do to you. It's about what you want me to do. You're unlike any female I've been with before, and perhaps that explains my momentary paralysis. I don't know what you expect of me, and I don't want to make assumptions and displease you. My only wish is to give you pleasure."

15

VANESSA

Vanessa's heart swelled with a surge of happiness.

Mo-red wouldn't have been so hesitant and cautious if she wasn't important to him.

Attractive, confident males didn't get nervous about hookups. If their performance wasn't top-notch, it wasn't a big deal. They could do better with the next one. But when they cared about a woman and wanted her for more than just casual sex, they sometimes got anxious.

On occasion, it got so bad that they couldn't get hard even though they were with the object of their desire.

Not that that had happened to Mo-red. He was so aroused that the hard length pressing against his zipper was about to win the war and burst through.

His eyes were still glowing red as well.

Nevertheless, it must be discomforting for him to feel anxious about his performance. The last time it had happened to him was probably his first when he was still barely out of boyhood.

Given how reserved the Kra-ell were about their feelings

and their refusal to show any weakness, his admission was precious.

Taking his hand, she brought it to her lips for a kiss. "You have no idea how much I appreciate your honesty, and I want you to know that this is perfectly normal and also incredibly flattering to me."

He frowned. "How so?"

"You wouldn't have performance anxiety if you didn't care about me. Males don't get anxious about performing with a female they don't intend to be with again."

A small smile lifted his lips. "I don't know what you mean by performance anxiety."

Mo-red was well-read, and Vanessa doubted that he didn't know what it was, but she was okay with spelling it out for him. "You worry about failing to please me before you've even tried. In your case, it's not motivated by fear of humiliation or rejection, but the fear of disappointing me."

"Is that your professional opinion, or are you speaking from personal experience?"

"Does it matter?"

"It does to me. I want to know that you've been treated right by the males you've been with and that they did their best to please you."

"Most of them did, but given that they were all human, what they could offer an immortal female was limited by their physiology." She leaned closer. "It's a matter of stamina. None of them could have climaxed twelve times in a row."

He chuckled. "Neither could I, but I gave it a serious try." He brought their conjoined hands to his lips and brushed them over her knuckles. "Thinking of you, I almost made it, my lovely Vanessa."

"I like it when you call me yours."

He shook his head. "You're not mine yet. I have to earn you first."

"Then I have to earn you too."

"You already did. You bought me with a kiss."

She laughed. "Don't sell yourself short. Tell me how you want to be earned."

He shook his head. "You go first."

"Just be yourself."

"Back at you, my lovely Vanessa."

She looked into his big eyes and saw the insecurity lurking in their depths. "You don't need to do anything special to win me over. You did that while tied to a chair, so now that you are semi-free, it should be a walk in the park."

"It's not. I'm out of my element." He lifted his other hand and brushed his fingers over her cheeks. "Is that pleasing to you?"

"Yes." She leaned into his palm.

"What else?"

Vanessa wondered how to progress from there.

She could take the initiative and show Mo-red what she liked, but she'd done that with most of her human lovers, and she was ready for something new.

What she'd fantasized about with him was very different, but she couldn't show him or tell him, or it would ruin the experience.

Perhaps she could hint?

Or better yet, she could start slow and let things unfold naturally.

"It's a new experience for both of us, and we will probably fumble a bit, but we will find our way. I'm much stronger than a human female, and I'm more resilient than both humans and pureblooded Kra-ell. I can't offer you a fight for dominance like a Kra-ell, but you don't need to fear hurting me, either. I'm very hard to break. So just be yourself, and I'll be myself, and we will learn each other like a couple of teenaged virgins fumbling about their first time."

16

MO-RED

Vanessa's words, combined with the scent of her arousal, released the coil Mo-red had wound down so tightly inside of himself that it had been stuck in the locked position until she'd given him permission to be himself.

His natural dominance surged forward, and his hand itched to touch her, to grab her hair and kiss her hard until her sweet lips were puffed up and swollen, ripe to take his erection between them.

Despite her insistence that she could take him in his natural state, he fought the urge to do what he'd just imagined. Perhaps he should warn her.

"Are you sure you are ready for the uncensored me? I'm not going to be gentle. I'm going to take you hard until you fully submit to me."

"Fates, oh, yes." She closed her eyes, and as he scented the flare of her arousal, he got the final confirmation he'd been hoping for.

This was precisely what Vanessa wanted from him.

But he had to hear her say it, and get her verbal consent, so there would be no misunderstanding about what they both wanted.

"Say it, Vanessa. I need to know that you understand what you're consenting to."

Her tongue snaked out, licking over her lips. "I want you just the way you are. And you don't have to worry about taking it too far. If it becomes too much for me, I'll let you know." Leaning closer and scrambling his senses with the delightful aroma of her arousal, she put her hands on his shoulders and whispered in his ear, "The cameras are off, but the AI is listening. If I say the word halt twice in a row, it will activate the magnetic field in your cuffs. So, you'd better stop whatever you're doing after the first time I say that word."

With that, the last of his fears were obliterated. If he got too rough with her, she could stop him with one word, and if he failed to respond, the second word would disable him. The question was what she would do if she couldn't talk, and given what he planned to do with her mouth, that wasn't hypothetical.

"Understood." He grinned. "That's perfect, save for one thing. What if your mouth is occupied, and you can't say that word?"

The blush that suffused her cheeks was precious. "I'm fine with that. A little danger enhances the pleasure, and the idea that I'm not in control thrills me."

Reckless female.

He wouldn't hurt her. If she displayed even the slightest distress, he would stop immediately, but she didn't know him well enough to place such blind trust in him.

"That's not good enough." He cupped her cheek. "You are used to being with men who you can overpower with ease, but that's not the case with me."

Her eyes softened. "I trust you, Mo-red. It wasn't my idea to program the AI with an emergency word. It was William's, and the only reason I brought it up was that it seemed like you needed it. I'm a hundred percent sure that I will never need a safety precaution with you. You will never hurt me." She smiled. "Unless I want you to."

Mother of All Life, have mercy. The female is wicked.

Wrapping his arm around her back, he pulled her against him and took her lips in the hard kiss he'd been fantasizing about just moments ago.

As she let herself get lost in the sensations, her body slackened against his chest, and he held her up effortlessly with one arm around her middle and the other gripping her hair.

Despite her assurances, he didn't want to cause her pain, and he didn't pull on the soft tresses, just used them to hold her in place for his kiss.

He could have kept ravishing her mouth forever and never gotten his fill of her taste, but there was so much more that he wanted to do, to touch, to taste.

Moving his lips to the column of her neck, he trailed soft kisses over the smooth skin, alternating with gentle scrapes of his fangs.

Vanessa moaned, and as she arched into him, he could feel her hard nipples rubbing against his chest through the layers of their clothing.

That needed to change.

Leaning away, he gripped the bottom of her loose shirt and pulled it over her head, and a split second later, she did the same to his and put her hands over his pecs.

"Fates, I've wanted to do that since I first laid eyes on you." She leaned down and kissed his chest. "Your skin is so smooth. So warm." She licked his nipple, and he saw stars.

Picking her up in a move that startled her, he rose to his feet and deposited her on the bed. "Take off your bra for me."

The garment looked delicate and expensive, and he was too impatient to take it off her without tearing it apart.

She looked at him with a challenge in her eyes. "I want you to take it off."

"As you wish."

He gave her a slight push, and when her back hit the mattress, he grabbed her leggings and pulled them off with one smooth move.

They'd come off along with her panties, and as her core was bared, the scent of her arousal permeated the small space, sending his primal urges into overdrive.

Her beautiful bra didn't stand a chance.

17

VANESSA

Vanessa knew that if she didn't take the bra off, Mo-red would obliterate it, but she didn't really care about the garment despite the obscene amount she'd paid for it. He could shred it to pieces as far as she was concerned.

But he'd asked her to take it off, and she was in the mood to oblige him. Smiling, she reached behind her, released the clasp, and pulled the cups down without bothering with a slow reveal.

Mo-red didn't have the patience for that.

His eyes were entirely red now, and his fangs were fully elongated. He looked like a sexy demon, and she couldn't wait for him to get rid of his jeans and show her the hard length she'd seen and felt struggling against his zipper.

Lifting her hand, she stopped him from advancing on her. "Your turn. Take off your pants."

He popped the button but didn't push them down. "You want this?" He cupped himself over the jeans.

"Yes."

"Then spread for me. I want to see all of you."

Ah, naughty, naughty male.

Spreading her knees just a fraction, her hand lowered to her center and hesitated there.

She'd never touched herself in front of another.

"More," Mo-red commanded. "I want to see you playing with yourself, pushing your fingers where you want this to go." He smoothed his hand along the hard ridge that was still covered by too much fabric.

The naughty thrill of obeying his command broke through the last of her hesitation, and she spread her knees wider, baring her lower lips to his hungry eyes, and put her pointer finger on top of her throbbing clit.

He hissed and then uttered a word she was sure was a Kraell curse.

"Your pants," she reminded him.

Between one blink of an eye and the next, they were down on the floor, and Mo-red's huge erection was pointing straight at her exposed center like a heat-guided missile.

He was larger than any male she'd been with before, but then she'd never been with a guy who was over six and a half feet tall.

He palmed that bad boy in his large hand. "Keep touching yourself, Vanessa. I want to see you making yourself wet while feasting your eyes on my shaft."

Who could have imagined that polite, charming Mo-red could be so blatantly sexy?

As she caressed her moist flesh, she moved her gaze to his eyes, and the need she saw in them ignited her desire more than the fingers on her core ever could.

Drawn to what he was so aptly watching, Mo-red inched toward her, and when he was within her reach, Vanessa shifted to her knees and put her hand on the part of him that wasn't covered by his hand.

Looking into his eyes, she lowered her head, extended her tongue, and licked the head as if it was an ice cream cone.

The pained groan that left his throat gave her an erotic thrill and encouraged her to continue.

Tightening her hand around him, she kissed and licked while working her hand up and down, and then she took as much as she could into her mouth and started bobbing her head up and down.

Mo-red growled, and as his hand fisted her hair, she had a moment of fear, expecting him to ram that huge thing down her throat, but she should have known he would never do that.

Instead, he pushed a little further and then retracted, taking her mouth in measured thrusts that pushed her to the limit but not beyond.

She was just getting into the rhythm when he pulled out and pushed her back on the bed.

"My turn, sweetheart." He gripped her thighs and pulled her to the edge of the bed, then knelt between them. "Oh, yeah. This is what I want." He lifted his red eyes to her. "Do you want to watch me take you with my tongue?"

As his words elicited a new flood of moisture from her core, she braced on her forearms so she could see the wicked things he could do with his super-long tongue.

Whatever she'd imagined, it wasn't the whip-like sensation of his tongue flicking over her engorged clit.

Seeing stars, she cried out, but as he flattened his tongue over the abused nub, the throbbing pain turned into such intense pleasure that she was hovering on the verge of orgasm before he even started.

His next move was to fold that monstrous tongue of his into a spear, and as he penetrated her with it, nearly reaching the end of her channel, Vanessa erupted with a scream.

18

MO-RED

Vanessa's body was still quaking when Mo-red mounted her and pushed just the tip of his shaft inside of her. She was slick from her release, but she was surprisingly tight for a female who had given birth.

Perhaps she hadn't been with anyone in a while.

He tried to go slow and give her time to adjust, but her words from before still reverberated in his mind. She didn't want him to hold back, and she was even more resilient than a pureblooded Kra-ell female who would have sneered at him if he didn't penetrate her in one brutal thrust.

With a groan, he surged inside of her until he was fully seated and then stilled.

Vanessa's nails scraped his back, but when he looked at her face, her expression wasn't one of pain but of ecstasy.

Taking her parted lips, he retracted and surged back in, and as she undulated her hips under him, he increased the tempo.

Mo-red was kissing Vanessa hard, and she was kissing him back with the same urgency, and soon her body was shaking with the need to climax again.

She consumed him with her kiss, the harsh moans she

emitted into his mouth, the nails she dug into the hard muscles of his ass—claiming him as completely as he was claiming her.

He couldn't get enough of her.

With her eyes glazed over and her breath panting, Vanessa was wild in her lust, and the more demanding his thrusting became, the more she writhed under him.

He was nearing his peak, and it was a spur-of-the-moment decision to flip her over, pull her hips up, and push into her from behind.

Looking at him over her shoulder, Vanessa gave him a feral smile worthy of a pureblooded Kra-ell female and a challenging look that said—that's all you got?

He was up for the challenge.

Gripping her hips, he shafted into her, and as he hit the very end of her channel, she cried out his name.

"Vanessa," he groaned as he kept going like a male possessed.

She turned her head and looked at him again. "Kiss me, Mored."

He draped himself over her, and as he crushed his mouth against hers, his fangs itched with the need to draw her blood.

When her sheath tightened around him, he knew he wouldn't last. Letting go of her mouth, he licked her neck and struck with his fangs.

The moment her potent blood hit his senses, his seed exploded into her with the force of a volcanic eruption.

It was like nothing he'd tasted before, and he knew that he would never again take the vein of another female.

As he kept drawing her essence into him, he was filling her with his at the same time, and the exchange was exhilarating.

Perfection.

When he was spent, he retracted his fangs, licked the puncture wounds closed, and dropped to his side, pulling her with him and spooning behind her.

For long moments, the only sound in the small room was their panting breath, and then Vanessa turned in his arms and faced him with a satisfied smile. "That was amazing. Can we do it again?"

He barked out a laugh. "Mother of All Life, save me." And yet his shaft stirred into life against her belly. "Give me a moment."

Human females usually blacked out from the analgesic and euphoric component of the venom his fangs released to ease the incision and immobilize them for the duration of the blood drawing, but pureblooded females didn't, and apparently, neither did immortals.

Lifting her hand, she cupped his cheek. "Did you hold back?"

"I didn't."

"Liar."

"Just a tiny bit."

"You don't need to. I can take everything you have to give and more."

"No kidding." He caressed her soft hair. "You're incredible, Vanessa. I've never come so hard with anyone before."

Her smile was full of bliss. "Same for me. I've never had anyone satisfy me as thoroughly as you just did. We were made for each other."

Despite her generous compliment, despite the two orgasms he'd given her, and despite her satisfied smile, he still had a feeling that it hadn't been enough. The night was young, though, and they had many more hours to perfect their sex game.

Pushing Vanessa onto her back, he entered her again and started thrusting slowly, teasing her. When she closed her eyes, and her lips parted on a moan, he dipped his head and took her nipple between his lips.

He hadn't paid homage to them during the first round, and he was going to rectify his oversight in the second, the third, and the fourth.

She bucked under him, spurring him to go faster, but he wasn't done feasting on her sweet berries and switched to her other breast.

When she kept bucking, he clamped a hand on her hip and gently bit down on her nipple.

She hissed, but the renewed slickness coating his shaft betrayed how much she enjoyed this new game. He repeated the same torment on the other side, and her response was the same.

When he kissed her, she retaliated, biting his lip until she drew blood.

He wanted her to take more, to suck on the wound she'd made and drink him as he had drunk her, but it wasn't her way, and she licked the small hurt away.

When Vanessa smiled and licked his blood off her lips, it was like pulling a trigger. The discharge was as immediate and as explosive as the first. Only when his tremors had subsided did he realize that he'd failed to make her climax alongside him. Shame flooding him, he groaned and dropped his head.

19

VANESSA

Mo-red was just as dominant as Vanessa had hoped he would be, and he'd more than satisfied her, but there was so much more she wanted to explore with him.

Not tonight, though. She could easily keep going, but he seemed totally drained.

They could experiment tomorrow night and, hopefully, for many more nights to come. Heck, sex wasn't limited to nighttime, so they could experiment during the day as well.

"I'm sorry," he whispered into the crook of her neck.

"For what?" She caressed his slim and yet very muscular back.

Was it her imagination, or was he much heavier than his build implied?

"You didn't orgasm this time." He lifted his head and looked into her eyes.

She chuckled. "As I said, we have the whole night ahead of us, and I can function on three hours of sleep. That leaves plenty of time for many more orgasms."

He smiled. "You're going to be the death of me, but what a way to go...."

She cupped his ass and gave it a squeeze. "I'm just trying to help you get that record you're after. Two down and ten to go."

"I don't need much sleep either, but I need a few minutes to recuperate."

"I have an idea. How about a shower and a coffee break?"

They hadn't spent enough time talking and getting to know each other as people.

"Wouldn't it break the spell?"

She tightened her arms around him. "I can put a new one on you any time I want."

"That's true." He was still inside of her and seemed reluctant to leave.

Then she felt him hardening and wondered whether her coffee break idea had been premature.

"Are the few minutes you needed up already?" she asked.

"It would seem so." He dipped his head and took her lips in a soft kiss. "All it took to get me hard again was thinking about the exquisite taste of your blood."

"Was it different than others you've tasted?"

"Very different." He started moving slowly inside of her. "It's like comparing water to vodka. One is necessary for survival, but the other one has one hell of an unforgettable kick."

It wasn't the best analogy she'd heard, but given Mo-red's limited palate, he probably couldn't come up with anything better.

Looking at his handsome face, feeling him inside of her, it was easy to forget that they weren't even from the same species. She could never cook a meal for him or take him on a date to a restaurant, and given that it was a big part of how humans and immortals socialized, it would be difficult.

Still, Jade and Phinas seemed to be doing fine despite their culinary differences, so it wasn't an unbridgeable problem.

"Hey." He nipped the tip of her nose. "Where have you gone? Stay with me."

"I'm sorry."

In a swift move, he pulled back while lifting her with him, and she found herself sitting on him face to face.

He kissed her as he shafted up into her, and soon she couldn't remember what she'd been thinking about that had gotten her distracted. When his hand reached between their bodies, and he pressed his finger to her clitoris, she moaned into his mouth and dug her fingers into his muscular shoulders.

He was all hard, solid planes, and she felt softer and more feminine in his arms than ever before. Being tall and slim, it wasn't something she experienced often. She could get used to this.

"Vanessa," he murmured into her mouth. "I want you to come for me."

She was close, but after orgasming twice, she wasn't sure she could do it again.

But then he bit the spot he'd bitten before, and the bite of pain, along with the effect of his venom, sent her over the edge. As he kept sucking on her blood, a string of gentle climaxes rolled through her, and her tether on reality snapped.

She soared on a euphoric cloud, passing over alien landscapes with a kaleidoscope of colors that were not part of her reality, and she had the passing thought that she was in a different dimension.

The sensation lasted for what seemed like hours, and when she finally came back down to earth, she was snuggled under the blanket within the protective shield of Mo-red's strong arms.

"Welcome back," he whispered.

"How long was I gone?"

"Not long. Fifteen minutes or so."

"Wow. It felt like I've been soaring for hours." She looked at his eyes that no longer glowed red but blue-green. "I didn't know that your venom could do that."

"Was it good?"

"It was amazing." She closed her eyes and nestled closer into his warm chest. "I don't think I have any energy left for nine more rounds."

He chuckled. "Thank the Mother. Neither do I."

20

MO-RED

Mo-red stayed awake long after Vanessa had fallen asleep. Full of wonder at the boon the Mother had bestowed on him, he was afraid to close his eyes, in case he opened them again only to discover that it had all been a dream.

Miracles like this didn't happen to males like him. He didn't deserve a female like Vanessa. A goddess, or as close to a goddess as he could have ever gotten.

What did she see in him?

Why had she chosen him?

He hadn't done anything to deserve her trust.

Eventually, he drifted off to sleep, and when he opened his eyes again, Vanessa wasn't in bed with him.

He had a moment of panic, thinking that he'd dreamt it all after all, but then he heard the shower running and smelled the fresh scent of coffee she'd brewed in the coffee maker.

As his heartbeat slowed back down to normal, he considered joining Vanessa in the shower. But perhaps she enjoyed having her showers in private and wouldn't appreciate him barging in on her.

He'd never showered with a female before, and he definitely didn't know the clan females' preferences and what the proper boundaries were.

If he had dared to impose on a pureblooded female like that, she would have clawed his eyes out. Humans were amenable to sharing their bathing time, but he hadn't been inclined to spend such intimate time with them.

Well, that wasn't true.

It would have been inappropriate of him to do so in the compound. He hadn't had a private bathing chamber, and to bring a woman to the one he was sharing with two other purebloods would have been frowned upon or worse.

Igor wouldn't have approved for sure.

He wondered what was going on with the compeller and whether he'd been forced into disclosing information about who he really was. Igor had always been an enigma, a puzzle that Mo-red hadn't been able to figure out.

Perhaps now that he and Vanessa had gotten closer, he could ask her. Then again, he didn't want her to think that he was with her because she was a source of information or because he needed her help to keep his head attached to his neck.

When the bathroom door opened, and Vanessa walked out with a towel wrapped around her body, he inhaled her scent, and all his anxious thoughts vanished. "Good morning."

"Good morning to you too." She leaned down and kissed him on the lips. "Did you sleep well?"

"I couldn't fall asleep for a long time. I was afraid that I would wake up and discover that it was all a dream."

She emitted a throaty laugh that sent an electric bolt straight to his balls.

"All you had to do was sniff the sheets to reassure yourself that my presence was not a dream."

He did as she suggested and lifted the blanket to his nose. "Oh, yeah. I see what you mean."

"You want to say that you smell what I mean." She took the mug of freshly brewed coffee from the stand and came to sit next to him on the bed. "Thank you for last night."

"No, thank you." He pushed up on the pillows. "Do you have to be anywhere this morning?"

She took a sip from her coffee. "Regrettably, yes. I have a full day of meetings."

"Can I ask with whom?"

She nodded. "Edna and I have postponed evaluating Valstar, but it's time we got around to him. If nothing else comes up to interfere with our plans, we will do it today with Kian watching through the surveillance feed."

"Be careful. Valstar is not a compeller, but he's smart and manipulative."

She nodded. "That's what Jade says. But don't worry, I can see through the layers of pretense people put up to shield their true nature. Then again, I'm not there to judge his character. I only need to determine whether he was Igor's victim or his willing accomplice."

Mo-red let out a breath. "Does it matter? We are judged based on our deeds, not our intentions. That's why I don't have much hope for the results of my trial to be anything other than a guilty verdict. I am guilty."

She put a hand on his thigh. "These are very special circumstances, and I'll work with Lusha to make sure that she presents your case as it should be presented. Your will was taken away from you, and you had to do what Igor told you. You were just a tool in his hands, or rather his mind."

"When is Lusha getting here?"

"Today." Vanessa rose to her feet and put her coffee cup

away. "I didn't ask, but do you drink coffee? I know that Jade does."

"I do."

"Do you want me to make you some before I leave?"

"I would rather enjoy it with you." He threw the blanket off, dropped his feet over the side of the bed, and stood up.

Vanessa's eyes traveled over his body. "Oh, my. You're making it difficult for me to leave."

"Then don't." He palmed his erection. "We still have nine rounds to go."

She laughed. "We stopped and went to sleep, so the count starts anew tonight, lover of mine."

He pulled her into his arms. "Can't you stay just a little bit longer?"

She wound her arms around his neck. "I can stay ten more minutes and have coffee with you."

"I'm okay with skipping coffee in favor of a much more pleasurable activity."

He might be running out of time, and he wanted to spend as much of what life he had left enjoying Vanessa.

"Hmm. Ten minutes." She looked at him from under lowered lashes. "Go to the bathroom to wash up, and I'll meet you there in two."

21

KIAN

"Good morning." Kian greeted Bridget and Turner and directed them to the conference table. "Is Julian joining us?"

After all, the young doctor was the one who had experience with the so-called truth drug.

"He's on his way," Bridget said. "After you called me last night, I did some research on the subject, and those drugs are highly unreliable." She turned to her mate. "Victor agrees."

"They have their uses." He popped the lid on his thermos and took a sip.

"The question is whether they would work on Igor." Bridget let out a breath. "Victor is confident that his chemist can cook up a combination that will make the Kra-ell sing, but I'm not sure he's right. We are not dealing with just a compeller. He also has an incredibly strong mind and was probably trained to withstand interrogation."

As a knock sounded at the door, Kian rose to his feet and opened it for Julian.

"Good morning." The doctor gave him an apologetic smile.

"I'm sorry I'm late, and I can't even use traffic as an excuse." He chuckled. "Although I have to say that I've never seen the café busier. I had to elbow my way through the crowd to get to the building's front door."

Julian was exaggerating for comedic effect, but it was true that the café was overcrowded.

The Kra-ell purebloods didn't eat sandwiches or pastries, but they enjoyed sipping coffee or just plain water and mingling with each other and the clan. Many of them had never before gotten to enjoy such freedom and relaxation, and Kian was glad that they were venturing out of their homes and making an effort to socialize with their new community.

As always, his gut had been correct, and it was the right decision to invite these people to join the clan.

He'd done a good deed, and hopefully it wouldn't bite him in the ass and prove his motto that no good deed went unpunished.

"We should enlarge the café," Turner said. "The grassy area we use for celebrations could be outfitted with tables, and Jackson can get a mobile cart with all the equipment that's needed to double the café's production capacity. Some of the young Kra-ell can be recruited as servers and get training from Wonder and Aliya."

"Excellent idea." Kian clapped Turner on the back before sitting down. "The more everyone mingles, the faster the integration. But let's get back to the subject at hand. We need to find a way to break into Igor's mind and get the truth out of him. Jade suggested that we can lower his resistance with drugs, which might help Toven break through, especially if he uses Mia's enhancing powers." He looked at Julian. "You used those drugs on Eleanor. What's your take on them?"

"We used them on Eleanor to make her forget us and what

we did to her. Denying her bathroom privileges was effective enough in getting her to talk. But don't forget that the stakes were much lower and that she was human at the time. Revealing Jin's location was not all that detrimental to Eleanor, so her resistance was more out of spite and stubbornness than fear for her life."

"True." Kian rubbed his jaw between his thumb and forefinger. "But since Eleanor was already immune to compulsion and thralling, she wasn't a run-of-the-mill human. She's also tough, smart, and stubborn, but she hadn't been trained to withstand torture, which was why denying her bathroom privileges worked."

"It's still worth a try," Julian said. "Worst case, it doesn't work."

"But how would we know that it doesn't?" Bridget asked. "The problem is not to get Igor to talk but to get him to tell the truth, and since we don't have a way to prove or disprove his claims, we have to be sure that he can't lie, and that's where the drugs can be effective. Telling the truth doesn't require a sharp mind, but making up stories does. Hopefully, when Igor's mind is muddled enough, he won't have the faculties to fabricate stories." She turned to Kian. "One of the first questions you should ask him is why he drank your blood, and the second is whether he has a way to transmit information to his handlers. We assume that they are on Anumati, but they could be anywhere. For all we know, they could be hiding on the dark side of the moon."

"You're right." Kian raked his finger through his hair, annoyed that he hadn't thought of that.

Since Earth had satellites orbiting the solar system that could take and transmit pictures from the dark side of the moon, Bridget had meant it metaphorically. Still, the gods could have technology that would camouflage their settlement and make it invisible to the satellite's cameras.

Julian nodded enthusiastically. "They could have a cloaking device like the one the Klingons used in *Star Trek*. Igor's handlers are gods, so they are probably still alive even seven thousand years later, and since they have interstellar travel capabilities, they could be anywhere in our solar system or others that are closer to us than their home planet."

Or they could be around the corner and communicating telepathically with Igor—

Cold sweat slithered down Kian's back. "Ella and Vivian can communicate telepathically regardless of distance or barriers. What if Igor can communicate telepathically with someone on Anumati? Mind waves, or however else telepathy works, are not the kind of transmissions we can detect."

There was a long moment of silence as everyone processed Kian's words.

"Crap." Turner snagged his thermos off the table and popped the lid. "That's the first question you need to ask Igor, not the second."

Bridget nodded. "I feel stupid for not thinking about this possibility sooner."

Julian huffed. "I'm Ella's mate. It should have occurred to me as soon as I learned about Igor."

"It's not a competition for who's stupider," Kian said. "Telepathic communication is such a rare ability, even rarer than compulsion or immunity, that it didn't occur to any of us that Igor might have it." He looked at Turner. "How soon can your chemist supply us with the drugs?"

"I can put in a rush order and have it delivered by tomorrow morning."

"Good. Do it, and ask for a large quantity. We will need to

test it on Jade first and probably on a couple of other pure-bloods as well."

"I don't think we should rush anything." Bridget shifted in her chair and crossed her legs. "Even if Igor communicated with someone on Anumati and informed them that he found a god and a group of hybrid descendants, it would take them centuries to get here."

"We don't know that," Kian said. "Their technology might have advanced dramatically since the settler ship left, and as you said before, they could have teams or whole settlements that are close to us that they could deploy on a moment's notice." He closed his eyes and leaned back in his chair. "We might have to come up with better ways to hide after all."

"Igor doesn't know where he is," Bridget said. "If the gods come looking for us, they have the same chance of finding us here as anywhere else. Ella and Vivian can talk to each other in their minds, but they don't have a built-in GPS. If you put them underground somewhere, they wouldn't know where they are."

"His handlers might know," Turner said. "We didn't remove the tracker from Igor before bringing him to the keep. That location is compromised, but the village is still safe."

Kian let out a long breath. "If the gods have monitored the signals, they also know about Safe Haven. That's two locations that are potentially compromised."

"I don't get it," Julian said. "If they've known where Igor was all along, why haven't they intervened?"

"They had no reason to." Kian gave him a tight smile. "They don't care about the Kra-ell. All they care about are Ahn's descendants, and as far as they know, there are none."

"So we are safe here," Julian said.

"Not really." Kian cast a sidelong glance at Turner, who looked as somber as Kian felt. "They might decide to clean up what's left of the settler gods. And if they found out about us, they might start searching. In today's world, it's very difficult to hide from those who know what to look for."

Bridget lifted a brow. "So, what are you suggesting, that we move to a different world?"

"I'm not suggesting anything. Contrary to popular belief, I don't have the answers to everything."

22

MARCEL

"Finally, it's done." Marcel put the phone he had just finished programming into the box next to William's desk. "This was the last one."

They'd literally worked day and night to prepare phones for the Kra-ell that would allow them to communicate within the village and surf the internet but block them from calling or transmitting any information outside of it. The programming hadn't been complicated, but there had been a lot of devices that needed to be modified.

William winced. "I'm not looking forward to all the questions we will have to answer. Most of these people haven't held a smartphone in their lives."

Kaia swiveled her chair around. "We should put the teenagers in charge of teaching the Kra-ell how to use their new toys."

"Awesome idea, my love." William beamed at his mate. "Can you call Cheryl and have her organize a team?"

She smiled indulgently. "Cheryl is in school right now, and so are Parker and Lisa."

"Right." He pushed his glasses up his nose. "I forgot."

"That's okay." Marcel lifted the heavy box and put it on his shoulder. "I'll get Sofia, and we will gather a few of the young Kra-ell. Those who served as guards are familiar with smartphones, so teaching them to operate these will be a breeze, and they can teach the others."

It was a great excuse to go home in the middle of the day and bother his mate.

After deciding to work from home, she'd applied to a couple of sites for freelancers and was immediately offered several translation jobs. There weren't many translators that were fluent in Finnish, Russian, English, and several other languages.

It was a shame that she hadn't allowed herself at least a couple of months of vacation, especially since they were working on her transition.

At the thought, Marcel's gut clenched, and he didn't know whether it was from worry that her transition was imminent or that it wasn't going to happen.

They had started five days ago, so there was no reason to get worried about it not happening yet, but Sofia was stressed, and that wasn't helping things.

Maybe the translation job she'd begun working on would help her to relax. Sofia was enjoying translating the Russian romance novel into English.

When Marcel got home, the first thing he noticed was how stuffy and warm it was.

Putting the box full of cell phones on the counter, he turned on the air conditioning and headed toward the guest bedroom that Sofia had turned into her workspace.

"Hello, darling." He leaned down and kissed her neck. "How is it going?"

"Slower than I expected." She wiped the sweat off her forehead. "What are you doing home so early?"

"The phones are finally ready, and I volunteered to distribute them. Since you speak Kra-ell, you can explain how they work to some of the young ones, and they will explain to the others."

Sofia didn't look happy about getting drafted for the job. "I'm a little under the weather today. You can get Pavel or Gordi or any of the other males who served as guards to do that. They know how cell phones work."

He'd stopped listening after the under-the-weather comment. "What's wrong? Do you have a fever?"

She put a hand on her forehead. "I don't think so. I've just been sitting here for too long with my head bent down over the book. Maybe I need to stretch my limbs and get some fresh air."

"Yeah, that's a good idea." He offered her a hand up.

She took it, which was a good thing because as soon as she pushed to her feet, she swayed and would have fallen backward if he hadn't been holding onto her.

He pulled her toward him and held her against his chest. "I think you should see Bridget, or rather she needs to see you."

Sofia lifted a pair of hopeful eyes to him. "Do you think it's the transition?"

"It might be. Bridget will know. I hope."

"Oh, wow." Sofia lifted a shaky hand to her forehead. "What about the translation?"

He chuckled nervously. "Don't worry about it. I'll find someone to do it for you if need be. But who knows? Maybe you can get back to it sooner rather than later. Some take only a couple of days to get back on their feet. You might be one of the lucky ones."

Neither of them believed his pep talk, but Sofia nodded. "I

hope so. Should I pack a bag? You know, in case Bridget decides that I need to stay in the clinic?"

"That's a good idea. Although I should probably pack it for you." He wrapped his arm around her middle, led her to the bedroom, and gently sat her down on the bed. "Just tell me what to put in the bag."

23

JADE

Onegus regarded the three young males Jade brought with her with a critical eye. "So, Jade tells me that you all served as guards in the compound."

"Yes, sir," Pavel said.

Gordi and Dugmon nodded.

"Did you volunteer to help us guard the prisoners, or were you recruited?" He glanced at Jade.

Gordi's English was barely passable, so Jade translated.

"I was recruited," Gordi said.

Onegus shook his head. "I can't use him until he learns more English."

The guy looked relieved.

"How about you, Pavel? Did you volunteer?"

"Yes, I did, sir. Everyone knows that my father is one of the prisoners, so my motives are clear. I want to spend more time with him in case, you know—" He swallowed. "In case my campaign fails."

Onegus arched a brow. "What campaign?"

"My brothers and I are making the rounds, trying to convince our people that our father was as much a victim of

Igor as the rest of them. My logic is that the more we repeat it, the more they will internalize it."

Jade respected that, and she wondered what Drova had to say about her friend's campaign. He was trying to save his father by blaming everything on hers.

Was she okay with that?

Onegus leaned back and crossed his arms over his chest. "That's admirable, but letting you guard your father is a conflict of interest. What if you help him escape?"

It was such an absurd notion that Jade had to stifle an eye roll.

Gripping Pavel's hand, she lifted his arm so his cuff was in Onegus's face. "There is no way he can help anyone escape, and you know it. Why are you taunting him?"

"Because I'm in charge of security, and that's my job. Right, Pavel? You understand why I have to do this?"

"Yes, sir. I do. But even if I wanted to bust my father out or had the means to do that, he wouldn't want to be busted out."

"And why is that?"

Onegus had to know about the therapist shacking up with Mo-red in a cell in the dungeon. He probably wanted to get Pavel's reaction to that.

"He moved in with the clan psychologist," Pavel said. "I'm sure that's not news to you."

"It's not. How do you feel about this development?"

Pavel shrugged. "It's very nice of Vanessa to give him affection at a time like this. I'm sure he's grateful."

Onegus smiled. "I'm sure he is, but my question was how you felt about it."

"I'm happy for him."

For a moment, Onegus just looked at the young male, and Jade wondered whether he was trying to sniff his emotions.

The immortals were good at that, but the Kra-ell were even better at hiding their emotional scents.

The trick was not to let their emotions surface. As long as they were buried deep within, they didn't produce discernible smells.

"Good." Onegus turned to Dugmon. "What about you? Is your father down there?"

"My grandfather is, but you won't find any males unrelated to Igor's inner circle. Half of those who were born in the compound are related to one or more of the prisoners. The other half is related to those who Jade and Kagra killed."

"Which one is your grandfather?"

"Volpath."

Gordi cleared his throat and asked in Russian, "Can I go?"

"Yes." Jade waved him off. "You're dismissed."

He dipped his head and turned on his heel.

"Is it okay if I let him find his way to the surface by himself?" she asked Onegus.

"Yeah. Between the compulsion he is under and the cuff, he can't get into any trouble." The chief picked up the receiver off the boxy phone on his desk. "I need to check with Kian to make sure that he's okay with these males assisting the Guardians."

"Of course," Jade agreed. "Do you want us to wait outside?"

"No need. It will only take a moment."

There was only one guest chair in Onegus's small office, and she debated whether to sit down or wait with the two males for Kian's verdict.

She knew Kian would approve because she'd run the idea by him already, but Onegus was following proper protocol, and she had no problem with that.

"This is just a formality," she told Pavel quietly.

"Good afternoon, boss," Onegus said. "I have Jade here with two young Kra-ell males who want to help the Guardians down in the dungeon. One is Mo-red's son, and the other is Volpath's grandson. Do you think it's a good idea?"

As he listened to the reply, which for some reason she couldn't hear, Jade wondered if Onegus's office phone was specially configured to keep the sound of the speaker on the other side from leaking out.

"Yes, I see. Okay." Onegus returned the headset to the receiver. "Kian said it was fine. You can bring them with you when he picks you up later today, and they can get oriented while you are there. They will return to the village with you."

"Will I be able to speak with my father?" Pavel asked.

"I don't see why not. I'll call Magnus and approve it."

"Thank you, sir. I appreciate it."

24

SOFIA

"Bridget is not in at the moment," the nurse said as Sofia walked in with Marcel. "I assume that you are here because you suspect you're transitioning?"

Sofia nodded. "Marcel had to practically carry me over here. I'm dizzy, and I feel weak."

"Let's settle you in a room, then." The nurse opened the door to one of the treatment rooms and motioned for Marcel to take Sofia inside. "I'm Gertrude." She offered Sofia her hand. "Don't worry. I'll take good care of you."

A series of basic tests ensued. Her temperature was taken and recorded, her blood pressure measured, and while the nurse took several vials of blood from her, Marcel typed furiously on his phone.

"Who are you messaging?" she asked.

"A couple of my friends, asking them to find your father, your aunt, and Helmi, to let them know that you are in the clinic."

"Isn't it too early? What if I just caught a bug?"

"Then they will escort you home, we will put a couple of pizzas in the oven and have a nice family get-together."

"I just don't want to get everyone's hopes up." Herself included.

Sofia didn't get sick often. In fact, she hadn't been sick in a long time, so maybe this was the transition. But who knew? She could have caught something during the voyage.

Yeah, that wasn't likely.

She'd been surrounded by immortals and Kra-ell, who didn't get infected with human viruses and didn't transmit them.

When Gertrude was done, she patted her shoulder and stepped out of the room, leaving Sofia and Marcel alone.

"Let's place some bets." Marcel sat on the bed next to her. "Who do you think will get here first, Bridget or your father?"

He was trying to distract her so she wouldn't get stressed, and she loved him for it. "It depends on who gets the news first and where they are when they hear it. My father is most likely with the animals, while Bridget might be in the office building."

"I still bet on your father. If I win, you owe me a kiss."

"Wait, I didn't bet against him. I just said that it depended on where he and the doctor were at the moment."

"So place your bets."

She closed her eyes. "I bet that Helmi will get here first because she will run while my father and Bridget will not. My father because he has bad knees and Bridget because she's too important to rush on my account. If I win, you owe me a foot massage."

As the door flew open a moment later and Helmi stood in the doorway out of breath and panting, Sofia laughed. "I win!"

"What did you win?" Helmi put a hand on her side and ambled into the room. "I was afraid that you'd be unconscious when I got here." She leaned down and kissed Sofia's cheek. "I've heard horror stories about people losing consciousness."

"Who did you talk to?" Marcel asked.

"Oh, many people." Helmi sat on the bed. "I was in the café today, training to become a barista."

"That's great." Sofia took her cousin's hand and gave it a squeeze. "When do you start working there?"

"Tomorrow. Wonder and Aliya wanted me to put an apron on and start right away, and I would have said yes if not for Percy, who told me that you were in the clinic. How did I miss you getting here? I should have seen you from the café."

Sofia shook her head. "Who's Percy?"

"A Guardian," Marcel said. "One of those I asked to find your family."

"Hello, Sofia." Bridget walked through the open door and cast Helmi a stern look. "I'm sorry, but you will have to step outside and wait in the reception area. Only one person is allowed to be with the patient inside her room."

The doctor had her white medical coat on, but it was open, and underneath, she wore a tight red skirt, a white blouse, and four-inch red spiky heels. She looked like one of those fake doctors on television, but the air of authority she carried around her like a shield was real.

"Yes, ma'am!" Helmi scurried away.

"Can I stay?" Marcel asked.

"You can." Bridget pulled a small tablet out of her coat pocket and turned to Sofia. "Your blood pressure is elevated, and your temperature is only slightly higher than normal. Any aches or pains?"

Sofia shook her head. "It's only a general feeling of weakness and dizziness."

Bridget nodded. "At this stage, all we can do is wait and see what happens next. I'm waiting for the results of the blood tests to rule out infections and other possible causes." She smiled. "Just to be safe, I told Gertrude to check for pregnancy."

Sofia's throat dried out. "We only stopped using condoms five days ago. I wouldn't be displaying symptoms yet."

"Condoms are not fail-proof, and you could have gotten pregnant before."

Sofia had read the statistics, and ninety-eight percent was pretty fail-proof in her book. Although that was only if they were used correctly, and she was sure Marcel had been as meticulous about that as he was about everything else.

Marcel cleared his throat. "You might have forgotten, but we didn't use condoms in the beginning."

Sofia had a moment of panic before remembering that she'd had her cycle since.

"I've gotten my period, so I obviously didn't get pregnant then."

"It was just a standard precaution," Bridget said. "Your symptoms might be due to a common cold or some other medical reason, or you might be transitioning. I just don't want you to get your hopes up."

"I haven't been sick in years. The last time I remember getting anything was strep throat, and it was during my teens."

"Then there is a good chance that you are transitioning. We will know for sure soon."

"How soon?" Marcel asked.

"Within the next twenty-four hours."

25

KIAN

After Jade had left the young Kra-ell in Magnus's care, she, Kian, and the brothers headed to Kian's old office, where Edna was already waiting for them.

"Can I see him first?" Edna asked. "I just want to know who to expect when I walk into his cell."

Jade pulled out a chair next to her. "Didn't you read his file?"

"Vanessa didn't prepare one for Valstar. We decided that I should probe him first."

"I see." Jade leaned back. "And where is the lovely therapist? Is she in Mo-red's cell?"

Kian cast her a stern look. "Do you have a problem with her and Mo-red being together?"

"Yeah, I do." She crossed her arms over her chest. "I didn't want to say anything in front of Pavel, but that's highly unprofessional of Vanessa. She's supposed to be an impartial observer and offer her professional opinion. If she were a Kra-ell, I would dismiss it as nothing more than sexual curiosity because we usually don't get emotional about sex, but your females are different. She must have developed feelings for him, and that disqualifies her from giving her opinion on his culpability in the crimes he committed."

The problem was that Kian couldn't argue with her about that because she was right.

"Vanessa thinks that it will help his case rather than hinder it. Her involvement with him will signal more than anything she could say in his favor that she thinks he's innocent."

"That might be," Edna said. "But she can't testify on his behalf. I suggest that she doesn't go on the stand at all. I'll read through her reports, and that should be the extent of her involvement."

As the door opened and Vanessa walked in, all eyes went to her, and she stiffened. "Is my lipstick smeared?"

"You look perfect," Jade bit out. "Perfectly...rested."

Kian had to agree. Vanessa looked like a well-satisfied female, and he was glad of it. She'd been all work and no play for too long. He just wished that her male wasn't facing a trial for murder.

If his people sentenced him to death, it would devastate Vanessa, and the clan would lose its only therapist.

Perhaps he shouldn't have allowed her to move in with the prisoner.

Anandur rose to his feet and pulled out a chair for Vanessa. "Don't mind Jade. She's in a bad mood today."

"I'm not." Jade crossed her arms over her chest. "I'm in a great mood. I finally have a phone."

"Congratulations," Vanessa said. "It's about time."

"Yeah, it is." Jade uncrossed her arms and leaned forward. "Look, I'm not one to beat around the bush. Your relationship with Mo-red is a problem. You're not impartial."

Vanessa cast her a cold look. "I'm never impartial. That's Edna's job, not mine. I get involved, and I don't try to hide my feelings or my opinions. Mo-red is a good male who was abused and victimized by Igor like the rest of you. Madbar is just an average schmo, but he's not inherently bad, and neither are the other prisoners I have interviewed. The only one I'm not sure about is Balboth."

Jade glared at her for a long moment but then nodded. "You are not wrong, which is why they are still alive. I don't know what's the right thing to do with them. Based on Kra-ell customs, they are guilty and should be executed, but that doesn't mean that I agree with that law or think it's just." She shifted her gaze to Edna. "What's your opinion, judge?"

"I need more information to form one, but our law prohibits executions. That being said, entombment is an extreme punishment as well, and we reserve it only for the worst criminals."

"Like Igor?"

Edna shrugged. "I don't have all the information yet about him either, and until I do, I'm not going to decide his fate even in my mind. My job is to evaluate the evidence and come up with a verdict based on it. My personal opinion is irrelevant."

Kian flipped his laptop open, scrolled through the surveillance feed until he found Valstar's cell, and turned the device toward Edna. "This is Valstar."

"May I?" Edna pulled the laptop closer to her.

"Of course."

"He looks resigned."

Jade huffed. "Of course, he does. He knows there is no way out for him. The only reason Valstar is still alive is that we needed him in case Igor called the compound, and after that, Toven didn't allow me to kill him because Valstar convinced him that he was a victim like the rest of us."

Edna lifted her intense gaze to Jade. "Toven is very old, and he is not naive. If he believes that Valstar deserves to be heard, I wouldn't make light of it."

"Valstar is a master manipulator, and Toven has a good heart." Jade winced. "I can't believe that I'm saying that about a god. Toven must be one of a kind." She cast Kian a sidelong glance. "Is your mother as kind-hearted as he is?"

"Even more so. My mother is all heart."

It was only a slight exaggeration. Annani could be ruthless when necessary, but she seldom showed that side of herself.

"A word of warning. Never mention my mother to Igor. As far as he's concerned, Toven is the only surviving god."

"He's not stupid," Jade said. "He knows that you are the descendant of a different god."

"Yes, but he doesn't know which one or whether that god is still around."

"Why is it important?" Jade leaned forward. "Igor is not going anywhere, and he's not going to tell anyone."

"I wish I was as convinced of that as you are." Kian pushed to his feet and offered Edna a hand up. "Let's get it over with. I'll escort you to Valstar's cell. The rest of us are going to watch you from the control room."

Vanessa pushed to her feet. "How come he is not being taken to the interview room like the others?"

"He doesn't have a roommate," Anandur explained. "So, there is no need to take him out to a different room, and because he's considered high risk, the less we move him around, the better."

26

JADE

As they entered the control room, Jade scanned the monitors looking for Valstar. Next to her, Vanessa did the same thing.

"What is Mo-red doing back with Madbar?" the therapist asked.

"He asked to spend time with him." Magnus vacated his chair and motioned for her to take it. "It's boring to be alone all day long."

"I should bring him some books," Vanessa murmured under her breath as she sat down.

When Kian offered Jade the only other chair in the room, she shook her head. "I would never dream of sitting while you're standing." She leaned against the desk and crossed her feet at the ankles.

"My mother would be appalled if I let you stand while I sit." He waved a hand at the chair. "Please, sit down."

Jade crossed her arms over her chest. "You're the leader. You should be the one sitting."

He grimaced. "You are a stubborn female, Jade."

She smiled. "I know, but you like me anyway."

The therapist watched their exchange with an amused expression on her pretty face. "You two are getting along much better than I would have ever expected."

"It's my charming personality," Jade deadpanned, catching from the corner of her eye a rare smile lifting Brundar's lips.

Vanessa laughed. "You two are too much alike. Who would have thought?"

"Not me." Anandur leaned against the desk next to her. "But here we are. She even laughs at my jokes."

"Not all of them." Jade nudged his shoulder. "Some are funny, and some are not."

"Most are not," Brundar murmured.

"You just don't have a sense of humor, brother."

On the screen, Edna took hold of Valstar's hands, and her expression turned pained.

Jade uttered a curse that, thankfully, none of the others understood. "She's encountering resistance."

"She'll be fine," Kian said. "Edna is tough."

As the minutes ticked off, and Edna and Valstar just stared into each other's eyes, Jade became impatient.

"Did you speak with Bridget about the drugs?" she asked Kian.

"Yes. Turner is getting them for us tomorrow. Are you still volunteering to be our test bunny?"

"I am." She uncrossed her arms and gripped the desk on both sides. "What better way to prove that I have no more secrets from you?"

Kian smiled. "Actually, it would be better if you had some. Otherwise, how will we know whether it works?"

Vanessa frowned. "What are you talking about?"

As Kian explained, Vanessa's frown deepened. "I strongly advise against using Jade as a test bunny." She turned to Jade. "These drugs are especially dangerous for people with PTSD.

They can worsen your symptoms. I suggest testing them on a couple of young purebloods who haven't suffered a trauma."

"I don't have PTSD." Jade looked down her nose at the therapist. "I suffered a trauma, and it affected me, but I'm fine now."

"Do you still have flashbacks? Do you have nightmares? Do you get anxious?"

"Yes, on the flashbacks. I no longer have nightmares, and I'm not anxious."

Vanessa shook her head. "Your heart rate accelerates every time you need to face Igor, and it's not because you are attracted to him. That's an anxious response."

Jade let out a huff. "I lived in fear for decades. What do you expect?"

Vanessa's eyes softened. "I'm not judging you. I think you are incredibly brave. But you shouldn't be subjected to that class of drugs. Let someone else be the hero for a change."

When Jade opened her mouth to argue, Kian lifted his hand to stop her. "Enough. I'm accepting Vanessa's professional recommendation. Find other volunteers."

Kian seemed more short-tempered than usual, and the therapist seemed to share Jade's opinion. "What's bothering you, Kian?" Vanessa asked softly.

He let out a breath. "I had a very disturbing thought this morning while I discussed Jade's idea with Turner and the doctors. We didn't detect any signals coming off of Igor, but there is a form of communication that doesn't emit any signals that we can pick up and is distance-agnostic." He looked at Vanessa. "The kind that Ella and Vivian share."

The therapist sucked in a breath. "Do you think Igor is a telepath?"

"I don't know that he is for sure, but he might be. If he has a connection with someone on Anumati, he can transmit information in real time, and we wouldn't be any the wiser."

"Kra-ell aren't telepaths," Jade said. "We can't read thoughts."

"Most of us can't either." Kian raked his fingers through his longish hair. "But Vivian and her daughter can conduct conversations telepathically, and their communication is not hindered by distance. They are the only two we know of who can do that, but that doesn't mean they are the only ones in the universe. There might be gods who can communicate that way, and since they are masters of genetic manipulation, they could have given Igor the ability. If the gods on Anumati know that at least one god survived and that the gods left plenty of hybrid descendants, what will they do with that knowledge? Will they come to finish the job?"

"Aren't you getting ahead of yourself?" Anandur said. "You came up with a hypothesis and went straight to talking about it as if it was a fact. We don't know whether Igor can do that."

"We don't, but it's crucial that we find out." Kian let out a breath. "So far, my paranoia has proven to be more foresight than delusion."

27

VANESSA

As they waited for Edna to be done, Vanessa's mind churned.

What if Kian was right?

Vivian and Ella were proof that it was possible to transmit thoughts across vast distances, so it wasn't a big stretch to assume that the gods were aware of it and had even figured out how it worked and what genes were responsible for the ability.

The implications were staggering, and not just in regard to Igor and what information he could potentially pass to the gods.

If the ability was innate in all the humanoid species that the gods had created with the help of their genetic material, and everyone was broadcasting on some level without being aware of it, it could explain so many previously inexplicable phenomena.

It was possible that telepathic transmission worked on the quantum level and was independent of time as well as of distance, which would explain foresight and remote viewing. It could also explain how breakthroughs and innovations tended to sprout at the same time in disparate locations.

It also reinforced Vanessa's belief that all intelligent life in the universe was interconnected on some level.

Talk about a mind bend.

Heck, it wasn't even limited to humanoids. What about dogs who knew when their owners were coming home, the moment the desire to come home arose, and before a single step was taken to begin the journey?

Her mind was spinning with the implications. It was ironic that the information had been there ever since Vivian and Ella had joined the clan, but no one had thought of their ability as anything more than a curiosity, a nifty trick, or in Lokan's case, a way to exploit their talents for his own benefit. It just showed how a slight change in perspective could lead to new discoveries, new possibilities, to new ways of thinking about things.

"Edna is taking a long time," Anandur said. "She's going to be exhausted."

Kian nodded. "She doesn't look good."

It took another ten minutes or so before Edna finally released Valstar's hands and leaned back in her chair.

She looked like she'd been through a battle, while he just looked anxious.

"So, how did I do?" Valstar asked.

Edna lifted her hand. "I'm still processing. Give me a moment." She looked up at the surveillance camera. "Do you want to come in?"

"That's a good idea." Kian pushed to his feet. "Edna looks tired, and we can save her the trouble of repeating what she sensed."

"We can't all fit inside that cell," Anandur said as he fell in step with Kian.

"If we fit inside Igor's cell, we will fit inside Valstar's."

As they passed by Mo-red and Madbar, Mo-red rushed to the bars and mouthed hello.

Vanessa cast him a quick smile and waved. "I'll see you later."

Thankfully, Jade had no more snarky comments and kept quiet until they reached Valstar's cell.

Pavel and Dugmon stood guard across from the door, looking somber. They were unarmed, but Alfie, who stood next to them, had two guns holstered at his hips. Vanessa wasn't an expert on weapons, but she assumed that one was a firearm and the other a tranquilizer.

The cell door was open, as were the bars, and Valstar was chained to a chair in a way similar to how the prisoners Vanessa had interviewed had been.

Edna sat on a chair across from him, and the only other place to sit was his cot.

Vanessa preferred to stand, and so did the others.

"Valstar was a victim," Edna stated.

Next to Vanessa, Jade seethed. "He fooled even you."

Edna lifted a hand. "Just like the others, his free will was compromised by Igor. He wasn't happy to be under the compeller's control, but being smart and opportunistic, he realized it was an opportunity to better his status by becoming useful to Igor above and beyond being a mindless tool. Valstar is neither inherently bad nor good, but that's true of most people. He feels guilty and ashamed about some of the things he did and proud of others, but my probe is not sufficient to determine which carries more weight."

"So basically, it's useless," Jade said.

The female had a thing or two to learn about talking to people without being offensive.

"It's not useless," Vanessa said. "Edna determined that Valstar is not a monster."

"I beg to differ." Jade pushed off the wall and stormed out of the cell.

"She hates me," Valstar murmured. "But she hates Igor more."

"Can you blame her?" Kian asked.

"No. I earned her hate. But maybe she would hate me a little less if she knew that I helped her."

"How?" Kian asked.

"When Igor read her emails and consulted with me about them, I did my best to make them seem unimportant. The truth was that I didn't know what game she was playing, but knowing her, I suspected that she was plotting something. I thought it was an escape. I could have never guessed that she was planning a coup."

When Kian looked at Edna for confirmation, the judge shrugged. "He seems to be telling the truth, but I don't have Andrew's talent. Besides, I don't think it will change Jade's opinion of him. She'll probably think that he was happy to get rid of her, and that's why he didn't share his suspicions with Igor."

Valstar nodded. "And she would be correct. That female was a thorn in my side."

"And yet you wanted to bed her," Edna said.

"Of course, I did. My Kra-ell instincts identified her as the best female in the compound to have offspring with, but Igor didn't allow anyone to invite her to their bed during her fertile cycle. Not that anyone dared to do so at other times. I didn't issue my invitation until she accepted Pavel's."

Didn't he know that it had been a ruse?

Should someone tell him?

Kian turned to look at Vanessa. "Do you want to interview Valstar now or later?"

She cast Valstar a quick look and shook her head. "He's been tied to this chair for too long. He needs a break. I can wait until he rests a little."

"No problem." Kian walked out of the cell. "We can take a lunch break."

28

MO-RED

"Hello, Father." Pavel stood on the other side of the bars. "How have you been?"

Mo-red approached the bars and put his hands over his son's. "I'm well. And you? How are the immortals treating you?"

"Very well." Pavel smiled. "Their village is beautiful. They have a square with a playground for the kids and a café for the adults. The immortals are still a little awkward and suspicious around us, but they are not hostile. There is also a language barrier. Many of our people don't speak English, and none of the immortals I've met so far know Russian or Finnish. It will take time, but it was a good move to join them." He cast a look at Alfie, who was patrolling the corridor. "We need to make ourselves useful, though. They opened their homes to us, gave us beautiful houses, and brought animals for us to feed from. We need to start repaying their kindness."

"Is that why you volunteered to assist the Guardians?"

"Yeah." Pavel smiled and leaned closer. "And so I could visit you whenever I want. I heard that you and the therapist became friendly. How did that happen?"

"The Mother works in mysterious ways. I feel as if we were destined to meet."

Pavel looked at him with surprise in his eyes. "You talk like a human from a romantic movie. We are Kra-ell. We do not bond with one partner."

"I was told that Jade has taken an immortal as her exclusive consort, so maybe things are changing for us."

Pavel snorted. "I don't know what Jade was thinking. It's almost as bad as what Igor did."

Startled by the vehemence in Pavel's voice, Mo-red frowned. "How so?"

"It goes against our biology. Don't get me wrong, I would love to have a female to myself and not share her with anyone, but that was exactly what Igor tried to do by murdering the other males, and that's why you are in prison right now, waiting for your trial. Our society cannot function without every female having several consorts. This is how it has been for hundreds of thousands of years, and that's how it needs to continue until our biology changes and we start having an equal number of male and female births. Jade choosing an immortal as her sole consort is irresponsible and selfish. She's our new leader, and she should lead by example by selecting several Kra-ell partners."

Mo-red couldn't argue with that, but it didn't apply to him. "You are correct with respect to Jade, but in my case, the opposite is true. Even if I were a free male, choosing an immortal female as my sole consort means one less male competing for our scarce pureblooded females. But even if I accept that we should all abide by the rules that have governed our society since time immemorial, I most likely don't have much time left, and I don't need to concern myself with what's good for the Kra-ell society at large. I'm just enjoying what is left of my life with an incredible female."

Pavel deflated. "Don't talk like that. Elias, Vasily, and I are telling as many of our people as we can about you and how kind you were to us and to our mothers throughout the years. The secretive smiles, kind words, and gifts were nice, but what made them so valuable to us was knowing what you were risking. You could have gotten in so much trouble with Igor if he found out, and yet you continued doing that even after my brothers and I were adults, and you were no longer inviting our mothers to your bed."

Mo-red felt tears prickling the backs of his eyes, but he would never allow himself to shed them in front of his son or any other Kra-ell, for that matter.

No self-respecting Kra-ell over the age of four, male or female, would ever allow himself such weakness. He was breaking traditions, but there was a limit to how far he was willing to go.

"Thank you." He forced himself to take a step back. "I appreciate it."

Pavel nodded. "I asked my mother to do what she can as well, and she promised she would speak to the other females."

Mo-red doubted Borga would do that. She'd never shown him any warmth, not because she didn't like him or was indifferent to his fate, but because she was a loner who didn't like being around people.

"Send my regards to your mother, and thank her for me."

"I will." Pavel let out a breath. "You look good, so I guess Vanessa is good to you."

"Very good!" Madbar said. "You should have seen his smile this morning. I've never seen such a big grin on your father's face."

Mo-red chuckled. "Don't listen to him. He likes to exaggerate."

"I'm not exaggerating," Madbar insisted. "He was glowing."

Pavel chuckled. "I'm happy for you."

"Speaking of happiness, are you still spending time with Drova? Her mother might not appreciate you two being together."

Pavel frowned. "Drova is just a kid. There is nothing going on between us."

That was a relief. "So why are you spending so much time with her that even the Guardians noticed?"

"She's smart, and I enjoy talking to her. We mainly talk about how Jade is messing up and what she should be doing instead. Besides, Drova is not going to stay sixteen forever, and when she comes of age, she might remember me fondly."

Laughing, Mo-red shook his head. "You are a natural politician, always thinking ahead and positioning yourself just right. But a word of advice—don't get involved with Drova. Do you really want to produce offspring that will have Igor's genes?"

A grimace twisted Pavel's lips. "That's a very good point."

29

ANNANI

"I feel restless." Annani looked out her window at the waterfall.

People were splashing in the water, but there were no children in the sanctuary, and without their joyful squeals, that beautiful tropical landscape, the waterfall, and the pond seemed like a waste of effort.

She had seen this same view for years, and so had the rest of the sanctuary's residents. It was no longer exciting unless they could share it with children.

Alena smoothed her hand over her protruding belly. "The sameness gets to me too. Especially when considering how exciting things are right now in the village."

Orion was so engrossed in the book he was reading that he had not lifted his head in hours, and Annani wondered whether he had fallen asleep.

"We should go on a trip," she said. "We have not traveled just for fun in a long time. What do you think about Thailand?"

"It's beautiful there, and the people are friendly, but it's not the vibe you are usually after. You prefer major modern metropolises where there is ample shopping and robust nightlife."

The hint was not lost on Annani.

It had been so long since she had last enjoyed a male, and her restlessness was no doubt the result of her coital hiatus. But Alena could no longer accompany her on those kinds of excursions, and going alone with just an Odu for company was depressing. She needed a new companion who was not mated and not pregnant.

The problem was that she could not take just anyone with her. She was the Clan Mother, and clubbing with a random member of her clan felt inappropriate.

Alena had been the perfect companion. Discreet, nonjudgmental, and had usually found her entertainment for the night before Annani had found hers. They had been comfortable with each other. They still were, but now Alena was mated and pregnant, and her hunting days were behind her.

Maybe she should go back to the way things used to be when it was just her and the Odus. Back then, she had pretended to be a priestess or a witch and seduced the men who came into her tent.

"I am not in the mood for a big city this time. I would like to tour nature."

Alena chuckled. "Yeah, I can just see you trudging through the jungle in your silk gown and matching slippers. Do you even own a pair of pants?"

"Why would I? They are terribly uncomfortable and restricting. I do not understand why women wear them when they can wear comfortable loose dresses."

"Not every woman is as perfectly shaped as you are, Mother."

Annani waved a dismissive hand. "I would not wear pants even if they enhanced my appearance. I am not willing to sacrifice comfort for looks, which is why I do not wear tall heels despite my diminutive size."

When her phone rang, Annani hunted for it in the hidden pocket her seamstress included in each of her gowns, and when she fished it out, she smiled at the picture of Kian on the screen.

"Hello, my son. Would you like to switch the call to video so I can look upon your handsome face?"

"I'm in my old office in the keep, and I don't have a lot of time."

She laughed. "Our conversation will not take longer just because I can see you as well as hear you."

"Right."

When he activated the video feature, Annani frowned. "You look troubled. What is it?"

"I had a disturbing thought, but first, I wanted to ask you if any of the gods had a telepathic talent like Vivian and Ella's?"

"As far as I know, none could communicate through verbal telepathy with other gods, but they could send their thoughts to the minds of humans and immortals. Why do you ask?"

"Remember our conversation about Igor and your concern about him transmitting information to someone on the home planet?"

"I do. You assured me that Igor had been thoroughly examined and that he emitted no signals."

"He doesn't, but what if he has a talent like Vivian and her daughter and transmits telepathically? We can't detect it, and it is not hindered by distance and perhaps even time. He could be broadcasting what he found all the way to Anumati, and since, in theory, his transmission could travel through space-time, the gods might have received the message a long time ago and deployed a ship. Or maybe they are already here? And what if they arrived during the conflict with Mortdh, and it wasn't him that bombed the big assembly but the gods who were sent to destroy the Eternal King's heir?"

Alena shook her head. "Your paranoia is out of control, Kian. You should speak with Vanessa about it."

"I love you too, sister of mine. Time travel is probably physically impossible, but thoughts are a different matter. How else could seers predict the future? How else would precognition and post-cognition exist? We know they do. We just don't know how they work."

"That's a fascinating thought experiment," Orion said. "Have you discussed it with Toven? Those kinds of philosophical questions are right up his alley."

It seemed that Alena's mate had been listening all along and had just pretended to be absorbed in his reading.

"I haven't," Kian said. "It first occurred to me this morning, and it has been twisting my gut ever since. Jade had an interesting idea for forcing the truth out of Igor, so I might find out whether my paranoia was, in fact, a prediction."

"What's her idea?" Alena asked.

When Kian was done explaining, Annani rose to her feet and started pacing. "I am the best thraller you have. I should return to the village and enter Igor's mind while he is weakened by the drugs. I can search his mind for the answers."

"I know you can, but I don't want you anywhere near him. Especially now that I suspect he can telepathically transmit information through time and space. Do you want your grandfather to know that an heir of his survived?"

A shiver went through Annani's body. "No, I do not." She sat back down. "But if Igor is drugged, how would he even know who is in his head? He will assume it is Toven."

Kian let out a long breath. "I called you because you demand that I keep you in the loop, not for you to jet over as soon as you can. First, we need to test the drugs on other purebloods to see if they have any effect on them, and if they do, we will try them on Igor while Toven gets inside his head. If Toven fails, I'll consider you."

Annani arched a brow. "Will you?"

"I'll think about it."

That was as good as a no.

30

VANESSA

Vanessa had learned only a little more about Valstar than she'd known from Edna's probe and Toven's assessment of him.

The guy was intelligent, well-spoken, and quite charming in a way that was somewhat disturbing. Nevertheless, she could understand how he'd gotten Toven to intervene on his behalf.

Valstar seemed to truly believe that he'd done the best he could under the circumstances and that he was not responsible for any of the evil deeds that had been done on Igor's commands.

He'd admitted to enjoying the fruits of Igor's master plan of creating a male-dominated Kra-ell society, but Mo-red had admitted the same thing.

The difference was that Mo-red's sons were doing all they could to intervene on their father's behalf, while Valstar's daughter was doing nothing. It wasn't an argument that could be used in court, but it spoke volumes about the difference between the two males.

Sofia had said that she and her mother had visited Valstar during the sea voyage, but when Vanessa interviewed Joanna, she hadn't had anything positive to say about her father. In fact, Sofia was more favorably disposed toward her grandfather than his daughter was.

It was possible that Joanna feared her association with Valstar would be detrimental to her, and that was why she distanced herself from him.

Vanessa needed to speak with the female again and get her to say more than the two sentences she'd dedicated to her father during the initial interview.

When Vanessa collected her things, he asked her the same question he'd asked Edna, "How did I do?"

"You did well." She smiled. "Do I think you are a benevolent angel? No. But I don't think you are pure evil either."

He arched a brow. "Have you seen pure evil?"

"Regrettably, I have." She put her notebook and pen in her satchel. "When I'm not evaluating you and your people and assisting them with managing the trauma they have suffered, I am in charge of a sanctuary for the rescued victims of trafficking. Do you know what that is?"

"I've heard the term. It refers to the practice of moving women from one place to another and using them as sex slaves."

"That's right. Some of those so-called women are taken from their families at the age of eleven."

"I agree. That's true evil."

"So is butchering males in front of their mothers and mates."

He winced. "I had no choice."

"I know. The evildoer was Igor, and you and the others were the swords he wielded, but then he was a tool in the hands of the gods, who took their orders from the Eternal King. So maybe he is the ultimate evil."

Except, the Eternal King was Annani's grandfather and

Kian's great-grandfather, and given how good his descendants were, she found it hard to believe that he was purely evil either.

Besides, if his people deemed him cruel and abusive, they would have taken him down.

"Good day, Valstar," she said as the door opened.

"Thank you, doctor," he called after her.

As soon as the door closed behind her, Vanessa took a deep, centering breath.

Everything she'd told Valstar also applied to Mo-red, and it made her uneasy. Why was Valstar treated differently than the other prisoners? Only because he was Igor's second-in-command?

The fact that he was more capable or knew how to make himself useful didn't make him worse or better than the others. He'd committed the same crimes for the same reasons.

It was good that she wasn't the one to judge him.

Those who had been under his rule knew better, and Jade's disdain for him wasn't a good sign. She didn't regard the other prisoners with such deep-seated hatred.

When Vanessa entered Kian's office, Edna and Jade were still there, and so were the brothers. Hopefully, that didn't mean that she would have to spend the entire afternoon analyzing her and Edna's impressions of Valstar. She still had a couple of interviews scheduled in the village, and she didn't want to reschedule them for the next day.

Except, why was she rushing?

At first, she'd rushed to be done as quickly as possible so she could return to the sanctuary. But now that Mo-red was in her life, she had no intention of leaving him before his trial ended and his verdict was passed.

"So?" Kian arched a brow. "What did you learn?"

She put her satchel on the conference table and sat down. "More of the same as Edna has found. Valstar is smart and capable, and even though he tries to appear modest and self-effacing, nothing could be further from the truth. He thinks most people are beneath him, and that includes Igor. Valstar thinks that he's smarter than Igor, but he fears him because of his compulsion power." She shifted her gaze to Jade. "How am I doing so far?"

"Right on the money." Jade crossed her arms over her chest. "Valstar is a conceited bastard who thinks he can manipulate the Mother herself."

"He said that he covered for you," Edna said. "He suspected that your emails to Safe Haven weren't innocent, but he made light of them when Igor asked his opinion."

Jade shrugged. "Maybe yes, maybe no. Igor sent a spy to Safe Haven with two hybrids to monitor her. He wouldn't have done that if he didn't suspect something. So Valstar either lied about that or wasn't very convincing."

"I have a question for you," Vanessa said. "Why do you hate him more than the other prisoners?"

Jade's eyes blazed red, and her fangs elongated. "He was there when my sons were slaughtered. I vowed to kill everyone who took part in that genocide. The others' hides belong to the females whose families they murdered." She leveled her red glowing gaze at Vanessa. "For your sake, let's hope that those females are more forgiving than I am."

31

JADE

It was an odd moment to have an existential crisis out of the blue like that, but it had all come crashing down suddenly, and Jade felt like someone had popped her balloon.

What did it matter whether Valstar lived or died? What did it matter if she lived or died?

It mattered to Phinas, and maybe it mattered a little to Drova and Kagra, but in the grand scheme of things, none of their lives mattered.

They were part of the ebb and flow of the universe, one generation replacing the other, and in time, they would become a distant memory and then fade entirely.

Except for the gods.

Those bastards had found a way to cheat death and live forever, but even they could be killed.

Was there really a place the soul went to after it was freed from the body?

"Jade?" Kian asked. "Are you with us?"

"Yeah, I'm sorry. What were you saying?"

"If your people accept Edna and Vanessa's assessment of Valstar, what compromise would you be open to?"

"What are the options?"

Kian looked surprised that she was asking, and Jade was surprised as well. A few minutes ago, she would have said that Valstar losing his head was the only acceptable outcome, but she was so tired, so exhausted by this never-ending process. If Igor was still alive, what did it matter if his minions lived or died?

"We can't put him in stasis," Kian said. "We can sentence him to spend time in the dungeon, but then we would need to figure out who would guard him. I don't want to waste Guardians on him, but since some of your people want to join the Guardian force, we could probably figure something out."

She closed her eyes for a moment and then opened them and looked at Edna. "You are the judge. What do you suggest?"

Edna pursed her lips. "It's a unique situation, but perhaps I can use the old laws the gods had for humans. They didn't have jails back then either, so if a death was deemed accidental, as would be the case of a brawl gone deadly or gross negligence, the perpetrator had to pay the family of the victim damages. If he had nothing to trade with, he paid with labor—meaning slavery. There were laws to protect slaves from abuse, so it was basically the equivalent of an indentured servant."

That was an intriguing concept. "Are you suggesting that Valstar become my slave?"

"Basically," Edna said. "But you can't abuse him, which means that he will get an adequate place to sleep and at least half a day off every week. You also can't make him do things that have no utility, like moving rocks from one pile to the other and back. But you can have him scrubbing toilets, collecting manure, or any other task that is beneficial in some way."

"Can I beat him up if he's not doing his job?"

"You can, as long as you don't cause him permanent damage."

When Vanessa grimaced, Edna lifted her hand. "It's not my law, and I don't condone it. I'm only describing the old laws the gods put into place. We can use them as a base and modify them as needed."

"I kind of like them the way they are." Jade felt her momentary ennui dissipate. "I can work with that. Naturally, I'd prefer his head, but if the other females whose families were slaughtered on his watch are more merciful, I'm willing to compromise." She turned to Kian. "You see? I'm always reasonable."

Vanessa huffed. "We are living in the twenty-first century, people. What you are describing is barbaric."

The therapist was probably thinking of her lover and what his sentence would be.

"Compared to the Kra-ell way, what Edna described is too merciful, but as far as I'm concerned, that's good enough for those of the accused I don't care about." She leveled her eyes at Vanessa. "Don't worry about Mo-red. His sons are working very hard on his behalf. I don't see Joanna making the rounds for Valstar."

"Yes, I've noticed. Any insight into their history that you care to share?"

Jade shrugged. "Valstar treated Joanna with the same indifference Igor treated Drova. But unlike Drova, who sought her father's approval, Joanna did everything she could to get back at Valstar for his disregard, including taking a human to her bed and getting pregnant with Sofia. Though to be frank, Jarmo was probably a better choice than the pureblooded peacocks who wanted her in their beds because she was Valstar's daughter."

Anandur smiled. "What could a puny human offer a hybrid Kra-ell female? She could squash him with her little finger."

"True, but perhaps Joanna needed something that the pure-bloods who grew up under Igor's tutelage couldn't give her, like respect and adoration. Contrary to how it seems to outsiders, it's not all about dominance games."

"It's not?" Anandur pretended innocence. "I thought it was."

That was funny coming from him. She'd heard about his mate's unique talent. Wonder had the strength of a Kra-ell female, but she didn't like using it for some reason.

"I hear that your mate could squash you with her little finger too. Does she?"

"Well." He crossed his massive arms over his barrel chest. "Wonder is not into those types of games. She's a delicate flower on the inside, and she likes to be treated as such. I always make sure that my mate gets whatever she wants."

Kian chuckled. "We all do. Human, immortal, god, or Kra-ell. All a good male wants is to make his mate happy."

32

GILBERT

"How was your day at the university?" Gilbert leaned to kiss Karen's cheek.

The twins were on the floor, playing with their toys while watching a kids' show on the television, Idina was probably in her room, and Cheryl was either in her cabana or hanging out with her new friends at the village playground.

It was a rare opportunity for a few quiet moments with the love of his life, and he should be thankful, but he was in a bad mood and didn't even know why.

Karen called it his man-period, and maybe she was right. His bad moods were cyclical, descending on him out of nowhere and for no good reason.

Karen shifted, making room for him in the oversized armchair.

"It was great. I love working at the university. It's such a pleasant change from my previous job, and the boys love Julia. She's so sweet with them."

"So that's her name." He squeezed next to her in the armchair and wrapped his arm around her shoulders. "I was trying to remember it all day long. For some reason, when I think of Julia, I see Meryl Streep in *Julie and Julia*. A twenty-two-year-old babysitter shouldn't be named Julia. She should be named Heather, or Mila, or Paisley."

"Paisley?"

"Yeah, that was the name of one of the buyers I met with today. We sold another house."

"Congratulations!" She clapped her hands. "Eleven down and forty-nine to go."

He grimaced. "Way to make my small victory seem like a failure."

Her eyes widened. "I didn't mean it that way, and you know it. I'm just happy that you sold another house. I know how difficult it is to find qualified buyers who can afford a mortgage payment with these record-high interest rates."

"Especially with all the layoffs in the tech sector. People are moving out of the Bay Area, not in."

"We will weather this out like we did all the other times." She smiled. "Like you always say—what goes down must go up, and what goes up must come down. We just need to ride the swells and not let them swallow us."

"I don't know." He sighed. "This time around, it feels like it's all going to hell. I've lost faith in things getting better."

"Come on, Gilbert." She took his hand. "This is so not like you, and especially not after a sale. What's going on?"

"Nothing. Let's talk about you."

"Na-ah. Tell me what's bothering you."

"I spoke with Gabi today."

"And?"

"And she asked me a bunch of questions about what I'm doing and what's going on with Eric and when we are coming to visit her. I hated telling her half-truths, but I couldn't tell her anything over the phone either."

"Why don't you and Eric fly to see her? Kian is okay with

you coming and going as you please, and you can tell her what's going on in person."

"That's the thing. I can't. Not unless we take someone who can compel her to keep quiet about it, and I don't think that Eleanor, Toven, or Kalugal are willing to do that. We need to bring her to us. She said that she's dying to meet Kaia's new boyfriend, so I can use that as leverage."

"Go for it." Karen patted his thigh. "But first, you should ask Toven to induce you. It will be much easier to explain things to Gabi when you are post transition."

"Right." He winced. "Toven is back, and I'm out of excuses. I should remind him that he promised to do that."

"Then it's good that I invited him and Mia for coffee and cake later this evening. Eric and Darlene are coming too, and William said he would do his best to get out of the lab in time to join us. He has been working so hard to supply the Kra-ell with cuffs and phones, but he's finally done with that." She chuckled. "Now he and his team will have time to assemble the two new Perfect Match machines everyone is waiting for."

"What's the occasion for the get-together? Did I forget someone's birthday again?"

He hoped Karen hadn't organized it just to get him to ask Toven to induce him.

"No, you didn't forget. I met Mia on my way home, and I said that we should get together, and then I thought, why not today? It's not like they have to travel far or make special arrangements. That's the beauty of living in the village. Your friends and family are within walking distance. After I got home, I called Darlene and invited her and Eric, and naturally, I invited Kaia and William too." She cuddled closer to him. "I'm baking your favorite chocolate cake."

"I smell a rat. You've planned this to force me into talking to Toven about the induction."

Karen made a mock angry face. "My chocolate cake doesn't smell like a rat, and you are too busy and preoccupied with work to take care of this, so I did it for you. You're welcome."

"What happened to the Karen who wasn't sure she wanted me to attempt transition?"

"She grew a pair."

"Oh, no!" He affected a horrified expression. "Not my Karen! Will I have to start calling you Kenny?"

Laughing, she punched his arm. "You're such a Neanderthal."

"Uggahaa!" He beat his chest.

33

TOVEN

Toven crouched in front of Mia. "Are you sure you're okay to go?"

"I have to get out of the house. I took a bunch of painkillers, so I should be okay."

Her legs had hit a growth spurt in the few days since they'd returned to the village, probably because she'd finally gotten to relax and rest and get pampered by her grandparents.

"If at any time you feel like you need to rest, don't try to power through it. Let me know, and we will come back home."

"Yes, sir." She saluted him. "I called Bridget, and she said the same thing you did about the rest and relaxation, but she also added that the transition is no longer putting such a big strain on my body, so it can dedicate more resources to growing my legs."

"Makes sense." He opened the door, and she drove her chair through it and down the ramp he and Curtis had built over the stairs.

"My grandparents are at Merlin and Ronja's. The four of them are starting a bridge club. Do you know how to play it?"

He shook his head. "I was never into cards, but maybe I can

ask Curtis to teach me the rules so we can play with your grandparents sometimes."

"He would love that."

When they reached Gilbert and Karen's home, Toven lifted Mia along with her chair and carried her up the three steps that led to the front porch.

Karen opened the door with an apologetic smile. "I'm so sorry. I forgot to tell you to come through the backyard. There are no steps in the back."

"That's okay." Toven leaned to kiss her cheek. "It gave me an opportunity to be all manly and impress my mate."

Mia snorted. "As if it's possible to impress me even more than I already am. I'm mated to a god."

"Even a god has limits." He followed her inside. "Helping your grandfather build that ramp was a humbling experience. I was so bad at it that he asked me to step aside so I wouldn't hurt myself. I was just the muscle, holding the heavy planks while he cut them to size and then putting them down for him to nail in place."

"Hello, Mia, Toven." Gilbert bent to give Mia a quick hug and then offered his hand to Toven. "It's good to have you back."

"It's good to be back." Toven followed him to the living room. "Not that the ship was shabby, but the stress wasn't good for Mia. She missed the comfort of our home and her grandparents."

"What's going on with your besties?" Karen asked, motioning for Toven to sit down while helping Mia navigate the chair next to the side table that was loaded with things to nosh on.

"The Kra-ell rescue mission got in the way. William and his crew were too busy to finish putting together the two new Perfect Match machines, and with Toven and me gone, my grandparents couldn't organize opportunities for Margo and Frankie to meet potential mates. Now that we are here and William can come up for air, we will resume operation Perfect Match."

"Can you include my sister in your operation?" Gilbert asked.

The doorbell ringing interrupted the rest of the conversation, and as Karen opened the door, Darlene walked in with Gilbert's brother, Eric.

"Grandpa," Darlene said teasingly, walking over and giving him a hug. "Mom sends her regards."

"Thank you." He kissed her on both cheeks.

Geraldine and Shai, along with Eric and Darlene, had visited him and Mia the day after their return, but it had been a short visit, and Geraldine was planning a family dinner for Saturday night. Regrettably, Orion and Alena were still in Annani's sanctuary and wouldn't attend.

After tea, coffee, and a delicious chocolate cake were served, Karen nudged her mate, and Toven got ready for the request he'd been anticipating since he'd returned.

Not wanting to pressure Gilbert into attempting the transition, he'd waited for the guy to approach him about it.

"So, Toven." Gilbert's face had lost some of its color. "Are you still willing to induce me?"

"Of course. Whenever you're ready, I'm at your disposal."

Karen put her teacup down. "I spoke with Amanda, and she can get the gym ready for the ceremony tomorrow night. But if that's inconvenient for you, any other night is fine."

Given Gilbert's surprised expression, he hadn't known that Karen had arranged things with Amanda.

"I should have known that Amanda put you up to it," Darlene said. "What did she do to convince you?"

Karen smirked. "She told me to grow a pair, so I did."

As Darlene chuckled, Toven glanced around, searching for the small children. Karen was a proper lady, and she would have never said that in front of her kids. "Where are the little ones?"

"They are at Cheryl's." Gilbert motioned with his head toward the backyard. "It was her idea to babysit them in her cabana."

Toven didn't know which 'her' Gilbert was referring to, Karen or Cheryl, but it wasn't important. What was important was to get Gilbert's transition going.

"I'll gladly induce you tomorrow night. The less time you wait, the less anxious you'll become."

"That's true." Gilbert ran a hand over his balding head. "Apparently, my Karen wants me to have a full head of hair again, and she's willing to go to great lengths to get it back."

"I don't care about the hair." She leaned over and kissed his balding head. "I love you just the way you are, and you should be flattered that I want to spend eternity with you. Once we both transition, that's what awaits us. Are you ready for that?"

"Always." He leaned to kiss her back. "You are it for me."

"Perhaps you could even get married," Darlene said. "I hear that the Clan Mother loves to preside over weddings."

Gilbert and Karen exchanged glances, and then Karen shifted her gaze back to Darlene. "You must be very intuitive. There is another reason for my sudden rush, and yes, it has to do with something that Amanda said. If, by some miracle, both Gilbert and I transition before the wedding cruise, we can get married on the ship. We know that all the evenings are already taken, but we don't mind a small mid-day ceremony."

Toven wasn't sure that the cruise was still happening, but he didn't want to ruin Karen's mood. If Kian decided to cancel the plan, she would hear it from him.

Mia turned to look at him. "Is the ship going to be ready any time soon? Kian said that it needs a lot of work."

"I don't know. I haven't talked with him about it. But there is another problem. How is he going to leave the Kra-ell in the village without supervision?"

"Kalugal's men," Eric said.

When the doorbell rang again, Gilbert rose to his feet and opened the way for William and Kaia.

Toven didn't remember whether they were one of the couples who wanted to get married on the cruise.

Once the greetings were over, he asked, "Were the two of you planning on a cruise wedding?"

"Not this one," Kaia said. "I'm too young to get married. Maybe on the next wedding cruise."

Karen snorted. "Not too long ago, you were talking about having kids, and you didn't think that you were too young for that."

"I'm not. I practically raised Idina and the twins." Kaia scanned the room and frowned. "By the way, where are they? I know they are not asleep at eight in the evening, especially not Idina."

"They are at Cheryl's."

"Awesome. If you'll excuse me, I'll go to say hi to my sisters and brothers."

"I'll come with you," William offered. "I miss the little munchkin."

She chuckled. "Don't call Idina a munchkin to her face. She'll bite you."

When the couple left, Darlene and Karen exchanged amused looks.

"I think someone is ready for a baby," Darlene said.

Karen shook her head. "Kaia is too young. But if she wants a baby, she'll have one, with or without my permission."

34

JADE

As the doorbell rang, Jade looked at Phinas. "Are you expecting anyone?"

"Nope. My people call before they come. It must be one of yours."

Not every one of hers had gotten their phones yet, and even if they did, it would take them some time to learn how to use them. There were no phones in the compound, and people were used to just walking over to the person they wanted to speak to.

It wouldn't be Drova either, because she came and went through the sliding patio doors in her room—ghosting her mother.

Jade had learned this new human phrase, which applied to how her daughter was treating her.

Not that she had a problem with that.

At sixteen, Drova was supposed to be independent, but she was also supposed to train, which she hadn't done since arriving at the village.

At least not with Jade.

Perhaps she was training with someone else. Pavel?

Jade pushed to her feet. "It's probably Kagra."

"Yeah, probably," Phinas agreed.

When she opened the door, it was indeed her second-in-command.

Kagra saluted her. "Good evening, Jade. May I come in?"

Jade arched a brow. "Since when are you so polite?"

"Since I've been lectured by a snooty fifteen-year-old about proper greeting etiquette." She walked in and waved at Phinas. "We don't want these descendants of the gods to think that we are barbarians." She plopped on the couch and helped herself to Jade's cranberry vodka.

"You're welcome." Jade sat across from her. "So, what brings you to our abode this lovely evening?"

"I took the females I told you about to see Onegus, and they will start training with the Guardians tomorrow. He said that because we are inexperienced, we can't have the all-female rescue team we want, but once we complete our training and go on at least thirty missions, he might consider letting us raid a trafficking cell on our own. I think he's full of crap and has no intention of doing that, but we will see. Maybe I'm wrong."

"How many females are we talking about?"

Kagra took another sip before putting the glass down on the coffee table. "Twelve for now, but I think more will join once the initial group reports having a good experience."

"What about the males? Any volunteers?"

"We have the two that you took to the keep, and others are waiting to hear from them about how that went. They are mostly concerned about being treated with respect. You know, not as less worthy than the immortals. If that goes well, I believe most will prefer to serve on the Guardian force rather than do gardening or building or whatever else the immortals deem as work that's beneath them. Besides, the rumor is that

Guardians are paid very well, even those who are still in training, so that's a big draw as well."

Jade nodded. "I prefer for our people to serve in the Guardian force as well, but we will do whatever the clan needs, whether it's gardening or collecting trash. We owe them. And for the same reason, those who will join the Guardian force will not be paid by the clan but by me."

Kagra let out a long, exasperated breath. "As the humans say, you are digging your own grave. There is already enough resentment about you choosing Phinas as your sole consort and denying our males the chance to father Kra-ell offspring. When they hear that you're refusing the clan's money for the services they provide, they will be majorly pissed."

Jade had been Igor's exclusive broodmare the entire time she'd spent in captivity, and no one had objected, but now that she finally had a choice, they were yapping about that?

"Who said that?"

"All the young males. You know how it goes. When one starts complaining, the others join."

"Let them complain," Phinas said. "Jade is mine, and if anyone has a problem with that, let him challenge me."

As Kagra grinned and gave him the thumbs up, Jade rolled her eyes. "Don't encourage his caveman act." She turned to Phinas. "No one can challenge you even if they want to. Toven made sure that they couldn't aggress on any immortals. Though I wonder how that is going to work while they are training."

"Good point." Kagra emptied the rest of the vodka down her throat. "I should find Toven and tell him that he needs to modify his compulsion."

By now, everyone knew that Tom's real name was Toven, and Jade still didn't understand why he'd kept it a secret before.

Had he really thought that giving himself a plain human name made him seem less otherworldly?

The doorbell ringing again put an end to that line of thought.

"Who is it now?" Jade glanced at Phinas.

"I'll get it," he offered.

"That's okay." Jade rose to her feet. "It's probably for me anyway."

Phinas was very patient and accepting about his home turning into the Kra-ell village headquarters. He shouldn't act as her assistant as well.

"You should consider getting an office in the office building or in the underground," Kagra said.

"It's eight in the evening." She cast her second-in-command a hard look. "Everyone should know that business hours are over."

"There is no rest for leaders," Phinas murmured.

That was true, and it hadn't bothered her when she'd led her tribe before, but now that she was playing house with Phinas, Jade cherished their alone time together. None of the things Kagra had said were urgent, and they could have waited until the next morning.

Opening the door, Jade was ready to tear off the head of whoever was on the other side, but when she saw who it was, her ire subsided as quickly as it had risen.

"Good evening, mistress." Vrog dipped his head. "Forgive me for bothering you at such a late hour, but you wanted me to update you about my progress on our school plans, and you were gone most of the day."

That was actually something she wanted to hear as soon as possible. What her people had to say about her relationship with Phinas could have waited. She was still pissed off about it.

"That's okay. Come in, Vrog."

"Thank you, mistress."

"Please, call me Jade."

"As you wish." He dipped his head again.

He'd said that before and had gone right back to calling her mistress.

Oh, well, old habits and all that.

"Hi, Vrog." Kagra looked at him over her shoulder. "What do you have for us?"

Phinas pushed to his feet. "Who wants cranberry vodka?"

"I do." Jade motioned for Vrog to sit next to Kagra on the couch. "Someone finished mine."

"I can have more." Kagra lifted the empty glass.

"Vrog?" Phinas asked.

"Well, if everyone else is drinking, I'd love some."

They waited for Phinas to return with the drinks, and when everyone had a glass in hand, Jade turned to Vrog. "Go ahead. What did you manage to do so far?"

"I worked out a class schedule with Bhathian, who's in charge of organizing the Guardian training. He agreed to move some of their classes to the other facility and rearrange class time here in the village. All the classrooms in the subterranean structure will be available to us from nine in the morning until one o'clock in the afternoon. I can easily fit a curriculum that combines self-learning in that time frame. I am a big proponent of individual progress, so that works out great. The teacher's job is to guide and explain, and it's the students' job to read and practice and progress on their own. Naturally, the teacher should always be available to answer their questions, and we can establish additional hours during which it is okay to contact the teachers."

"That solves the classroom problem," Jade said. "What about teachers?"

"We can organize the children into groups of similar age

and divide class time between three people. Callie, Brundar's mate, is an accredited teacher, and she's willing to take on the kindergarten through fifth-grade kids. I'll take sixth through twelve, and I was hoping you could take the little ones. They will only need an hour or so a day."

Phinas put his glass down. "How is Callie going to manage to teach full-time while also running her restaurant?"

"Ah." Vrog smiled. "That's the other good news I wanted to share. Isla is taking over the kitchen at Callie's, and she convinced her sister to join her. Hannele will bring her daughter and Isla's daughter Lana with her, and the two will work in the restaurant after school."

"Did you check with Kian that it's okay to bring in the humans?" Phinas asked.

"Not yet, but I don't think he will object. The community needs them, and they need the community. Whether they are in Safe Haven or in the village, they pose the same risk of exposure to the clan, which in my opinion, is minimal."

"Good luck with that," Jade said. "If you need me to talk to him about the humans, let me know."

"Thank you." Vrog smiled and tilted his head in a semi-dip. "But I can approach Kian by myself. We've been bouncing educational ideas off each other for a while now. His door is always open to me."

"How nice is that," Kagra said mockingly. "You and the mighty Kian are buddies."

"I wouldn't go that far, but we are on friendly terms."

35

VANESSA

The two meetings Vanessa had conducted in the village hadn't boded well for Mo-red or the other prisoners, and as she waited for Alfie to open the cell for her, she struggled to put a smile on her face.

The Guardian had told her that Mo-red had returned to their apartment cell in the evening and that he'd been in a good mood. She didn't want to spoil it. They might not have many nights left together, and she didn't want to waste them feeling depressed.

As the door finished swinging open, she strode through, dropped her satchel on the couch, and wrapped her arms around Mo-red's neck.

Someone had given him a white button-down shirt, and with his dark olive-toned skin, he looked good enough in it to eat.

In fact, Vanessa intended to do just that.

"I missed you." She inhaled his clean scent.

"A bad day?" He caressed her back, his large hands giving out heat where they touched her through her clothing.

"It wasn't one of my best." She leaned away and started on the buttons of his shirt.

Smiling, he let her do the work and watched as she parted the two halves, pulled it down his arms, and let it flutter to the floor.

She took a moment to put her hands on his smooth pecs, and as she leaned in to kiss his chest, he reached behind her and unzipped her skirt.

As it fell down to the floor, she stepped out of it, popped the button of his jeans, and worked his zipper to reveal the magnificent length that had been eager to say hello to her.

"Hello." She smoothed her hand over the silky length, eliciting a hiss from Mo-red.

When she leaned to kiss his nipple, the hiss turned into a growl, and when she flicked her tongue over it, his head dropped back on his neck.

Ah, the power she wielded.

It didn't matter how strong Mo-red was. He would let her do to him whatever she pleased, and she would repay him in kind, but only after she pleasured him until he came harder than he'd ever come before.

She needed a success tonight, even if it was just to give this male more pleasure than he thought was possible.

Still working his erection, she sucked his nipple into her mouth and grazed it gently with her blunt front teeth. She might not have functional fangs, but her canines were long and pointy enough to draw blood.

When it seemed that his knees were about to give out, she halted her assault only to push him onto the bed. There were advantages to living in the cramped space. The bed was never farther than a couple of steps away.

A strong tug took care of his jeans, and as he lay sprawled on the bed, naked and aroused, she drank in the sight of him.

"You're the sexiest male I've ever seen."

He chuckled. "Your eyes must be clouded by desire, but I'll take the compliment." He pushed back against the pillows and palmed his erection. "Take off your clothes."

Using her immortal speed, she was naked in five seconds with her clothes neatly folded on the couch. The space was too small to make a mess.

"You're gorgeous." Mo-red's eyes roved over her body. "I want to be inside of you so badly." He began stroking his shaft while she advanced on him.

Feeling like the predator she was, Vanessa put her knee on the bed and got between his spread legs.

Her eyes riveted to the shaft he was leisurely stroking, she licked her lips, lowered her head, and rubbed her cheek against the velvety head.

Mo-red's hips bucked up, and as she extended her tongue and licked him, the sound of his heartbeat thundered in her ears.

She wasn't a Kra-ell female who could wrap her long tongue around his girth and squeeze it hard, but given how he'd responded to her pleasuring him like that the day before, she doubted Mo-red had enjoyed that particular form of intimacy with the purebloods often if at all.

After all, allowing fangs around his most vulnerable flesh required a level of trust that he couldn't afford while fighting them for dominance.

Evidently, though, he trusted her.

"Vanessa," he hissed her name as he threaded his fingers in her hair. "You're killing me, but what a way to die."

Ugh, did he have to say those words right now?

Talk about a mood killer.

She had to take her mind off the topic, and the best way to do it was to get down to business. Sucking him into her mouth, she took as much of him as she could until he was filling her so completely that she couldn't breathe.

Pulling her head up to take a breath, she dipped down once more, taking impossibly more of him into her throat. It was still just a little over half of the length, and his hand had a death grip on what remained outside her mouth.

Damn. Why did she have to think about that word again?

Attacking his shaft with renewed vigor, she reached with her hand between her legs and massaged her engorged nub with the same urgency she was bobbing her head up and down Mo-red's arousal.

In moments, they both reached the point of no return and as Mo-red shouted her name and exploded in her mouth, her own climax erupted.

36

MO-RED

Spent and boneless, Mo-red sagged into the mattress. "Mother of All Life, Vanessa, this was—I just have no words."

Her satisfied smile was bright enough to illuminate not only the cell but the entire dungeon level.

Holy Mother, it was bright enough to illuminate the entire city.

He might not have the right words to express what he felt verbally, but he could show her.

Just as soon as he caught his breath.

Three heartbeats later, he had her on her back with her hands locked over her head. "My turn."

The room was already permeated with the scent of her arousal, but as soon as he'd taken control of her body, it not only flared but caught fire, and if that wasn't a sure sign that this was precisely what she wanted, the glazed-over look in her eyes confirmed it beyond a shadow of a doubt.

His hold on her wrists was so light that one tug would have freed them, but Vanessa had no wish to get free, and she left her hands where they were.

Perhaps he could tie her up for an even more powerful effect.

Tugging on the string that held his hair back, he pulled it off and used it to loosely tie Vanessa's wrists together.

"Your hair is amazing," she murmured. "I want to touch it."

"Don't move your hands from where I put them," he commanded.

"Yes, sir." She smiled coquettishly.

Gripping the ends of his long hair, he brushed them over her nipples. "How does it feel?"

"Like silk."

He flicked the strands over her breasts, making her moan and arch for more.

He had to kiss the lips that emitted that moan, the lips that had been wrapped around his shaft and had given him such unimaginable pleasure. Dipping his head, he kissed her as if this was their last kiss. It wouldn't be. There would be more, but they were numbered, and he had to make each one count.

How many more times would he get to kiss Vanessa before his life ended? To touch her and make her moan and scream his name when she orgasmed?

He shouldn't let her leave this room for any reason, but regrettably, it wasn't up to him.

She was free to do as she pleased, and he should be grateful for every moment she was willing to spend with him.

"Mo-red," she murmured against his lips. "I want to feel you inside of me. I need it."

He'd wanted to pleasure her with his mouth, but he couldn't deny her. She was the one making the rules in the game they were playing, including his display of dominance. He was hers to command, and she was his to please.

As he entered her in one swift move, Vanessa groaned, but

he didn't pound into her. Instead, he went slow and gentle, giving his hips a twist on every downward surge and enjoying the feel of her. He was in no rush to do more now that she'd taken the edge off with the first climax she'd given him.

Soon, she was bucking under him, urging him to go faster, harder, and as he obliged her, he snaked his hand between their bodies and added pressure to the seat of her desire.

When Vanessa exploded, he pulled out and dove between her spread thighs. Lapping at her, he prolonged her climax, and when her tremors subsided, he flipped her around and entered her from behind.

Vanessa's hands were still bound with the string he'd tied around her wrists, and in this position, she kept her arms outstretched in front of her, her head down on the pillow, and her glorious ass up in the air.

Taking his furious pounding, her body was a sight to behold, but he could only imagine the expression on her beautiful face, and he needed to see it as he took her like a beast—to watch her take all he was giving her and plead for more.

"Look at me, Vanessa!" he commanded.

She lifted her head and turned it to look at him over her shoulder. Her lips were parted, her eyes glazed over with passion, and the sight of her ample breasts swaying with each thrust and retreat was almost enough to send him over.

Draping himself over her, he cupped her breasts and then tweaked her nipples. He wished he could be everywhere at once, sucking on those turgid peaks while filling her with his cum, but that was the stuff of dreams, and this reality was better than any dream.

When his climax was near, he licked the spot where her neck met her shoulder and struck with his fangs. She tensed under him, but it lasted no longer than a second, and when he started to take long pulls of her blood, she tightened around him.

Mo-red erupted, replenishing what he was taking with what he had to give.

37

VANESSA

When Vanessa opened her eyes, the first thing she noticed was that Mo-red's magnificent hair was once more tied with the string, and her hands were unbound.

"How long was I out this time?"

"Not long. Maybe fifteen minutes. How long did it feel?"

"Longer." She kissed the underside of his jaw. "You are addictive. I will have a hard time leaving here tomorrow morning. All I want to do is make love to you."

He chuckled. "Funny, I had the same thought."

"Oh, yeah? What were you thinking?"

"That I need to keep you locked in here and spend every moment I have with you. But I'm not in charge of you, nor would I ever want to be. If by some miracle I am set free, I will be at your disposal whenever you need me, but not the other way around."

She frowned. "Why? Doesn't that make me in charge of you?"

"Yes. Which is the natural order of things according to Kraell traditions. I'm starting to see the wisdom of our ways even when males don't outnumber females four to one."

No human male would have ever uttered such a statement, and neither would her immortal male relatives. Most of them were great and believed in gender equality, but they were overly protective of their female relatives.

"That I would love to hear. Please elaborate."

"It's hard to explain. Females are just better leaders. They are more attuned to their people, and they see more than males do. I'd rather get ordered around by a female than by a male."

That didn't jive at all with the dominant streak he exhibited. Then again, the only place it ever manifested was during sex. He was very amenable outside of bed.

Wasn't he just pure perfection?

She could purr like a kitten if not for the axe hanging over Mo-red's head. It was just her luck to find the perfect male and to have to save him first.

It shouldn't be a big surprise that the Fates would orchestrate something like that for her. She definitely had a savior complex, so throwing a male who was in a desperate situation at her was a major ingredient in the Fates' recipe. The rest of the ingredients were precisely calibrated to her liking as well.

Mo-red was smart, respectful, accommodating, handsome, tall, not too full of himself, and a demon between the sheets.

Yep, the Fates made Mo-red perfect for her in every way so she would fall in love with him.

Was she in love with him, though?

Or was she confusing postcoital bliss with love?

Probably the bliss was the culprit.

Vanessa wasn't a young, naive woman who fell in love with the first male who gave her multiple orgasms. She was an immortal who had lived for over three centuries and had seen the worst and the best of people, including the most romantic loves and the worst, unimaginable sexual abuse.

"Why are you frowning?" Mo-red asked. "Was I too rough with you?"

"Oh, no. You were perfect. That was what I was thinking right now." She smiled. "It's like the Fates custom made you for me."

"The Fates?"

"The three Fates are the unofficial higher power our clan believes in. They are like your Mother of All Life, except that they don't determine where your soul will go after you die. Their main thing is matchmaking. We believe that they reward those who have sacrificed for others or suffered greatly with a truelove mate, and they are known to go to great lengths to arrange those pairings."

"I see." He lifted his hand and caressed her cheek with his finger. "I'm sure that you've earned the right to a truelove mate, but you deserve a virtuous prince, not a lowlife like me. Why would the Fates punish you like that? I'm probably the worst choice they could have made for you."

She hated that he thought so little of himself. But at the same time, it was one of the reasons she was so taken with him. Mo-red was humble despite being wonderful in every way.

"Why would you say such a thing?"

"Isn't it obvious? I'm a murderer on trial for slaughtering my own people. My future prospects are not good."

Vanessa closed her eyes and let out a breath. "Don't you see how that makes you perfect for me? What do I do for a living? What is the driving force in my life?" She opened her eyes and looked into his. "When you look for the definition of Savior Complex in Wikipedia, you will find my picture next to it."

His eyes widened. "Really?"

She chuckled. "It was a joke. You won't find my picture on Wikipedia or anywhere else. But I'm well aware of your predicament, making you the perfect candidate for me to fall in love with, and the rest of your wonderful attributes are just the cherry on top."

"Oh, yeah? What are those wonderful attributes that you are referring to?"

Evidently, Mo-red had an ego that needed stroking after all.

"Let's see..." Vanessa pretended to think about it while tapping a finger over her lips. "You are intelligent, kind, and handsome, but what I love most about you is what you can do with your tongue." When he looked taken aback, she cupped his cheek. "Just joking about the tongue. You are wonderful in every way, which is why I can't help but fall for you."

38

MO-RED

Had Mo-red heard Vanessa right?

Had she just said that she'd fallen in love with him?

Or had she meant that she was in the process of falling in love with him?

Or maybe she might fall in love with him because of all his wonderful attributes?

Mo-red wasn't supposed to believe in the concept of love, but he had long suspected that what the Kra-ell regarded as loyalty to the tribe was actually love for one's family. He hadn't been in love with the mothers of his sons, but there was no doubt in his mind that he loved his children, and the same was true for every Kra-ell parent.

Otherwise, why would they give their lives to protect their children?

This was the power of love, and there was no greater motivator in the universe. Well, unless one was a sociopath like Igor.

Was he in love with Vanessa, though?

Would he give his life to protect her?

The answer to that was a resounding yes, but was it really proof of love?

Every Kra-ell male was raised with the conviction that his two jobs in life were to protect his tribe and to sire strong offspring. It was so deeply ingrained that he might have projected it on Vanessa because, in his mind, she had become his new tribe.

"I don't know if I have misheard." He leaned away to look into her eyes. "Or whether you have misspoken."

A moment of confusion passed through her eyes, and then she closed them tightly. "Oh, boy. I should know better than to blurt out everything that crosses my mind. I must be still loopy from your venom. I can't be in love with you because we've just met, but I might be in the process of falling in love with you."

"Don't." He leaned down and kissed her lips. "Shield your heart. I'll only bring you pain."

"No, you won't." Fire ignited in her eyes. "We are going to win this trial, and you're going to live. I won't accept any other outcome. And once you are free, you can fall in love with me."

He laughed. "Is that an order?"

"Yes, it is, and I don't care about the Kra-ell's no-love clause. Forgive me for insulting your traditions, but that's bullshit. You are humanoids related to gods and humans, and just like them and us, you are capable of love."

"I'm not arguing with you. I think so too."

"Good." She let out a breath. "From now on, I want you to think positively and assume that you are going to win that damn trial."

"Is that an order?"

"It is."

"I'm not a great believer in positive thinking, but if you tell me to do it, I will. You are the boss."

"Such sweet words." She leaned in and kissed his lips. "And

you say that you're not perfect for me. You couldn't have been better if you had another two sets of hands to pleasure me with."

He arched a brow. "Don't tell me that you were thinking that while we were…making love?"

"Why? Does it freak you out?"

"No, it's just that I was thinking the same thing. Maybe we have a mental connection."

"Or maybe great minds think alike." She waggled her impressive brows. "I have naughty fantasies."

"About being with more than one male at a time?"

"No, I don't swing that way. My fantasies are a little stranger than that." Vanessa snuggled closer. "I have fantasies about an alien lover with an extra set of magical hands and other things to give me pleasure with." She chuckled. "You see? The Fates even took that into account when they found you for me. You are an alien, and you have a magical tongue."

"That's indisputable. But it's not the same as having another set of magical hands…or other pleasure-giving appendages."

Vanessa's pale cheeks got pink with a faint blush. "You are the only one I've ever told about this. I don't know why I feel so comfortable with you."

He pointed his finger at the ceiling. "The Fates."

"Indeed." She narrowed her eyes at him. "If you're game, there is a way for us to fulfill that fantasy together, you know."

"I don't know. What are you talking about?"

"Have you heard of Perfect Match?"

"Like the ones your Fates arrange?"

"No. It's a virtual fantasy that we can experience together. We have the machines in the village, so once you are free, I'm taking you on a virtual adventure with both of us having extra abilities to enhance each other's pleasure."

"I have no idea what you're talking about, but it sounds like fun."

"I'll show you." She slipped out of his arms, reached for her satchel, pulled out her phone, and returned to bed. "There is even a Krall adventure, and yes, it is loosely based on the Kra-ell. Kian's wife is a seer, and she came up with it without knowing that her made-up people were real." She pulled up the Perfect Match Studios' website. "The introductory video explains it quite well."

After watching the presentation, Mo-red had a good idea of what to expect, and he was also incredibly turned on. "You have a date. But in the meantime, let's see what I can do with the gifts the Mother of All Life gave me at birth."

39

MARCEL

Bridget put her stethoscope back in her pocket and turned to Marcel. "The good news is that Sofia is transitioning. Frankly, I didn't think she would. The bad news is that her blood pressure is high, and her heartbeat is irregular. Gertrude will get an EKG to check her for arrhythmia, and I will stay in the clinic to watch her closely until the critical stage is over."

The doctor had looked worried before checking Sofia's vitals, and her expression hadn't improved after the examination.

A lump the size of a boulder lodged itself in Marcel's throat, making it difficult to verbalize his questions. Forcing it down with a hard swallow, he cleared his throat. "What are her prospects? And please, don't give me false reassurances. I want your honest opinion."

"I would never lie to you. Sofia is young and healthy, so her chances of pulling through are excellent. That being said, she needs to be monitored closely. If her heart gives up, we will fight to keep her with us."

"Will giving her my blood help? I know that it was done for

the director of the paranormal program to strengthen him temporarily so he wouldn't die right then and there. It might give her the boost she needs."

Bridget's eyes turned calculating. "It might. The director wasn't transitioning, and he was fully human, so I'm not sure if it will work the same way on Sofia, but in the event there is nothing else we can do for her, we will try that as a last resort."

Meaning, if Sofia was dying, administering his blood would either save her or hasten her death.

On her way out, Bridget put her hand on Marcel's shoulder and gave it a light squeeze. "I'll tell her father that he can come in."

When Sofia had lost consciousness last night, Jarmo had refused to leave her side and had sat with her throughout the night.

Even Bridget didn't have the heart to kick him out of the room, and she'd only asked him to leave during the examination.

When the door opened, Marcel was surprised that Jarmo didn't walk in alone. Sofia's mother was with him.

"The doctor said I could see Sofia," she said as she approached the bed.

"Of course." Marcel rose to his feet and offered Joanna the chair. "Please, sit down."

"Thank you." She took his seat. "What's the prognosis?"

"Bridget says that Sofia is young and healthy, so her chances of transitioning successfully are very good. But she needs to be watched closely."

Joanna tore her eyes away from her daughter and turned to look at him. "Why does she need to be watched? What's wrong with her?"

"Her blood pressure is very high, and her heartbeat is irregular."

"What does that mean?"

"It means that her heart might give out," Jarmo murmured. "We have a history of heart disease in the family."

She cast him a baleful look as if it was his fault that Sofia was having a difficult time transitioning.

"If things get worse, I will give her a transfusion of my blood," Marcel said. "It might help."

"Or it might not." Joanna took Sofia's limp hand in hers. "I wish I could tell her how proud I am of her. But I was busy wallowing in my anger and resentment toward my father, and I waited too long. Now it's too late."

Marcel was starting to regret letting Joanna into the room.

What if Sofia could hear her?

The resignation in her mother's voice would make her think that she was dying.

"When Sofia wakes up, I will remind you of what you said right now." Marcel walked around the bed to where Jarmo was sitting on Sofia's other side. "You are a fighter, my love." He leaned down and kissed her forehead. "You are going to pull through and come back to me, you hear?"

He didn't expect a response, but he could have sworn that there was a slight change in Sofia's expression. It was as if she suddenly appeared a little more comfortable, more peaceful.

Jarmo smiled up at him. "You are good to my daughter."

Joanna huffed. "Is he? She's here because of him. What if instead of gaining immortality, she dies?"

"She's not dying or going to die." Marcel glared at her. "If you don't have anything positive to say, I suggest that you leave."

Casting him an indignant look, she pushed to her feet and walked out of the room without a word to him or to Sofia's father.

Jarmo sighed. "Don't be angry. Joanna is sad and scared. That is why she talks like that."

"You don't need to apologize for her." Marcel sat back in his chair and took Sofia's hand. "You are a good father, and your sisters stepped in and have been better mothers to Sofia than Joanna could have ever been, even if she tried her best. She's still a child herself."

Jarmo chuckled. "Yes. I think that too. How you say in English? Daddy issues?"

"Precisely."

40

KIAN

Kian opened the back door to the clinic and led Jade and the two male Kra-ell volunteers inside.

Sofia was transitioning, and her family was in the waiting room. He didn't want to advertise to the entire village what they were about to do.

Julian and Turner were already waiting for them in the operating room's reception area. "Good morning, and thank you for volunteering. I'm Julian." He offered his hand to Jade.

"I know who you are. Good to meet you."

Turner, true to form, remained quietly observant from where he was leaning against the wall.

Next, Julian shook the hands of the two male volunteers. "I have experience with this particular class of drugs. That's why I'm here and not my mother. Before we begin, I just want to warn you that one of the side effects is memory loss of the events preceding the administration of the drug. So, if there is anything important you need to remember about today or yesterday, I suggest that you write it down."

As the two males shrugged, Jade looked around. "I need a piece of paper and a pen."

Kian lifted his hand. "I thought we had an understanding, and you were not going to participate in the experiment. These two young males will suffice."

She glared at him. "I will not subject my people to anything I didn't try myself. Either I go first, or none of us does it. Make your choice."

Kian's fangs itched to make an appearance and challenge the infuriating female who refused to follow his orders, but he was a civilized male, and he wouldn't growl at her with his fangs on display like a beast.

Besides, he could totally empathize because he would have done the same.

"If you suffer a mental breakdown, don't blame me or Bridget because we've warned you about the possible side effects."

"I'm doing this of my own volition and taking full responsibility for the outcome." Jade waved her hand around. "You are my witnesses and can attest that I said that."

As the Kra-ell and Julian nodded, she looked to Turner who returned her gaze with a level stare of his own, not bothering to acknowledge her statement.

Jade extended her hand to the doctor. "Now, can I get a piece of paper and a pen, please?"

Julian frowned. "Didn't you just get a new phone?"

"I did, but what does it have to do with this?"

"You can record a message for yourself, or you can use the note application. You can even program the note to chime at a certain time so you will know to look at it."

"I don't know how to use any of these features, and now is not the time for a lesson. Just get me a piece of paper. When I put my hand in my pocket, I'll find it and read it. That will be my alarm."

Kian stifled a chuckle.

This was the difference between the older generations and the ones that grew up with a smartphone attached to their palms.

Patting his coat pockets, Julian looked at Turner. "You always carry that yellow pad around. Do you have something to write on?"

Turner shook his head. "I didn't plan on taking notes. I'm here out of curiosity."

"Maybe I can find something in my mother's office." Julian opened the door to the operating room. "In the meantime, make yourselves comfortable." When he saw the alarmed expressions on the Kra-ell faces, he chuckled. "I'm not going to operate on you. It's just the only private room in the clinic right now."

Jade cast a questioning glance at Kian.

"It is. Sofia is transitioning, and her family is up front."

Jade's eyes widened. "How come no one told me? This is huge news."

"Not really," Turner said. "You have no one else like Sofia. There will be no other transitions for your people."

"Not yet, but there might be in the future." She clapped her two companions on their backs. "This is a cause for celebration."

"Not for us," one of them said. "Our children can't transition unless we have them with immortal women or pureblooded Kra-ell females."

Was there a note of resentment in the guy's tone? Or was Kian imagining it?

The door opening put an end to the discussion.

"I have writing implements for all three of you." Julian

handed each of the Kra-ell a piece of white paper and a pencil. "While you write down the things you want to remember, I'll prepare the drugs."

Jade straddled one of the chairs Julian had brought in preparation for the test, using the hard back as her writing surface.

The two males followed her example, but while they were done writing their memories in under a minute, she was still scribbling vigorously while Julian waited with three syringes at the ready.

Evidently, she had a lot of memories from the last twenty-four hours.

When she was done, she folded the piece of paper and put it in her pocket. "Okay. I'm ready. What do you want me to do?"

"Roll up your sleeve, please," Julian said.

"Hold on." Turner lifted his hand. "The males should go first. What works on Jade might not work on Igor because of the size difference and other factors that have to do with their different genders."

Jade pursed her lips. "There isn't as much difference between Kra-ell males and females as there is between human men and women or even immortals. Gordi and Antony are not much taller or heavier than me."

"But we are stronger," one of them said. "We have more muscle mass. I should go first."

Kian didn't know which one was Gordi and which one was Antony.

"What if there are adverse effects?" Jade asked.

"Then we certainly should go first," the same guy said. "You are our leader. You can't afford to be out of commission."

41

JADE

Jade didn't want to get injected with the drug, but it was her duty as the leader and the one who had suggested the idea.

She hadn't told Phinas about what she was about to do because he would have tried to stop her, and thankfully, the village rumor machine had remained quiet on the subject. She would tell him later after it was over and she was back home unharmed.

Home.

It was so strange to think of his house as a home, but in the short time she'd shared it with him and Drova, she'd so easily started to regard it as her home.

Did Drova feel the same, though?

Her daughter wasn't around much, and even when she was, she projected hostility. They needed to talk, though.

Maybe she should invite her to visit Igor before they put him in stasis. Although, to be frank, she thought it would do more damage than good. Igor's parting words to his daughter might scar her worse than his indifference over the years ever did.

"I'm going first," Jade told the doctor in a tone that didn't leave room for argument. "If I don't have a severe adverse response, you can try it on Gordi next." She rolled up her sleeve and offered him her arm.

"Very well." He gripped her wrist with surprising gentleness, and as he struck her upper arm with the needle, the pain was minimal.

"You have a light hand," she complimented him.

"Thank you." He put medical tape over the prick point. "Now, we wait." He disposed of the syringe and brought over a chair. "Forgive me for staring at you, but I need to monitor your responses."

"About that," Kian said. "Why aren't you hooking her up to monitoring equipment?"

"There is no need," Julian said. "She is not in danger."

Turner frowned. "Jade is not immortal. We shouldn't assume that her body can take as much abuse as an immortal's would."

Julian smiled. "I know what I'm doing, Turner. You don't need to worry."

Jade chuckled. "Are you worried about me, Turner? That's sweet. I didn't know you cared."

"I care." He crossed his arms over his chest. "I might not be expressive with my feelings, but that doesn't mean that I don't have any."

Kian snorted, and Julian hid a smile.

"Your friends beg to differ." She waved at the two, and it felt as if her arm was moving in slow motion. "I think it's working." She waved it again and got dizzy. "I don't feel so good."

Julian's concerned face got too close for comfort. "What are you feeling?"

"I'm dizzy, and you sound like you're talking from underwater. Everything is in slow motion. Including you." She lifted her hand and touched his cheek. "You are very handsome. You look a lot like Kian but better because he's too perfect. I like more rugged men. Like my Phinas." She smiled and felt her face stretching as if her smile was too big. "He's handsome in a manly way."

"What about me?" Turner asked. "Do you find me handsome?"

"You have incredible eyes, so intelligent. I admire your mind, but even if I wasn't in love with Phinas, I wouldn't have chosen you. You are a full head shorter than me."

"I think it's working," Julian said. "I don't think she would have said any of these things without the drug."

Kian snorted. "I'm not sure about that. She has the tact of a bull in a china shop." He leaned closer. "If I wasn't married, and you weren't in love with Phinas, would you have chosen me?"

"No. I like you, but you're too pretty." She waved her hand again. "Amanda's mate is more my type. But I like you as a friend. You are honest and honorable, and you work hard for your people. I admire those qualities in you."

Turner's pale eyes appeared in front of her face. "We need to ask her something that she would have lied about if not for the drug."

"I don't know what it might be," Kian said. "I'll call Phinas. Maybe he knows."

"Wait!" Jade lifted her hand. "I didn't tell him about this. He's going to be mad."

"Try Kagra," Gordi suggested. "Maybe she knows something super embarrassing about Jade that she would have never admitted to anyone but her best friend."

"Good idea." Kian pulled out his phone and started texting.

Good thing that Kagra didn't know anything embarrassing about her.

"Wait." Julian lifted his hand. "I have a better idea. You don't need to ask Kagra." He leaned closer to Jade and smiled. "Tell us something that no one knows about you. Something that you are very embarrassed about."

There was only one thing, and she wasn't going to say it.

"Come on, Jade." Julian took her hand. "Do it for me. You like me, right? You trust me?"

She nodded because she liked him very much. He was so sweet.

Leaning forward, she put her hand on his arm. "Promise me that you won't tell anyone."

"I won't. I promise. You can whisper it in my ear."

"Okay." She leaned over so her lips were nearly touching his ear. "My real name is not Jade. It's Je-Kara, and it means precious. If you tell anyone, I will have to kill you, which is a shame since I like you so much." She patted his cheek.

As the door opened and Toven walked in with Mia driving through, Jade smiled. "Now, that's a beautiful face. You look like one of those mannequins they have in the stores."

Toven frowned. "Did you give her the drugs already?"

"Yes." Julian patted her shoulder. "She is all yours."

42

VANESSA

"Hello." Vanessa offered her hand to the plump blond woman waiting alongside her in the underground parking lot. "I'm Vanessa."

"No English." The woman patted her chest. "Isla."

"Oh, yes. You are Sofia's aunt."

"Sofia. Yes." Her expression turned grim. "No good."

"She's transitioning. She will be good."

They both nodded and then turned to look at the door to the large vehicle lift.

Lusha wasn't the only human arriving from Safe Haven. A couple of members of Igor's former compound had decided to move to the village, and they were the woman's relatives. Vanessa knew who she was, but the name eluded her.

William had promised to work on a new earpiece tech that would provide an instantaneous translation. The technology was available, but it was clunky, and everyone knew that William could do better if he only had the time to dedicate to the task.

But there was only one of him, and no matter how many new assistants he trained, no one seemed sufficiently capable to just take a new project and run with it without William having to be the brain behind it.

When the elevator doors opened, and the limousine pulled out, Isla released a happy squeak and rushed to intercept it.

Okidu hit the brakes just in time to avoid hitting her, and a moment later, the back door opened, and a teenage girl jumped out.

As the two embraced and tears started flowing, another woman and another teenager got out of the vehicle and joined the tearful reunion.

Vanessa guessed the older woman was Isla's sister and the younger teen was her daughter.

The last one to emerge from the limo was Lusha.

Dark-haired, short, with a pleasant round face and thick glasses, she looked more like a kindergarten teacher than a lawyer. The plain jeans and pink T-shirt added to the impression, but appearances could be deceptive, and the sweet exterior could cover a shark's personality.

Or at least Vanessa hoped so. Mo-red and the others needed a strong defender who wasn't easily intimidated.

"Hi." The girl walked around the tearful four. "I'm Lusha." She offered Vanessa her hand.

"I'm Vanessa. Welcome to the village."

"Thank you." She took a deep breath. "Hannele, Lana, and Jessica are so excited. They were a little disappointed with life at Safe Haven, and they missed Isla and Jarmo."

"I can imagine."

After living with the Kra-ell and being immersed in their culture, the free-love philosophy of Safe Haven shouldn't have been too foreign to the human females who had been having sex with the Kra-ell males without expecting any commitment. But perhaps they'd expected a more vital community and had been disappointed with how remote and isolated the place was.

"How about you?" she asked Lusha. "Did you like it at Safe Haven?"

"It was okay. A bit boring, though. The only jobs we could have there were housekeeping and gardening, and neither were what I wanted to do with my life." Lusha turned to look at Okidu, who was pulling everyone's luggage out of the trunk. "I should help him."

"Don't." Vanessa put a hand on her shoulder. "He will consider it offensive if you don't let him carry your luggage."

"Oh, really? Why?"

"It's just his way." Vanessa didn't want to explain about Okidu and that he was a cyborg who had been programmed to be helpful. She threaded her arm through Lusha's.

Discussing the girl's accommodations was more important at the moment. "I assume that you are not close enough to your father to want to stay with him."

Lusha's hybrid father had arrived with Jade in the village, while her human mother had chosen to settle in Safe Haven.

"I'm not," the girl said. "I mean, we are not strangers, and he acknowledges me, but we are not close." She smiled sadly. "My mother decided to stay in Safe Haven, and I'm going to miss her. I told her that I would come back after the trial."

"That's definitely possible." Vanessa glanced at the four females who had stopped crying and were now chatting excitedly and following behind her and Lusha.

She pressed the button for the elevator. "You have three options as far as lodging. You can stay at my place, or I can find you a room in another house, and you can also get a room where the prisoners are being kept so you will not have to commute back and forth."

"I thought that they were being kept here."

"They are not. We have another location that is about a forty-five-minute drive from here. As I told you over the phone, I spend my free time with Mo-red at the other facility, but I have to come to the village during the day to continue the interviews. If you stay at my place, you will have it all to yourself most of the time, and the Guardians or I can drive you back and forth as needed. The question is, where do you prefer to work?"

Lusha seemed lost. "I don't know. I want to spend some time in the village and get to know the people here, but I also need to start working on the defense."

"I have a suggestion." Vanessa led her into the elevator and held the door open until the others got in. "I'll take you to my place first so you can leave your things there, and then I'll give you a tour of the village. We will grab something to eat, talk strategy, and go to visit the prisoners. You can decide where you want to stay after seeing both locations."

"Thank you." The girl looked relieved. "That's perfect."

43

MO-RED

When the cell door opened, Mo-red's heart rate accelerated as it always did when he expected Vanessa to enter, but upon seeing her companion, it did that for a whole different reason.

"Hello, Lusha." He offered the young human his hand. "Thank you for agreeing to defend me and the others."

"You're welcome." She shook his hand. "I just hope I can actually help you."

Given Vanessa's somber expression, she didn't have much faith either in Lusha's ability, her chances of success, or both.

"Please, take a seat." She motioned for the girl to sit on the couch and sat next to her.

Mo-red wanted to pull Vanessa into his arms and tell her not to worry, but he didn't know whether she would be okay with him doing that in front of Lusha. Instead, he turned the chair around to face the couch and sat down.

"Lusha and I talked on the way," Vanessa said. "It's too complicated for me to do it justice, so I'll let her explain."

The girl cleared her throat, took a sip of water from the bottle she'd brought with her, and put it down.

"Naturally, I don't have any experience defending people charged with murder, so that's a problem, but I did some research on the subject before coming here, and I can work with what I've learned. The main issue, though, is that the Kra-ell are not bound by human laws, so citing them might not do us much good." She pushed a strand of dark hair behind her ear. "Under human law, I can use the insanity defense, but it's not really applicable. It requires the defender to be unable to determine right from wrong at the time of the killing, which we know is not true. You knew it was wrong but were unable to refuse the command. We can claim diminished capacity, but that's not a great line of defense either."

"Why not?" Vanessa asked. "The guilty deed was not the product of a guilty mind."

Lusha nodded. "I didn't say that it didn't apply. It's just not a strong line of defense because it is difficult to prove. Usually, it's used when it can be proven that the person is not at fault because their actions were a consequence of abnormal brain function."

Mo-red lifted his hand. "I think that's our best line of defense, and it's not at all difficult to prove. My brain, which controls my body, got hijacked by Igor. And if anyone doubts the power of compulsion, Tom can easily demonstrate it by compelling a member of the jury to do something that they don't want to."

Lusha scrunched her nose. "I'm sorry, but a demonstration is not good as proof. You have no way of proving that at the time of the murders, you were trying to resist the compulsion but couldn't. For all they know, you were a willing participant and as culpable as Igor. Whoever aids, abets, counsels, or benefits from the offense, will be tried, indicted, and punished as a principal offender, who in this case is Igor."

Mo-red's heart sank. "Then I'm doomed. Even if I can prove

that I wasn't a willing participant and that I was forced to do Igor's bidding, I can't claim that I didn't enjoy the fruits of the crime. I'm guilty."

Lusha smiled shyly. "Not so fast. As I said in my opening statement, the Kra-ell don't care about human laws, and in this case, I think it can work to our advantage. Instead of basing our defense on existing human laws that are beneficial to your case, we will bring up philosophical arguments which should be universal and not human-specific. That being said, humans have such a rich treasure trove of philosophy on the subject of moral responsibility that I have plenty of material to work with."

Mo-red frowned. He was only vaguely familiar with the most basic tenets of human philosophy, but from what he knew, moral responsibility was not about culpability. It was a more general term that applied to issues like the responsibility of the capable to defend or provide for the less capable.

Jade was a good example of someone who believed it was her moral responsibility to lead their people because she was best suited for the job. If she decided not to do it, and someone less capable took the leader's position, she wouldn't be put on trial for neglecting her duty or for inadvertently causing harm to the people, even if that other person caused them major damage.

"I don't understand how moral responsibility has anything to do with this," he said. "What we need to do is prove that I and the others had no choice. What we did does not reflect on our morality because our free will was taken away from us."

"Precisely." Lusha smiled. "The notion of free will is pivotal in determining whether people are morally responsible for their actions and in what sense. What's important for our case is that moral responsibility is not the same as legal responsibility. Sometimes they are one and the same, but in our case, we can separate the two and focus on the moral responsibility alone, proving that it does not exist without free will."

It was a clever twist, but he doubted that the Kra-ell could be manipulated into a philosophical discussion and to base their judgment on it.

"How is that different from Tom's demonstration of the power strong compellers have over their victims? Even if you prove that moral responsibility does not exist without free will, you can't prove that we were robbed of ours while the murders occurred."

"Ah." Lusha smiled conspiratorially. "It's different because it will give us time to expose the Kra-ell to a different way of thinking and fill their heads with philosophical questions. Hopefully, that will undermine the beliefs they brought with them from their home planet, so they won't demand a death sentence. Once that's done, we can ask Tom to demonstrate to drive the point home. The thing is, most human courts would have found you either not guilty or, at most, guilty of manslaughter. We need to get the Kra-ell to think more like modern humans who live in democracies that respect human rights. That will take time and clever maneuvering."

It was a smart strategy, but it was risky and could blow up in their faces if the Kra-ell lost patience. Then again, he couldn't come up with a better strategy to change his people's attitudes in a short period of time.

"Do you think it will work?" Vanessa asked.

Lusha let out a breath. "That's the best I've been able to come up with so far, but I would love to talk to the clan's judge and get her opinion."

44

KIAN

As Kian strode toward Igor's cell, he was accompanied by a small crowd.

Per his request, the doors to the other cells had been closed as soon as he and his entourage had arrived at the building so the other prisoners wouldn't be aware of what was going on.

Noticing that Turner needed to jog to keep up with his much longer strides, Kian slowed down. Despite the guy's brilliant mind and the admiration of everyone who knew him, Turner was supposedly self-conscious about his height.

Personally, Kian had never noticed Turner having insecurities, but he took Syssi's word for it. After all, he was well aware of his obtuseness when it came to feelings, and he trusted her assessment.

Julian had no problem keeping up, but he hung back, closing the procession with Edna, Toven, and Mia.

Jade strode as purposefully as Kian did on his other side, the effects of the drug long gone. "I hope it works on him as well as it worked on me and the two males so we can get what we need out of him and put him in stasis. Every minute that he's still awake is a minute too long."

Kian had no idea what Jade had whispered in Julian's ear, and the doctor refused to tell him anything other than that it had been personal and none of Kian's business. Toven had still struggled to get into her mind even though she'd offered no resistance, but with Mia's help, he'd been able to get into her latest memories, including what she'd told Julian.

The doctor had confirmed that what Toven had plucked out of her mind was correct, but they had done it in whispers, so Kian still didn't know what it was, and he was curious.

What could be so embarrassing that Jade had threatened to kill Julian if he told anyone?

"I can't argue with that," Kian said. "Especially if what I suspect is true and Igor is transmitting information about us to someone on the home planet."

He stopped in front of Igor's cell, where Magnus was waiting for them along with the two young Kra-ell volunteers. "Good afternoon. How is the prisoner doing?"

"He should be awake by now."

In preparation, the Guardians had shot Igor with enough tranquilizer darts to down an elephant, so they could go in and chain him to the iron cot, which was bolted to the concrete floor.

"Can't you see him through the surveillance cameras?" Jade asked.

"We can, but he hasn't moved a muscle since we tranquilized him, and he hasn't opened his eyes either."

Perhaps Igor had been weakened by hunger. After the truth drug idea had come up, Kian had instructed the Guardians not to feed him. His last meal should have been the evening of the day before, which would make him hungry or rather thirsty, but not starving.

The Kra-ell didn't need to feed every day, and when they fed, the quantities weren't large. Their bodies were incredibly efficient at processing the blood intake and extracting the nutrients they needed from it.

If their metabolism had also been engineered by the gods and was not innate, it was quite ingenious. The servants the gods had created were not a drain on their food resources. They didn't need to waste time preparing or cooking their food either.

He felt sorry for them for missing all the culinary treats, but he had to admit that the simplicity of their nutrition was enviable. As long as the Kra-ell could find game, they wouldn't starve.

"When was Igor last fed?" he asked.

"Yesterday morning." Magnus pulled out his phone and initiated the door-opening sequence. "Theo gave him a blood bag before you told us to stop feeding him."

"So he's not hungry." Kian let out a breath. "I hope the drugs will do their thing despite that."

Turning to his entourage, he signaled for Toven to come forward. "You and Mia should stay in the control room until you are needed." He looked at Edna. "Perhaps you should go with them. I don't want you anywhere near him until I'm sure the drugs are working."

She nodded. "I'll go with Toven and Mia."

Turner wanted to be there when they administered the drugs, and Kian had no reason to deny him.

As the three followed Alfie to the control room, the rest crowded inside the vestibule created by bisecting the cell with iron bars. Kian had no choice but to stand right next to the partition, and despite Igor being bound, a trickle of unease slithered down his spine.

Igor's attack had left a permanent scar on his self-confidence, but there was no way he would ever admit it to anyone other than Syssi.

He had an image to uphold.

Besides, he had nothing to fear. Magnus and the brothers were armed and alert, the two young Kra-ell had enough muscle power to subdue Igor, and they were all wearing earpieces.

He'd made everyone in his group double-check the fit before they entered the elevator.

"Open the bars," he told Magnus. "Let's do this."

45

JADE

As the doctor and Magnus entered Igor's inner cell, Jade stayed on the other side of the bars together with Kian, the brothers, and the two Kra-ell.

There was no space for more than two people standing side by side next to the cot, but even if there was, she was happy to stay out in the vestibule. She would be even happier when Igor become a distant memory.

He bared his fangs at his visitors. "Didn't you pump me with enough tranquilizers already?"

"We decided to try to improve your personality," Magnus said. "We have something new that will make you friendlier." He motioned for the doctor to do his thing.

Julian pulled a syringe out of his black bag and a vial of murky-looking liquid. Tearing the wrapper off the syringe, he stuck the needle into the vial and pulled three-quarters of it into the body of the syringe.

"Is that enough?" Jade asked. "That's how much Julian used on me and the other two volunteers. Igor probably requires more."

"The prudent thing to do is to start with the same dose and add more if needed."

It had been plenty enough for her, but she wasn't enhanced like Igor with god genetics. Toven hadn't been able to access her long-term memories, but it was enough that he'd succeeded in collecting her recent ones. All they needed was to determine that what Igor was saying was true.

When five minutes or so had passed, Julian stepped out of the cell and motioned for Kian to enter. "He should be more malleable right now."

"Let's see." Kian took a deep breath and joined Magnus next to Igor's cot.

The Guardian had his gun in hand, but Brundar wasn't taking any chances and held a couple of daggers that he was twirling between his fingers as if they were chopsticks or pencils.

For a moment Jade watched him, transfixed by the dexterity and skill, but then she remembered what had happened the last time she and Brundar had been focused on his knives and turned toward the cell.

"How old are you?" Kian started.

"Seven thousand, two hundred, twenty-two."

Igor didn't sound nearly as loopy as she'd been earlier that day.

"Who sent you?" Kian asked.

"The gods."

"Which one of them?"

Igor let out a breath. "You don't know him. His name is Ba'al-cock."

Jade had a feeling he was toying with Kian. Baal meant owner in ancient Semitic languages, and everyone knew what the second part of the name meant.

"Very funny," Kian said. "You see? It's already working to

improve your personality. There is nothing like a sense of humor to win friends and influence people."

"Haha." Igor affected a fake laugh.

"Why did you drink my blood?"

"I was curious. I wondered what you would taste like."

"Was it good?"

"Exquisite." Igor licked his lips. "Quality bouquet."

"It's not working," Jade murmured. "He needs a stronger dose."

Kian had either heard her or reached the same conclusion because he walked out and signaled for Julian to go back in. "Double it."

"He might black out," the doctor cautioned. "I'll give him the quarter that's left in the vial first."

"Fine." Kian leaned against the bars as he waited for Julian to administer the second dose.

When Julian stepped out, Kian returned to Igor's side.

"I'll ask you again. Why did you drink my blood?"

"Because I could. The scent of your fear was delightful."

Kian waited a few more moments before asking the same question again.

"My fangs were the only weapon I had," Igor said this time. "What else could I have used to threaten your people?"

"You didn't have to drink my blood. As far as I'm aware, you are heterosexual, so it wasn't because you wanted to turn me on."

Igor smiled. "Did you enjoy it?"

"You know I didn't. It was humiliating."

"Good. Then I achieved at least one goal with that ill-planned escape attempt."

Jade shook her head. "It's still not working."

Igor tried to turn his head to look at her, but the chains holding him down didn't allow for much movement.

"Yeah. I'll give him a little more." Julian pulled a new vial and syringe out of his bag.

Once again, he and Kian changed places, and when a few minutes had passed, Kian tried again. "Why did you drink my blood?"

There was no answer, either because Igor was tired of coming up with lies or he had passed out.

"Call Toven in," Kian said.

Anandur opened the door. "There isn't enough room for Toven and Mia to get in. Some of us will have to trade places with them."

Jade didn't want to leave, but she was the only one there who wasn't really necessary. She motioned for the two Kra-ell youths to follow her.

"Leave the door open," she told Anandur. "If he tries anything, we will jump right in."

Anandur nodded.

As she joined Edna outside, the judge asked, "How is it going in there?"

"Not good. I don't think it's working."

Edna nodded. "I had a feeling it wouldn't."

46

ANNANI

"Please, can you stop pacing?" Alena pleaded. "You're making me dizzy."

"I am anxious to find out whether the drugs worked on Igor. If my pacing bothers you, you can join Orion in the amphitheater."

Alena groaned. "I've seen them put on that performance a hundred times. I can't sit through it again."

"It is not the same show. Adarella wrote a new play."

"All her plays are variations on the same theme, and the same actors play in them." She put her book away and pushed to her feet. "It's the first time for Orion, so he is undoubtedly enjoying himself. Maybe I should join him just to see him having fun."

"That is an excellent idea."

Alena hesitated by the door. "Are you going to be okay here by yourself?"

"Yes, yes." Annani waved her daughter away. "Kian is going to call any minute now."

Alena nodded. "If he shares any exciting news, you know where to find us."

"Yes." Annani forced a smile. "Go, have fun with your mate."

She should not have dragged the pair with her to the sanctuary. They were bored, and they missed the village and the rest of their family, and the truth was that she missed that too. Perhaps Kian was right, and it was time to turn the sanctuary into a vacation retreat and move everyone into the village.

Even with the Kra-ell, there was still enough room for her people to settle there. Sari had no plans to join, so they would still have two separate locations for the clan, which was strategically advantageous.

Despite the quiet on Navuh's front, it would be foolish to assume that the Brotherhood was no longer a threat.

Areana claimed he had no plans to move against the clan and was busy shoring up the Brotherhood's income sources. These days, a bunch of hackers could do much more damage than an entire army of dumb soldiers, so there was not much use for mercenary armies.

When the phone clutched in her hand finally rang, Annani answered immediately. "How did it go?"

"It failed," Kian said. "Toven couldn't get into Igor's head even with Mia's help. We kept increasing the dose, and Igor just blacked out at some point before Edna could try it."

"Are you going to attempt it again?"

"Yes. Julian said that he now has a better feel for how much Igor can take. We will also try a different class of drugs. Maybe a different combination will have better results."

"And if it does not?"

"Then we put him in stasis and forget about him. Even if he can transmit information telepathically, he won't be able to do it while in stasis and buried in the catacombs."

"You should let me try it. I might be a stronger thraller than Toven. After all, I am Ahn's daughter, and Ahn was the most powerful compeller and thraller among the gods on Earth.

Ekin was a brilliant scientist, but he did not possess strong mind manipulation powers. What Toven and Mortdh inherited from the Eternal King was just an echo of that."

Kian was quiet for a moment. "I don't doubt you, but you've never used those powers to break through to someone as resistant as Igor. In fact, you've only used them very gently on Kaia and Aliya and a little less gently on Dalhu's men."

"I do not like using mind control, and I do not have much practice, but I know I have those powers within me. I really do not understand why it is okay for Toven and even Mia to get near Igor but not me. What are you afraid of?"

He sighed. "Besides the fact that you are more precious to me than Toven and Mia, and besides the fact that you are the heart of the clan, and without you, we will be lost, Igor does not know that you exist, and I want to keep it that way. I'm not a legitimate heir to the Eternal King's throne because I am half-human, but you definitely are, and as far as we know, you are his only heir. Need I say more?"

"I understand your concern, but there are ways to mitigate the risk. If Igor is drugged, chained, and blindfolded, how will he even know that I am near him? I will not say a word. You will ask him the questions we need answers for, and I will enter his mind to pluck the answers out in complete silence. You just need to tell everyone there not to mention my presence or to address me in any way."

The long silence on the other side was a good sign that Kian was actually considering it.

"Well?" Annani did not have the patience to wait for him to decide. "Are you going to use me, or are you going to lose sleep worrying that the gods might show up on our doorstep because Igor telepathically transmitted information about us?"

If he did not answer her right away, she would disregard his wishes and just show up at the keep.

"We will try again tomorrow, and if we fail again, I'll consider it seriously."

Stifling a groan, Annani closed her eyes. "I trust you will arrive at the right conclusion. Do not let your irrational fear for my safety endanger our people."

47

PETER

"Excited?" Kri elbowed Peter in the ribs.

"Why would I be excited?"

"I am," she admitted. "I'm also intimidated. Until now, I was the baddest badass female in the clan. Now, there are a whole bunch of them who can hand me my ass."

"What about Wonder? She's probably as strong as the Kra-ell females."

"Yeah, but she's as docile as a puppy. She doesn't like using her strength."

"I wouldn't call her docile. Delicate is a better term, feminine, gentle."

Kri snorted. "I don't need to be politically correct."

As the sound of female voices drifted down the hallway, Peter squared his shoulders and stood taller.

He'd heard the stories about Jade and Kagra's killing spree and how Phinas had saved Kagra's life. He'd also seen Kagra prancing around the village and was intrigued. Jade's second-in-command was unlike the other Kra-ell pureblooded females who were somber and radiated aggression.

From what he'd seen so far, Kagra was quick to smile and

laugh, which was uncommon for the Kra-ell, and she didn't seem to take herself as seriously as Jade did.

She was also hotter than sin.

Back in the day, he'd been attracted to Eleanor, who shared many characteristics with the Kra-ell, but Kagra was prettier, and despite being as slim as the rest of them, she had a round ass that he couldn't take his eyes off.

"Hello." The object of his fascination sauntered into the classroom with a bunch of other females following her inside. "I'm Kagra." She offered her hand to Kri.

"Hi." Kri shook it. "I'm Kri, and this is Peter. We will start with evaluating your level of training." She smiled. "Brute strength is great, but you also need to know what to do with it."

One of the other females released a derisive snort. "We've been training since we could walk. There is nothing you or your friend can teach us."

Kri advanced on the female. "I am a head Guardian, and you answer to me. I expect to be addressed with respect."

Kagra lifted her hand to stop the situation from escalating. "I apologize for Rishba. We are here to learn." She turned to the female. "The only words I want to hear from you are 'Yes, mistress.' Understood?"

The female seethed, but she dipped her head. "Yes, mistress."

Hell, why did that make him hard?

He liked Kagra's commanding tone of voice, and he liked how the other female submitted to her authority.

As Kagra shifted her eyes to him, he gave her a slight nod of approval.

Kri clapped her hands. "Today, I want to see your hand-to-hand fighting skills. Pair up, ladies."

As the twelve females paired up, Kagra looked Kri over. "I guess it is you and me." She shifted her gaze to Peter. "Unless you would like to take a tumble with me?"

Talk about double entendre. Was she flirting with him?

"I would love to."

Kagra grinned. "Perhaps you'd like to get one of those exoskeleton suits. You don't stand a chance without one."

"We will see about that." He got in position on the mat. "I might be a glutton for punishment, but I'm curious about your abilities."

With her fangs on display, her grin looked feral, but her eyes weren't red, so he knew she hadn't gotten in a real fighting mood yet.

"I'll try not to rearrange that pretty face of yours." She crouched. "I kind of like it the way it is."

Was she trying to unbalance him, or was she flirting for real?

Kri chuckled. "You're not playing fair, Kagra."

"All is fair in love and war," the female quoted. "Isn't that what humans like to say?"

Kri shook her head. "You're trouble, aren't you?"

"You have no idea."

Kagra pounced so suddenly that Peter hadn't even had time to brace for impact and found himself on his back with the hellcat straddling him.

"Hello." She caught his hands and pulled them over his head. "What do I get for winning this round?" She leaned over him, her face hovering an inch away from his. "A kiss?"

He was about to answer in the affirmative when Kri pulled Kagra off him by her shirt.

"Knock it off. This is not sex education 101. You can continue this somewhere private."

Kagra got free with a quick twist and bared her fangs at Kri. "Watch it, Head Guardian. The next time you pull something like this, you'll find my hands around your neck." She got in Kri's face. "And I won't let go that easily."

"Ladies." Peter jumped to his feet. "Please, let's continue in the same civilized manner we started." He put his hand on Kagra's shoulder. "There is no reason to fight over me. Kri is happily mated, and she's not interested in me. I'm single, available, and interested."

48

KAGRA

The immortal was deliciously handsome. He was dark-haired and olive-skinned like a Kra-ell, but he wasn't as tall. Then again, he packed much more muscle, and even though he wasn't as strong, he looked good, and Kagra liked the way he had felt under her when she'd straddled him.

That goatee of his was so cute, making him look devilish, and his full lips were just begging to be kissed and nibbled on.

He didn't seem to mind that she was stronger. On the contrary, it turned him on, and when the scent of his arousal hit Kagra's nostrils, she wished for everyone else to magically disappear from the room so she could have her way with him.

It was an uncommon reaction for the male descendants of the gods.

The ones she'd flirted with on the ship had been interested until she'd shown the first hint of aggression. Max had been avoiding her ever since she'd pinned him to the wall in a darkened hallway of the ship and shown him how a pureblooded female could kiss, and Dandor lost interest as soon as Max had, probably after he'd heard about the kiss.

Well, tough.

Kagra wasn't going to change who she was because those males couldn't handle her. She could be gentle if she wanted to, and she'd even tried a couple of hybrids back in the compound, but she wasn't going to hide who she was just to stroke some fragile male's ego.

"You're with me, Kagra." Kri assumed a fighting stance. "Come at me."

Looking disappointed, Peter took a step back and leaned against the wall to watch.

She winked at him before charging Kri.

The female managed to get a hold of her and threw her over her shoulder, but Kagra was up so fast that Kri hadn't had time to brace for the impact and found herself in the same position Peter had been in only moments ago.

"Oh, wow. You are something else." Kri took the hand Kagra offered her. "Are the others as skilled as you are?"

"They might not be as fast, but they are good." Kagra stood next to the Guardian and crossed her arms over her chest. "They can also outlast you and your Guardian friends."

For a few moments, the two of them observed the other females spar with each other, and then Kri lifted her hand. "I've seen enough. You are all qualified to join the program. How many of you can handle a gun?"

Only Kagra lifted her hand. "I trained before the abduction. None of us got to use firearms in Igor's camp. We trained with old swords and javelins, which were great for building strength but useless as far as weapons go."

Kri nodded. "So, I guess you know nothing about explosives either."

"I know they go boom." Kagra slanted a look at Peter. "What is your specialty?"

"Being charming." He pushed away from the wall. "I will gladly list all of my many attributes over coffee."

She smiled. "Are you asking me out on a date?"

Shaking her head, Kri stepped away from them and walked over to a pair of females locked in a grappling embrace.

He arched a brow, which enhanced his devilish look. "Do the Kra-ell date?"

"No, we don't. We are very straightforward in regard to sex. We issue an invitation, and a male either accepts it or not."

He grimaced. "That doesn't sound like fun. Where is the seduction? The mating dance? It's not just about the physical stuff."

"It's not?" Kagra asked mockingly.

"Nope." He leaned back against the wall, bending one leg at the knee. "Would you like to give it a try?"

"Yeah, why not. Is there a bar anywhere in your village?"

"Not yet. We had one built in the newest phase, but so far, no one has offered to run it."

"Interesting. Let me ask around. Not everyone wants to join the Guardian force. Maybe someone will be interested in operating the bar." She smiled. "We don't eat your food, so drinks and coffee are the only things we can share."

"What about dancing?"

She shook her head. "We have traditional dances that the males perform, but we don't have couples' dancing."

"Why not?"

She shrugged. "Doesn't really work with the way our society is structured. But hey, it's a new beginning for us, so maybe dancing is in our future."

He reached for her hand, and she let him grasp it. "I would love to teach you to dance. Regrettably, we don't have a club in the village either, and I can't take you to the city." He pulled her closer to him. "But I can teach you at my place."

She arched a brow. "Are we still talking about dancing?"

"Yes." He smiled. "I intended to play hard to get."

She knew what he meant. She'd seen enough American movies in which that phrase had been used.

"Why would you want to do that?"

"To make things more interesting." His expression turned serious. "I've never been interested in exploring things outside of bed with a female, but with you, I want that. I want to get to know you."

"Well, isn't that precious?" She leaned into him. "I want to get to know you too."

49

VANESSA

After leaving Lusha with Madbar, Vanessa returned to her and Mo-red's little nest within the dungeon and kicked her heels off.

"So, what's your impression of Lusha?" She plopped on the couch next to Mo-red.

"She's very intelligent." He chuckled. "I knew she must be smart to have been selected to study at the university, but she seemed so unassuming that I never thought much of her. It proves how wrong it is to judge a book by its cover."

Vanessa nodded. "When I saw her first, I thought that she looked like a kindergarten teacher. Then we started talking, and I realized that she is highly intelligent, but I still thought of her as a little timid. She's so soft-spoken and unassuming, but that illusion evaporates once she starts talking about law and philosophy. She's passionate about it, and she's not afraid to stick to her guns, so to speak."

Stretching her legs in front of her, Vanessa wiggled her toes. "She gives me hope."

He took hold of her calves, moved her around, and placed

her legs over his thighs. "Why do you wear such pointy shoes? They are obviously uncomfortable."

As he started gently massaging her toes, Vanessa closed her eyes and released a moan that was more appropriate for a very different sort of massaging. "They make me look good."

"You look amazing regardless of your footwear."

Mo-red's voice had dipped an octave lower, and when Vanessa opened her eyes, the evidence of his arousal stared her in the face. His irises had a red tint, and his fangs protruded over his lower lip.

"Was it the moan that did it? Or are you getting turned on by my toes?" She wiggled them again.

"Both." He pressed his thumb to her arch, eliciting another throaty moan.

"I hate to ask, but I feel compelled to. Where did you learn to massage feet like that?"

He smiled. "Not everything about Kra-ell sex is a fight for dominance."

Jealousy churning in her stomach, she arched a brow. "You told me that it starts with a battle, culminates in a climax, and that there is no snuggling or talking after it is done. Was that a lie?"

"No, it wasn't. But sometimes, it doesn't start immediately with a fight. Sometimes the female wants to be pampered first."

"That's such a waste. What's the point of getting a foot massage if, a few moments later, a savage fight for dominance erupts?"

Mo-red shrugged. "It's also customary for the male to bring a small gift when he's invited, but if he doesn't have a gift, he can substitute it with a nice gesture like a foot massage or a back rub."

The Kra-ell culture was fascinating.

It was a mistake to focus just on the main tenets of their

culture and assume that everything about them was simplistic and monolithic. There were many nuances to their interactions, which included ways to show affection without grand gestures or declarations of love.

Vanessa could appreciate that, but the lack of exclusivity wasn't something she could live with, not with Mo-red.

If he were not imprisoned, would he have wanted to be with more females?

Would he have accepted an invitation from a pureblooded female while they were together?

Would he have been okay with her inviting another male into her bed?

"I need to ask you something." She pulled her feet out of his hands. "If you were free, would you have sought the company of females other than me?"

He frowned. "Would you have wanted me to?"

"Don't answer my question with another question. Just tell me yes or no."

"No."

"Why not? Exclusivity is not part of your culture."

"It is not, but I don't wish to be with anyone other than you."

"That's because you are not free, and I'm the only one you can have. In normal circumstances, you would have been pressured to be with a variety of females."

He seemed offended by her words, and she regretted saying them, but something inside had pushed her to get the answers. Maybe it was an insecurity she hadn't known she had, or maybe it was the unsettling conversation with Lusha that had highlighted and sharpened the difficulty they would face proving Mo-red's innocence.

Hell, she couldn't even call it that. There was no argument that he'd committed those crimes. There had been witnesses. The only question was whether he was morally responsible for them and whether his people would make the distinction, separating the intent from the deed.

Mo-red leaned away from her as if she'd physically pushed him. "There is pressure on the females to have a variety of partners because there are so few of them, and if they choose to be exclusive with one male, it wouldn't be fair to the others. There is much less pressure on the males, especially if their chosen female is not Kra-ell. On the contrary, they remove themselves from the competition."

His answer should have been enough, and she should have stopped that line of inquiry, but she had to know what he felt for her and why.

"Wouldn't you suffer ridicule for disregarding the so-called Kra-ell way?"

"Probably." He chuckled, but the sound was more sardonic than humorous. "But why should I care what others think of me? They already deem me dishonorable. They call me Igor's puppet and a dozen other derogatory names."

"What if that wasn't your situation? Would you have still chosen to be with me and no one else?"

"Yes. A million times, yes. Even if it meant excommunication, the answer would still be yes."

50

MO-RED

What had gotten into Vanessa?

She seemed like such a confident female, but her line of questioning implied insecurity.

Had he done or said something to undermine her?

Mo-red shook his head. "What's wrong? Why are you asking me questions you should know the answer to?"

"Should I?" She lifted her legs off his lap and swung them over the side of the couch. "We've just met, and I don't know much about you other than the facts I collected." She pushed to her feet and walked over to the coffeemaker. "You have three sons from three different females, and they have only good things to say about you, which is great, but I don't know what to expect from you in regard to our relationship." She filled the machine with water from a bottle she took out of the refrigerator, popped in a pod, and turned around to face him.

He was at a loss.

"Did anything change in this regard from this morning? Did I say or do anything that was offensive to you?"

Letting out a breath, Vanessa closed her eyes for a brief moment. "Not really. I think it was the foot massage."

Now he was at an even greater loss. "I don't understand. Did I do it wrong?"

"No, you did it perfectly, and I allowed myself hope for more foot massages in the future, which I shouldn't have done."

"I understand. After talking with Lusha, you realized that I don't have a future."

Vanessa shook her head. "No, it wasn't that." She turned around to remove the cup from the coffeemaker and put another one under the spout. "Well, yes, that was the initial trigger. Lusha didn't agree with the line of defense I had in mind and explained why it wouldn't work, which got my gut twisted in a knot. But then she explained what she thought could be a good defense, and it gave me hope. What followed that was a string of thoughts that dealt with the long term, and that was when I realized I might be fooling myself. Even if the results of the trial are the best we can hope for, there might not be a future for us simply because of our different cultures. I want exclusivity, and you might not even know what it means."

She took the two cups, put them on the tiny coffee table, and sat down, but not close enough to touch him.

There was a chasm growing between them, and he wasn't sure it was a bad thing. Maybe they would save themselves a lot of pain by ending things now.

Could he do that, though?

Could he sacrifice these precious moments just so the pain of saying goodbye to her wouldn't compound the pain of saying goodbye to his life?

Mo-red wasn't a coward, and he wasn't afraid of pain, but he didn't want Vanessa to suffer. If he could shield her from torment, he should.

Except, he couldn't let her think that she meant so little to him.

"You're wrong." He took Vanessa's hand and clasped it

between his. "I want this with you. I want forever with you and only you, even if it means my excommunication from my people. But I'm a realist, and I know that allowing myself to feel everything my heart wants to feel will make losing it even more devastating than losing my life. Perhaps that's why you are pulling back, and I don't blame you for it, but I don't want you to think that you are just a temporary reprieve for me." He shook his head. "I'm not expressing myself well, and I'm making assumptions that I shouldn't. I don't know what you're allowing or disallowing yourself to feel for me."

As she looked into his eyes, her expression softened. "You are more insightful than you give yourself credit for. I let my fear of losing you to your people in a trial mushroom into losing you regardless of the result."

He chuckled. "If I'm ever set free, you will have a very hard time getting rid of me. I'm not going anywhere. Are you?"

He held his breath as he waited for her answer.

"I'm not." She squeezed his hand. "I don't know if we will survive this as a couple and if our differences will prove too much for us to overcome, but I don't intend to give up on you either."

It hadn't been a profession of love, not on his part and not on hers, but it was implied, and as someone who had never said the words to anyone before, he had been pretty damn close to saying them now.

51

GILBERT

Eric leaned over and whispered in Gilbert's ear, "Nervous?"

"What do you think?" Gilbert smoothed a hand over his thinning hair. "I'm not worried about the match with Toven. I know it will be over in a split second, and he won't hurt me, but I'm worried about what will happen next. I have five kids that will be orphaned if I don't make it. Karen has already lost a husband she loved dearly, and Kaia and Cheryl have lost a father. I can't put them through that again."

"I know." Eric pulled him into a fierce embrace and clapped him on the back. "You'll be okay. Otherwise, those Fates will have to deal with me."

"Stay with Karen during the ceremony, will you?"

"Of course."

They both looked to where Karen was sitting with Darlene and all their children.

Kaia looked anxious, and so did Cheryl, but Idina and the twins didn't know what was going on and were enjoying playing with the balloons the gym was bursting with.

Amanda had done a great job with the decorations, transforming the gym into an event venue. Round tables were covered in white tablecloths, the chairs had blue slipcovers and white ribbons tied around the backs, and each table had a centerpiece made from balloons and ribbons.

The Odus were distributing appetizers and putting bottles of whisky and ceremonial wine on the tables while the room slowly filled with people.

"I didn't expect so many to show up," he said to Eric. "Are they so eager to see me humiliated?"

His brother snorted. "That's what I thought, but they are just happy to see you finally do it. Bets were being placed on how long it would take you to summon enough courage to attempt the transition."

"Really?"

"Yep. Some were betting six months, others a year, but I bet on the shortest duration, which was two weeks." Eric grinned. "After tonight, I'm going to be twenty-three dollars and fifty cents richer."

"That's the entire pot?"

"No, but I wasn't the only one betting on two weeks."

"Who were the other ones?"

"Anandur and William. But don't look so offended. Many didn't even know about the betting, and they were a quarter each."

"Well, that's not so bad. I'm glad you believed in me. Frankly, though, I wouldn't be here tonight if not for Karen and Amanda ganging up on me. I hate to admit it, but I'm a chicken."

"No, you are not." Eric clapped him on the back again. "You're a family man."

That was a nice way of saying it, and it was true. Gilbert wasn't afraid of dying. He was afraid of leaving his loved ones alone and worried about what would happen to them without him.

As Kian and Syssi entered the gym, everyone hushed as if their arrival signaled the start of the ceremony. The only problem was that Toven hadn't arrived yet, and they couldn't start without him.

Syssi smiled, waved, and joined Amanda at the family table while Kian walked over to Gilbert and put a hand on his shoulder. "How are you feeling?"

"Nervous."

"That's understandable. Still, you couldn't have done better than Toven. A god's venom is almost guaranteed to get you where you want to be, which is on the other side of the transition, alive, well, and immortal."

"Amen to that." Gilbert released a breath. "Where is my inducer?"

'"He's outside the doors, waiting for my signal to come in."

"What's the signal?" Eric asked.

"This." Kian turned to face the crowd. "Hello, everyone," his voice boomed in the room. "Are you ready to celebrate Gilbert's induction?"

As clapping and cheers erupted, the gym door opened, and Toven entered with Mia and her grandparents.

Gilbert dipped his head, and so did Eric.

The god smiled and inclined his head as well.

Kian cleared his throat. "We are gathered here to present this fine man to the community. Gilbert is ready to attempt his transformation. Many who have gotten to know Gilbert and his family during the weeks since their arrival in the village are excited to be here tonight to witness his induction, and they are all vouching for him and his worthiness. Who volunteers to take on the burden of initiating Gilbert into his immortality?"

Toven raised his hand. "I do."

"Excellent." Kian turned to Gilbert. "Do you accept Toven as your initiator? As your mentor and protector, to honor him with your friendship, your respect, and your loyalty from now on?"

"I do." Gilbert dipped his head. "I'm honored and grateful for the privilege Toven agreed to bestow on me. I couldn't have asked for a better inducer. Literally."

As cheers and applause erupted, Kian waited until they subsided before continuing. "Does anyone object to Gilbert becoming Toven's protégé?" When no one raised their hands, Kian nodded. "As everyone present agrees it is a good match, let's seal it with a toast." He took the small wine glass Okidu handed him. "To Gilbert and Toven."

52

TOVEN

Toven got in position on the mat and planned his attack. The problem was making it look like Gilbert posed a challenge, so the guy wouldn't feel humiliated.

He hadn't thought to do that with Eric, but the younger brother was not as hard on himself as the older one was, and he had taken his quick defeat in stride.

As Gilbert assumed a fighting stance across from him, Toven had to stifle a chuckle. The guy was tall, still muscular, and in his youth he must have done some wrestling because his stance was correct, but he was pudgy around the middle, had a bald spot on the top of his head, and didn't look particularly threatening.

How was he supposed to feel aggression toward him?

Eric had mouthed off about Toven's mother, but that had only made him laugh, and then he'd insulted Toven directly and added that his entire gene pool was tainted, which had an element of truth to it, so the taunt had worked.

It didn't seem like Gilbert had prepared a similar strategy, though.

"Perhaps you should try to insult me," Toven suggested. "It worked for your brother."

Gilbert grimaced. "I could never bring myself to insult you. I'm too grateful to come up with anything negative to say about you."

The guy looked at him with nearly worshipful admiration, which made it even harder for Toven to summon aggression.

"I can come up with something." Eric stepped up to the mat. "Will it work if I'm the one issuing the insults?"

"It might." Toven gave him a smile to reassure him that there were no bad feelings between them despite Eric's irreverent attitude. "If I attack you, Gilbert will jump in to protect you."

"He will." Eric rubbed a hand over his clean-shaven jaw. "He's always done that. The problem is that you move so fast he will not make it in time to intercept, and I'm not in the mood for another bite, no matter how much I enjoyed the one you gave me." He waggled his brows.

Was that the angle he was choosing to pursue?

Toven hoped it wasn't. He was not attracted to other males, but he had never been offended by males who found him attractive, even those who hadn't been bashful about expressing their interest.

There was nothing wrong with it as long as it was done in a respectful manner and a refusal was accepted graciously.

Gilbert straightened and waved his brother away. "I'll do it the old-fashioned way." He walked up to Toven and punched him in the gut.

It was like getting hit by a child, and Toven had to work hard on not laughing. "You'll have to punch me harder."

A calculated look passed over Gilbert's eyes, and a moment later, he swung around with his leg, aiming for Toven's privates.

Naturally, he never made it, and as Toven caught his leg, Gilbert went down, landing on his ass.

Toven's fangs didn't even itch.

"Hey, Toven," Eric called. "If you and Mia have a baby girl, are you going to name her after your mother? What was her name, Elsa?"

As some people in the crowd laughed, Toven guessed there was a joke in there somewhere, but it was lost on him. Who was Elsa?

"It's no use." Gilbert lumbered to his feet. "It's not going to work. Oh well, it's the thought that counts, right?" He walked up to Toven and offered him his hand. "Thanks for trying. I appreciate it."

Would this be just one more failure to add to the long list of them? That Toven couldn't even summon aggression at will to induce a Dormant's transition?

He could imagine the smug look on Mortdh's face, mocking him for being too mellow, too accommodating, not ambitious enough, a mama's good boy—

The memory was enough to get his venom glands going and his fangs to elongate. Pulling on Gilbert's hand, he caught the Dormant's head with his other, tilted it to the side to elongate his neck, and struck.

53

GILBERT

Gilbert hadn't expected the attack to happen so fast and with no provocation. When Toven's fangs pierced his skin and then went so deep that he thought they would come out the other side of his neck, the burn was unbearable, but the god's hold on his head was so strong that he couldn't do anything other than submit.

When he felt like he was going to pass out from the pain, suddenly the burn subsided, replaced by a cooling sensation, and soon he was floating on a cloud of bliss the like of which he had never experienced before.

Was this what people felt on drugs?

No wonder there were so many addicts. The pot he had smoked as a teen was nothing, not even a blip on the scale of what he was experiencing now.

Thankfully, there was nothing sexual about the sensation, which had been one of his greatest fears. It was pure pleasure and calm, but then things changed, and he found himself soaring over psychedelic landscapes, marveling at colors he had never seen in reality and the translucent beings who were waving at him as he passed above them.

Were they angels? Occupants of other dimensions that had become accessible to him thanks to the venom?

How did that work? Had the venom unlocked blocks in his mind, allowing him to see things he normally couldn't?

It seemed like hours had passed with him floating over wondrous cities and beautiful valleys and mountains covered with flowers and trees in colors not found on Earth, and then he was floating back. He couldn't explain how he knew he was returning home, except for the tug on his heart that seemed always connected to Karen and the kids.

When he opened his eyes, the face that greeted him was as familiar to him as his own. "Hi, gorgeous." He tried to lift his hand to brush aside a dark lock of hair that cascaded down the side of her face, but his arm refused to move.

"Hi back to you." She dipped her head and kissed his forehead. "Are you okay?"

"I'm better than okay. I feel wonderful. How long was I out?"

"Long. I started to worry and wanted the doctor to check on you, but Vanessa said you were doing fine and to give you time."

"Vanessa? Isn't the doctor's name Bridget?"

Karen chuckled. "Yes. Vanessa is the psychologist, but she was right here while Bridget was on the other side of the gym. A moment later, you opened your eyes and looked at me." She let out a breath. "That was such a huge relief."

This time his hand obeyed his wishes when he tried to lift it and made it all the way to Karen's cheek. "I love you. I will always come back to you."

"Promise?" She smiled, but a lone tear slid down her cheek.

"I promise." He tried to lift his head so he could kiss her, but it was no use.

"Welcome back." Toven's voice came from his other side. "How are you feeling?"

With effort, Gilbert turned his head to look at the god. "I'm still floating. Thank you for the psychedelic trip."

"You're most welcome."

"Can I ask what finally spurred your aggression?"

Toven smiled. "I'm allergic to failure. I couldn't accept failing to induce you, and I forced myself to remember my brother mocking me for this or that. I hated him for always talking down to me."

Gilbert chuckled. "That would do it."

"How would you know?" Karen asked. "You are the oldest, and your younger siblings adore you."

"I know how important a good word from an older sibling is, and I also know the power of negativity. So much can be destroyed with a few hateful words."

The god nodded. "My brother's hate destroyed a world."

Karen lifted her hand. "Please, let's not allow negativity to impact this moment. This is a time to rejoice and hope for a better future."

"Amen," Gilbert said.

The god nodded. "Indeed. You are a wise lady, Karen."

"So, Toven." Gilbert managed to lift himself to a sitting position. "What does our new bond of friendship entail? Do we just send each other birthday cards, or is there more to it?"

Toven shrugged. "I don't have any expectations. You can do with it as you please."

"Can we at least invite you and Mia to dinner?" Karen asked.

"Always," Mia said from behind Toven. "But I hope this is more than that. I want us to be a family."

"I would like that too." Karen put her arms around Gilbert's shoulders.

54

MO-RED

As Mo-red paced the cell he shared with Vanessa, he contemplated asking the Guardian to put him back with Madbar until she returned.

He didn't like being alone, never had, but in the state he was in, he wouldn't be good company for Madbar or anyone else.

After their talk, Vanessa had seemed reassured about his feelings for her, but she couldn't stay, so he couldn't cement it by proving his feelings with worshiping her body.

She'd taken Lusha back to the immortals' village, and then she'd been supposed to take part in some ceremony that she hadn't elaborated about. She also hadn't told him how long it would take, and since it was after midnight, he was afraid she wasn't coming back.

He would have been okay with that if she was too tired to drive to wherever it was this structure was located, but he wasn't okay with her spending the night at her home because she'd had second thoughts about the two of them.

Was there any way he could convince her that his feelings for her ran deep?

He could tell her that he loved her, but those were just

words that humans threw around like they were nothing, and she might not believe him.

What else could he do?

How did the immortals know when they found their one and only? Did they even believe in that?

With a sigh, he took a coffee pod from the stack and popped it into the machine. Drinking alone held no appeal for him, but he had nothing else to do, and making coffee would keep him occupied for a couple of minutes.

There were five bags of blood in the refrigerator, but he wasn't hungry, especially not for bagged animal blood. The little he took from Vanessa during sex was not only exquisite in taste but evidently also contained all the nutrients he needed.

Talk about a symbiotic relationship.

Except, he had nothing to give her in exchange for everything she was giving him.

When the door's mechanism engaged, Mo-red's heart skipped a beat, and when it swung open, and Vanessa walked in, it swelled with emotion that he was sure was love.

So much for the Kra-ell being unable to feel it or recognize it.

"Hi." She hung her satchel on the back of the chair and then turned to him. "Why are you looking at me like that?"

"Like what?"

She chuckled. "Like you are awestruck."

"That's because I am." He put a hand over his heart. "When I see you, my heart swells. Is that love?"

She smiled, but it was more for him than out of happiness about what he'd said. "Right now, it's lust and infatuation." She walked up to him and wrapped her arms around his middle. "Did you just shower?"

Evidently she didn't want to talk about feelings.

"Yes, I did."

"You smell good." She put her cheek on his chest. "This is so rare for me to be with a male tall enough so I can do this even with my heels on."

Mo-red really didn't want to talk about all the other males she'd embraced in the past. Instead, he put his hands on her back and caressed it over her blouse. "How was the ceremony?"

"It was unusual, that's for sure." She kissed his cheek and then unwound from his embrace to sit on the couch. "I need to take off my shoes."

Sitting beside her, he wondered whether he should offer another foot massage. When he had done that earlier, the result had been an argument he was still upset about.

Catching him looking at her feet, Vanessa lifted them onto his lap. "If you want to give me another foot rub, it would be greatly appreciated."

"Are you sure?" He put his hands on both of her slim feet.

Her toenails were painted lilac blue, which was in contrast with her otherwise professional and conservative appearance.

"Yeah, I'm sure. I'm sorry for my earlier freak-out." She smiled. "Even psychologists sometimes get upset and act irrationally." She snorted. "Let me rephrase. Psychologists do that as often as everyone else and sometimes more. We live in our heads."

"I don't think you were irrational. I think you were feeling insecure for some reason. You have so much going for you that no one would ever imagine that you have any insecurities, but I guess that you never wondered before whether the males you were with had feelings for you other than lust. Am I onto something?"

55

VANESSA

Mo-red was either very insightful or understood her better than anyone else.

Heck, he understood her better than she understood herself, and that was saying something. Maybe he could do so because he was in the same situation.

"I bet you never wondered whether the females you were with had feelings for you either."

"I did not." He kneaded her toes with gentle fingers. "I focused on satisfying them, which was my duty as a Kra-ell male, but the encounters were so short that nothing meaningful could have developed." He paused what he was doing to her feet. "When I was a young male, I had heretical thoughts about having one female all to myself, but they were more about plentiful sex than emotional bonding. When I got older, I banished those thoughts as well."

"What about now?"

He smiled. "Now I'm old and jaded, and I can say to hell with all that posturing. I don't care what my fellow Kra-ell think and say about me. Most of them hate me anyway. If not for my impending trial, I could allow myself to explore what my heart can feel without limitations, but given that I might not be here for long, perhaps I should throttle down those new feelings welling inside me."

Vanessa sighed. "On the contrary. I think now is the perfect time to let yourself feel everything you possibly can. I don't even want to think of an outcome that would rob you of your life, but on the remote chance that it would, you should let yourself go wild."

His expression turned pained. "How can I? Saying goodbye to my sons is going to be bad enough. Saying goodbye to you will be worse."

She swallowed. "I know, but like everything else in life, depriving ourselves of something because we fear losing it is not smart. If I never allow myself to love a male because I'm afraid of losing that love, then I'm bringing the same outcome about anyway. You can't lose what you don't have."

"Precisely," he agreed.

"The fear of loss is stronger than the hope of gain. It was most evident in the ceremony today. Gilbert was terrified of getting induced because he feared losing his life more than he wanted to gain immortality. In the end, though, his mate helped him to overcome his fear."

When Mo-red stared at her with an uncomprehending look on his face, Vanessa realized that he had no idea what she was talking about. He and the other prisoners had been isolated while his people had learned about Dormants and their ability to transition into immortality. He had no idea that it was possible.

Should she tell him?

Kian had such strict rules about what was allowed to be said and to whom, but who would Mo-red tell? For better or worse, he would never be set free to go wherever he pleased. The best possible outcome they could hope for was house arrest in the village and a long community-service sentence.

"I'm sorry." She put a hand on his forearm. "I forgot that you don't know about Dormants and transition."

He shook his head. "What are Dormants?"

"Dormants are human carriers of the immortal godly genes. They transfer from a mother to her children. The sons can't give it to their offspring, but the daughters do, even if they were never activated. Immortal males have venom that can activate Dormants, male and female, but not in the same way. The other limitation is age. Older human bodies might not be strong enough to survive the transition. Gilbert and his mate are both Dormants, and both are not young, hence the fear."

Mo-red still looked at her with miscomprehension in his eyes. "I thought that only the sons and daughters of gods with humans could be immortal and that everyone in your community were the children of gods."

"We are the great-great-grandchildren of gods, and many of us are many times removed from the original god or goddess who started their line."

A lie of omission was still a lie, but Vanessa had no choice.

She was taking liberties with what she was telling Mo-red, but given Kian's suspicions about Igor's mission and capabilities, she couldn't tell him about Annani's part in the creation of the clan. That needed to remain a secret for now.

"What happened to the gods?" Mo-red asked. "Where did they go?"

"Most of them died."

"Did the humans kill them?"

Vanessa shook her head. "One of their own did that, or so we think. No one knows for sure what happened. All we know is that the gods were assembled in one place to cast a vote, and a bomb exploded over their assembly hall, killing them and the one who we think dropped it. We assume that he was flying a small craft that was not designed as a bomb carrier, and he was caught in the blast or the deadly cloud that ensued."

Up until recently, everyone in the two immortal factions—the clan and the Brotherhood—believed that it had been Mortdh who'd dropped the bomb, but now with what they had learned from Igor, Vanessa was no longer sure of that.

Once the Eternal King had realized that the settler ship had malfunctioned and drifted in space for thousands of years, he could have sent another team of assassins.

A new team arriving with weapons of mass destruction to eliminate all the gods at once made more sense than Mortdh going on a suicide mission.

From everything she'd learned about him, he wasn't the suicidal type. He had just happened to be at the wrong place at the wrong time.

56

MO-RED

Mo-red had a feeling that Vanessa was giving him a censored version, but that was okay. She probably couldn't tell him everything even if she wanted to, but maybe she could tell him a little more and satisfy his curiosity.

"So if all the gods died, where did the immortals come from? And what about the compeller?"

"Not all the gods died, and immortals existed long before the bombing." Vanessa leaned back against the couch armrest. "A large community up north led by Mortdh's immortal son escaped the deadly cloud. It started with several thousand and grew from there. Other immortals were scattered around, and the females produced the next generation of Dormants. They knew about the activation and used it to turn Dormants into immortals."

"The Kra-ell can't activate their second-generation offspring. If my hybrid sons have children with humans, their kids will be human."

"That's true, but if a hybrid female had a child with a human, that child could be activated." She smiled conspiratorially. "Sofia is transitioning as we speak."

Mo-red sucked in a breath. "Don't toy with me. Is she really becoming Kra-ell?"

Vanessa nodded. "Her immortal boyfriend induced her transition, and she is in the clinic. She's lost consciousness, but our doctor is not worried. Sofia is young and healthy, and she should do just fine. We don't know how the transition will affect her, but we believe she will grow fangs and venom glands like your hybrid females. She will also be long-lived like them, or so we hope."

Sofia was the only child in the entire history of the compound born to a hybrid mother and a human father, and given that the longevity gene was transferred from mother to daughter, it made sense that she was the only one who could be induced. The question was whether she could have been induced by a Kra-ell male. If she could, it was a game changer for their community.

"I don't know whether Sofia ever engaged with a pure-blooded male before meeting her immortal boyfriend. Do you?"

"She didn't," Vanessa said. "But even if she did, it wouldn't have done her any good. Your venom is not potent enough to induce transition. Only our males can do that."

Great, one more area where the gods and their descendants had an advantage over the Kra-ell. Did the immortal venom provide more pleasure as well?

Vanessa wouldn't know. She'd never been with an immortal male, but it made sense that the more potent the venom, the more powerful its effect. What the immortals didn't have, though, was a dexterous tongue that could do things to a female that none of them could.

"What has gotten you excited?" Vanessa regarded him with a smile. "Suddenly, there is a red gleam in your eyes, and your fangs got longer."

"I felt a little intimidated by all the advantages immortal males have over us, but then I remembered a few things that they don't have, and we do."

"Such as?"

He flicked his tongue over his fangs.

As Vanessa's scent of arousal tickled his nostrils most deliciously, Mo-red reached to unbutton her elegant trousers. "Let me remind you." He pulled her pants down her thighs, dragging her panties along for the ride.

When she was bared before him from the waist down, he drank in the sight of her.

"Beautiful."

She cupped her mound. "Are your females also bare down here? Or are they like humans?"

"They are bare but not nearly as beautiful as you are."

She laughed, the sound sending a zing to his shaft. "I'm sure our anatomy is quite similar."

"It's not." He removed the hand that was covering what was his. "Your petals are so delicate." He folded himself so he could take position between her legs, quite a feat considering how small the couch was. But he was unwilling to waste time by moving things to the bed.

She slid down, resting her neck on the sofa's arm and parting her thighs to give him better access. "I have to admit that tongue of yours is the stuff of the most wicked dreams."

"Is it, now?" He lifted her foot and kissed her just below the fold of her knee, teasing her as he advanced where he wanted to go.

"Yes." She moaned. "If the world ever learns about your existence and accepts you, I bet you would star in every kinky porn flick. You would make a fortune."

"Would you share me with an audience?" He kept kissing

the inside of her thigh, then switched to the other side, tormenting them both with sweet anticipation.

"No." Her fingers threaded in his hair, loosening it from its binding. "You are mine. My kinky secret lover."

Her words of ownership made him happy beyond reason. He wanted to be hers, to pleasure her, master her the way she liked it, and satisfy her like she'd never been satisfied before.

Closing his mouth over her moist petals, he sucked them in before extending his very long tongue and spearing it inside her.

Vanessa detonated like a firecracker, shouting his name and pulling on his hair so hard that he was sure clumps of it would remain in her hands.

It was so worth it, and as he kept working her with his tongue and fingers, she orgasmed again and again until she could orgasm no more and pushed on his head instead of pulling it to her.

He treated her to a few more gentle licks, cleaning her up, and then kissed those silky petals before looking up at her flushed face.

57

VANESSA

Exquisite. That was the only way Vanessa could describe the experience. Well, wicked was a good description too.

She still wanted to take Mo-red on a Perfect Match fantasy trip and explore her darkest desires with him, but she had to admit that he came pretty close to fulfilling them in the real world.

She wasn't shy about her needs and wants. In fact, she'd been quite forward with the human males she'd been with, but for some reason, she was a little hesitant to show her darker side to Mo-red.

Perhaps it was because there was an element of danger with him, which hadn't been a part of the experience with humans. She could easily overpower most men, but Mo-red could do whatever he pleased to her. She trusted him, but he was so incredibly strong that he could really hurt her without meaning to or even realizing that he was causing her pain beyond what she considered arousing.

Erotic pain straddled a razor-thin line between sexy and harmful, and Mo-red wasn't skilled in the art. He was used to super-strong Kra-ell females who could give him a proper fight for dominance, not a make-believe one meant to arouse more than cause pain.

Still, if she didn't communicate her desires, how would he know to give her what she needed?

Smiling, she pulled away from him, turned around, and leaned over the couch armrest, thrusting her ass up for him to do with as he pleased.

The breath he sucked in was a good start.

At least he liked the view.

"Take off your blouse," he commanded. "I want you naked."

"Yes, sir." She lifted her torso and pulled the blouse over her head.

Her bra was off next, and when she was fully naked, she lowered herself over the armrest again.

She felt the couch dip as Mo-red climbed on his knees and positioned himself behind her.

When she felt just the tip of his shaft at her entrance, she rocked her hips, trying to get more of it inside her.

It earned her a hard slap on her upturned behind. "Patience, my lovely Vanessa."

She almost came from just that.

Was Mo-red perfect, or what?

How had he guessed what she wanted? What she needed?

Swiveling her hips again, she courted more of what he had given her, and once again, he didn't disappoint, delivering another hard smack to her other butt cheek.

The guttural moan that escaped her throat was all the confirmation he needed that she liked the game they were playing, and as he delivered several more in quick succession, she orgasmed so hard that she saw stars.

"You like this, don't you, you wicked girl?" He kissed her

heated bottom. "So damn sexy, I'm about to shoot my load all over your pinked ass."

"Yes." Her sheath muscles fluttered in anticipation.

As he entered her with one hard thrust and then pulled back and thrust back in, she let her head roll back on her shoulders, and then he was folded over her, his mouth on her throat.

"You are my salvation, Vanessa," he murmured against her skin as he pounded in and out of her. "Whatever the future holds for me, I can die a happy male holding the memory of this moment in my heart."

Tears welled in her eyes, but she refused to let them flow. He would smell them and think he had hurt her when nothing could be further from the truth.

Vanessa had never known such pleasure, not even when he'd bitten her, and his venom had sent her soaring over the clouds. This was real. The other stuff was not.

She rocked her hips as he pumped inside her, the world and its tribulations fading away along with any self-conscious thought she had. She wanted to tell him how he made her feel, but all she managed were soft moans and throaty groans.

Hopefully, those primitive sounds communicated what was on her mind and in her heart. She was his, and he was hers, and the world outside this room could go to hell. She lived for this moment with Mo-red, a communion of body and soul.

When he roared, she tensed and moved her head to the side, giving him access to her vein, and when he struck, the burning pain of his fangs breaking skin detonated another explosion, sending her soaring over the clouds even before his venom could trigger the euphoria she was so well acquainted with by now.

"Mo-red," she whispered his name as if it was a prayer.

He didn't answer.

58

SOFIA

The first thing Sofia became aware of was that everything hurt. Her legs, her arms, her back, her throat, and even her jaw felt as if it was being stretched.

What was happening to her?

Oh, right, she was transitioning.

Despite the pain she smiled, or tried to. Her facial muscles refused to obey her brain's commands, and she panicked, thinking she was locked in an unresponsive body, experiencing pain but unable to communicate her distress.

Focusing, she tried to lift her eyelids, and then, after what seemed forever, she managed to move them enough to see a sliver of light, and her relief was so profound that tears welled in that little window to the world she'd managed to create.

"Sofia?" She heard the concern in Marcel's voice but could do nothing to reassure him. "You're crying." She felt his finger wiping the tears from under her eyes, which was a relief too. "You're awake." She felt his lips brushing over her forehead. "I'll get Bridget."

She wanted to tell him not to leave her side, but she couldn't open her mouth or lift her hand. All she managed was to blink several times.

"Don't worry, love." Marcel kissed her again. "I'm not leaving. I'll just use my phone to call Bridget."

How did he know what she'd meant by that furious blinking?

Her man was a mind reader even though he claimed not to have that paranormal ability.

As she felt herself drifting away, Sofia struggled to stay awake, but it was a hopeless battle. Her eyelids refused to stay even slightly parted, and her exhausted and aching body couldn't handle being awake.

The next time she came to, the back of the bed was raised so she was semi-reclined, and her face felt as if someone had put lotion on her skin. Was it the nurse?

She doubted the doctor would have been so considerate.

"Try to open your eyes, Sofia." The doctor took her hand.

She knew that because Bridget had small hands with delicate long fingers, and she recognized the doctor's touch.

When she managed to force her eyelids to lift once again, Bridget gave her hand a gentle squeeze. "That's good. Now try to open them all the way."

"Is that normal?" Marcel said from somewhere in the room.

"Every transition is different," Bridget said. "Sofia has been out for several days, and she's exhausted from everything her body has been doing in the meantime."

Oh, Mother of All Life, had she grown even taller?

Forcing her lips to part, she croaked what was supposed to be 'what' but came out as a 'wa?'

"I'll get you some water." The doctor let go of her hand and walked over to the sink.

Sofia barely dared to blink for fear her eyelids would drop and refuse to lift again.

A moment later, Bridget returned with a cup and a straw and put the tip of the straw between Sofia's parted lips. "Take small sips."

As if she could do more than that. She could barely close her lips around the straw to suck up the water.

The little she took provided much-needed moisture to her mouth, so she could say something the others would understand. "What happened to me?"

On the other side of the bed, Marcel leaned over and kissed her cheek, looking happy and relieved, so whatever changes she'd undergone couldn't be too bad. "You are transitioning, sweetheart," he said.

"I mean, what changed about me?"

He looked at the doctor. "Maybe you should explain."

That didn't sound good.

Bridget pulled her compact tablet out of her coat pocket and swiped down with a well-manicured finger. "You grew one and a half inches in height, which makes you six feet and a quarter of an inch tall, and the growth was spread out proportionately. I'll spare you the details of what got longer and by how much. You are also growing venom glands and fangs, but it's too early to tell whether your fangs will be functional for the purpose of drinking blood. So far, it doesn't look like your body is developing the rest of the system needed to process blood intake. I also didn't notice any change to the shape of your eyes, but I'm sure your vision and hearing have improved dramatically. Your olfactory senses are most likely enhanced as well."

That didn't sound too bad. She could do without the additional height, fangs, or venom glands, but it was a small price to pay for a significantly longer lifespan.

"How long was I out?"

"It's Sunday," Marcel said. "You started transitioning on Wednesday and lost consciousness the same night."

"That's not so bad, right?" She looked at the doctor.

"Not bad at all." Bridget turned to Marcel. "I'll leave you two alone. If Sofia stays awake for several hours, we will take it from there. In the meantime, you can give her small sips of water."

"Can I see my family?" Sofia asked. "They are probably worried about me."

Bridget smiled. "They are all camping outside the clinic because I didn't allow more than two people inside at once. When you are ready, Marcel can call them in, and I'll pretend that I don't know they are crowding your room."

"Thank you," Marcel said.

"You're welcome. Just don't let them stay so long that they tire Sofia. If she wants to get out of here anytime soon, she needs to stay awake."

He saluted her with two fingers. "Yes, doctor."

59

ANNANI

Annani looked out the window of her private jet even though there was nothing to see, with the fluffy cloud cover obscuring the view.

When Kian had called the day before to tell her that Toven had failed again, she had not been surprised. In her gut, Annani had known that only she could succeed, but Kian had to try everything he could before finally conceding defeat and agreeing to let her try.

Igor would be drugged and blindfolded, and she would not speak to him, only enter his mind and look at his memories. Hopefully, that would be enough to determine which part of the story he had told was truth and which was falsehood.

She was not looking forward to taking a look inside a sociopathic murderer's mind, but she was excited about going back to the village and holding her two new granddaughters. Childhood was so fleeting, especially those precious first months, and she hated losing even a day in their lives.

The Fates knew babies were a rare treat for the clan, and she was blessed with four if she counted Ethan and Darius.

Phoenix was no longer a baby, but she was still in that

delightful age of innocence when children still adored their parents and thought the entire universe revolved around them and their immediate family.

Later, when they realized it wasn't so, the joy of childhood started to fade. There were peers to impress, teachers to contend with, and other adults that didn't share their parents' opinion that they were the best gift anyone could have ever hoped for.

Naturally, not all families were happy, and some were so miserable or even abusive that the outside world was a respite in comparison.

Annani sighed. If she were an actual deity, not just an alien female with incredible mind-control abilities, she would have fixed everything wrong with the world and made every home a safe haven.

"Are you tired?" Alena asked.

Annani turned to look at her daughter. "I thought you were sleeping."

Alena had brought her favorite pillow with her, turned the seat into a bed, and her steady deep breaths had implied that she was sleeping. Orion had done the same, but he was asleep for sure. His mouth was slightly open, and his eyelids fluttered as he dreamt.

"I was." Alena turned on her back and lifted the back of her seat. "But you know me. I'm a light sleeper, and you are a loud thinker."

Annani laughed quietly, so as not to wake Orion up. "Did my heavy thinking wake you up?"

"I guess. What else could it have been? What's bothering you, Mother?"

"I am not bothered. I am contemplative."

"Okay." Alena adjusted the pillow behind her neck. "What were you contemplating so hard?"

"I have decided to move into the village for the next two to three years. I do not want to miss another day with my granddaughters." She glanced at Alena's rounded belly. "Or this little guy when he gets here. I know you and Orion want to live in the village, not the sanctuary."

Alena frowned. "You sound as if you know for sure that Orion and I are having a boy. Did you have a vision about our baby?"

Oops...

Alena and Orion did not wish to know the gender of their baby before he was born, and Annani had made sure to refer to the baby in gender-neutral terms, but she had been preoccupied and had slipped up.

"Since Amanda and Kian both have girls, it is statistically probable that you will have a boy."

Alena lifted one brow and lowered the other, looking amused. "Right. Since when do you rely on statistics? You know what they say about it. There are three types of lies—lies, damn lies, and statistics."

That was funny, but Annani did not laugh. Looking at her daughter down her nose, she affected a huff. "It is simple logic. The chances of having a boy or a girl are fifty percent."

"In the general population when taking into account large averages. It did not work in my case. I had many more girls than boys."

"Thank the Fates for that. Imagine what would have happened if you did not. Our clan would have been half the size it is now."

"True, but you are still trying to avoid answering me. How do you know we are having a boy?"

"I do not. It was just a guess."

"Fine." Her daughter fluffed her pillow, turned on her side, and closed her eyes. "Be like that."

Alena did not look like she was okay with that answer, but she would have to be because Annani did not have a good reason for the strong feeling she had about the baby being a boy. She was not a seer like Syssi, and her less-than-mediocre remote-viewing ability was only good for seeing things in the present and perhaps just a short time into the future or the past. She could not remotely see the baby's birth in four months or so.

"Who is going to run the sanctuary?" Alena asked without opening her eyes.

"Belinda can do that. Nowadays when everything can be done via video calls, messages, and emails, there is no reason for me to be physically present to lead my people there. The only problem is one of morale. I expect many would want to relocate as well."

"What about your idea to open the sanctuary to clan members who want a quiet vacation away from everything?"

"Nothing is preventing them from going anytime they want now. I always welcome guests."

Alena chuckled. "It's a little difficult for people to accept your hospitality when they have no way of getting there. Your Odus are the only ones who know where the sanctuary is and can fly people there."

"All the Odus can do that. They share information. What one learns, the others can do as well. Okidu and Onidu can fly people from the village to the sanctuary, and Ojidu can fly people from Scotland."

Alena turned on her back. "I didn't know that they could do that."

"It took me some time to realize that as well, but I am convinced I am right. I do not know how they communicate with one another, but I suspect that it is like a Bluetooth connection. They airdrop information to one another when they are close."

"Huh." Alena pursed her lips. "We need to test that."

Annani nodded. "I plan to do so when we arrive at the village."

60

KIAN

Kian waited alone in the parking garage for the limousine carrying his mother, sister, Orion, and two of his mother's Odus.

One had remained behind to provide piloting services for the sanctuary's residents.

When the limo came to a stop, he opened the back door and offered his hand to Annani. "Welcome home, Mother." He kissed her on both cheeks.

"Thank you." She smiled and didn't react to him calling the village her home.

Was it a good sign?

Was she warming to the idea of moving her permanent location to the village?

"I'm so glad to be back," Alena said, following their mother out. "I love the sanctuary, but it gets boring after a while." She looked lovingly at her mate, who followed her out of the vehicle. "Orion pretended that he was having a good time, but he was bored out of his mind and itching to get out of there."

"Not true. It was a very relaxing vacation." Orion shook Kian's hand. "I read some good books, watched a Broadway-style production performed by superb actors, and spent time lazing in the warm pools. But the truth is that I need to get back to work, or I'll lose all my contacts."

Alena pouted. "I don't want to start traveling as soon as I'm back. I want to spend some time in the village." Her lips tilted up with a hint of a smile. "Although if you want to go to Europe, I wouldn't mind visiting my kids in Scotland."

"We don't have to go right away, and my destinations are France and Belgium." Orion wrapped his arm around Alena's shoulders. "We can stay a few days here, then you can spend fun time with your family at the castle while I go on short purchasing excursions, and then we can come back in time for the cruise." He cast Kian a sidelong glance. "Is that still happening?"

"I hope so." Kian offered his arm to his mother. "Let's see how things go with Igor." He started toward the elevator. "But that's a discussion for later. Right now, Syssi is waiting for us with dinner."

"Is Amanda coming?" Alena asked.

"Of course. The entire family is going to be there to welcome you back." He patted his mother's small hand. "We missed you. Allegra keeps asking about Nani."

"Oh," Annani cooed. "I cannot wait to kiss her cheeks and hug her. Has she grown in the time I was gone?"

Kian chuckled. "You were gone ten days. She grows fast, but not that fast."

"It felt longer." Annani stepped into the elevator. "I missed her and Evie fiercely, and also Ethan and little Darius. How is he doing? Is there any improvement with his colic?"

"I don't know," Kian admitted. "With all the drama going on, I haven't talked to Kalugal in days."

"Maybe you should," Annani said as they stepped out of the

elevator. "He is a smart boy. He might have some clever suggestions."

"Well, he's coming to dinner tonight, so we can ask him what he thinks." He helped his mother climb into the golf cart waiting for them in front of the pavilion.

Annani frowned at the fabric canopy that was closed on all sides. "Is my visit a secret?"

"I don't want it getting out that you are back." Kian offered his hand to Alena, but she smiled and climbed in without his assistance.

"It will not remain a secret for more than five minutes." His sister sat behind their mother. "Unless you want to hide Mother in your house."

"That's not a bad idea." He climbed into the golf cart and sat next to Annani. "Would you mind staying with us?"

Annani rearranged the folds of her gown and turned to look at him. "With Alena and Orion back, everyone will know that I have also returned. So, unless you want to hide all of us in your house, including our Odus, that is not going to work."

"We have room for everyone."

"House party." Orion climbed in next to Alena. "If Okidu prepares all of our meals, I don't mind."

"Why hide us, though?" Alena asked.

"Frankly, it's just a gut feeling that I should keep Mother a secret, at least until we resolve the Igor problem." Kian raked his fingers through his hair. "Other than Jade and Kagra, the Kra-ell don't know that any gods other than Toven are still living, and I prefer to keep it that way for now."

Annani shrugged her delicate shoulders. "I can wear jeans and a T-shirt and pretend to be a visiting immortal from Scotland. The only problem would be to get our people to keep the charade going. It will not work if they start bowing to me."

Annani laughed. "The more I think about it, the more I like it. It has been so long since I pretended to be just a regular girl."

Behind them, Alena chuckled. "We would have to work on your speech patterns, Mother. You need to start using contractions and some slang."

"I can do this." Annani cleared her throat. "What's up, girlfriend?"

It sounded like a queen trying to mimic a commoner, and Kian could barely hold back laughter. "That was good, but it still needs some work."

Annani snapped her fingers and repeated the exact phrase without much improvement. "Was that better?"

"Not really, Mother," Alena said. "We will practice after dinner."

"Jeans," Orion murmured. "I cannot imagine the Clan Mother wearing jeans and a T-shirt. And what about all that majestic hair?"

"I can braid it," Annani said in a perfect Californian accent.

Kian shook his head. He shouldn't be surprised that his mother could mimic any accent she pleased, but it still sounded strange hearing her speak like a native.

61

SYSSI

Syssi bounced Allegra on her knee as she looked over the gathered people around the table.

Most of her family was there, which made her heart swell with gratitude for all the wonderful people in her life, but as always, there was a smidgen of sadness over those who were missing.

Sari and David should be at the table, and so should her parents. Sari didn't want to move into the village, and Syssi's parents were happy doing their thing, but there was always a chance that all of them would arrive for a special occasion, like the wedding cruise that she hoped was still happening, given everything that was going on.

The brother she'd lost, however, could only join them in spirit, and the same was true for her grandparents, who she still missed even though they were long gone.

If only she had found Amanda sooner, or Amanda had found her, she would have found out about her godly immortal genes before Jacob's accident, and he would still be here today. If he were immortal, he would have survived the accident. His body would have healed the damage.

"Mama?" Allegra looked at her with a pair of worried eyes.

"Yes, sweetie. Mama loves you." She kissed the top of her daughter's head.

Kian was right. She shouldn't let herself get depressed because it affected Allegra. But was it healthy to always push those thoughts out of her mind?

It was a question for Vanessa, but the clan's psychologist had enough on her plate at the moment. Then again, Syssi could have talked with the therapist about those thoughts before but had chosen not to, so that was just an excuse.

The truth was that she didn't even talk with Kian about it. In part, it was because she didn't want to add to his already heavy burden, and in part, it was because talking about Jacob made her so sad that it took her days to recover.

So perhaps her coping mechanism was all wrong, but it worked. All that mattered was that she could be there for her husband, daughter, and extended family.

Everyone carried pain inside of them, and everyone had their own ways of dealing with it, and not everything could or should be solved with therapy sessions.

Syssi was sure that Kian still thought about the daughter he'd had with his first wife, who had died of old age centuries ago, but he hardly ever talked about her, probably for the same reason she rarely mentioned Jacob.

Heck, she didn't even talk about him with Andrew. Her older brother was probably still struggling with the loss as much as she was, and the same was true for her parents. Perhaps her mother's undertaking the mission in Africa had been her way of coping with the loss. She was so busy, working long days without breaks, that she had no time to think about the son she'd lost, and the fulfillment she got from helping others soothed some of the pain.

"I think Syssi's jeans would fit me," Annani said.

It was such a strange thing for the goddess to say that it instantly pulled Syssi out of her head.

Annani was so petite that she would probably swim in her pants, but Syssi had a couple of stretchy leggings-style jeans that might work. The question was, why would Annani want to wear pants when all Syssi had ever seen her wear were floor-length silk gowns?

"I would gladly loan you any item of clothing I have, and I might have a few options that will fit you, but why do you want to wear jeans all of a sudden?"

Annani cast an accusing glance at Kian.

He smiled sheepishly. "We talked on the way about hiding Annani's presence in the village for a while, mainly from the Kra-ell. She suggested dressing up in modern clothing and pretending to be just another immortal female visiting from Scotland. She thinks that jeans and a T-shirt will be good enough to disguise who she is."

"It will," Annani said. "It is all in the appearance and people's expectations. No one will expect a goddess to wear jeans, so even if they notice something strange about me, they will just think that I have some special paranormal talent."

Syssi shook her head. "I'm sorry to disappoint you, but that won't do the trick any more than it did for Toven. He wasn't wearing anything fancy when he met Jade for the first time, and she knew immediately that he was a god. The Kra-ell know what the gods look like, and your perfection cannot be explained as anything other than godly."

"You can try to shroud yourself," Amanda suggested.

"Or Eva can make you less beautiful," Jacki said. "That woman is a genius with makeup and wigs. She made me and Jin look so drab that no one gave us a second glance."

"Not true." Kalugal put his arm on the back of her chair. "I knew there was something special about you from the very start."

"That was the affinity between immortals and Dormants at work. If I were a run-of-the-mill human, you wouldn't have looked my way."

"I would like to believe I would have noticed you despite the disguise. Beauty is not everything."

Smiling, she leaned toward him and kissed his cheek. "That's sweet, but that's not how we are wired. It's shallow as hell, but we are programmed to respond to physical beauty. Maybe it is something the gods put into us?"

"I wouldn't put it past them," Kian said.

62

KIAN

Kian found it surreal that they were all talking about inconsequential stuff and dancing around the issue of why Annani was back and what she was about to do.

But even more surreal was that he was allowing his mother to get near Igor.

Maybe no one wanted to bring it up so he wouldn't find a reason to cancel the plan and ask Annani to return to Alaska.

The truth was that he was tempted to do just that, but it was probably too late to back out now. First of all, they really needed to know what was in Igor's head and whether what he had told them was true.

Secondly, Annani wouldn't have it.

If Kian told her now that he changed his mind, she would overrule him and go to see Igor whether he approved the visit or not. He was well aware that she didn't need his permission to do anything, and the only reason Annani was accommodating his paranoia was that she didn't want to undermine his authority.

However, that wouldn't stop her now when her people's

safety was on the line. Igor's suspected ability to communicate with the gods on the home planet had to be proved or disproved.

"My son," Annani addressed him in a more formal tone than usual. "I wish to inform you that I plan to stay in your village until further notice." She smiled at Allegra. "I am not willing to miss any more time with my granddaughters."

The announcement seemed to catch everyone by surprise, and for a long moment, no one said a word.

Kian was surprised as well, but he shouldn't have been. Before he'd asked Annani to return to the sanctuary, she had stayed at the village far longer than she ever had previously and had not shown any signs of getting restless and wanting to leave.

Amanda clapped her hands. "I'm so happy, I could cry." She pushed to her feet and went to hug their mother. "With you here, I'm not afraid to get pregnant again."

Kian didn't want to burst her bubble and remind her that when her son died, Annani hadn't been far away. She couldn't have saved him even if she had been right next to him when he'd broken his neck.

Death had been instantaneous.

"What about your people?" Kalugal asked. "Will they be okay without their shepherdess?"

Annani smiled indulgently. "In today's world, the shepherdess can be on a different continent and provide leadership and guidance remotely. I love technology and innovation and the way they change our lives for the better."

"If that was true, I could have taken my wife and daughter on a proper vacation more often." Kian set his cup down. "I can work remotely, but it's not the same as working from my office."

"That is because you have a business to run and a community to defend." Annani steepled her slim fingers. "In the sanctuary, I am just a figurehead, and my people can get by just fine without me. My only concern is that they will feel neglected. The sanctuary is isolated, which suits many of its inhabitants, but without me there to provide excitement, some might wish to move out."

"They are welcome to come here," Kian said. "I don't think Sari has room in her castle or its additional buildings for more members."

He was still upset over his sister's refusal to unite their clan in one location and split the responsibilities of managing it between them. He did not dismiss the importance of having three different strategic locations, but perhaps it was time to change their mindset from the persecuted, who chose a defensive position, to the persecutors, who chose to go on the offensive. There was strength in numbers, and with the Kra-ell joining the clan, it was truer than ever.

"Sari might still decide to move here," Amanda said. "As soon as she gets pregnant, she will want to be near Mother. She will also want her child to grow with her or his cousins."

"It might take centuries for Sari to conceive," Annani pointed out.

Alena chuckled. "Statistically speaking, Sari should conceive anytime now. The three of us did so in quick succession, so I believe our fourth sibling is due for a baby."

"Since when are you talking statistics?" Amanda asked.

"Since Mother started basing her predictions on them, I thought that I should do it too. It sounds more convincing than gut feelings, precognition, remote viewing, and all the other things Kian calls mumbo jumbo."

When Syssi raised a brow, Kian lifted his hands. "I used to call them that. I don't anymore. I'm a believer." He turned to his mother. "So, what is your gut telling you about Igor? Is he communicating telepathically with someone on your home planet?"

"I do not know, my son. But what I do know is that I will succeed where Toven failed. I will get into Igor's head."

As a stunned silence stretched over the table, Kian let out a breath. "I know this comes as a shock to you, but that is why the Clan Mother is back. Toven failed to thrall Igor even with the help of powerful drugs and Mia's enhancement, and Annani is our last hope."

"Just put the bastard in stasis," Kalugal said. "Even if he can communicate telepathically with someone on Anumati, he has already done it, and the gods know that we exist. But frankly, I don't think they needed Igor to learn that. Do you really think that they didn't send anyone else to investigate?"

"That's exactly what led me to believe that Igor can communicate with them. The reason they didn't send anyone else was that he reported that the gods were gone. Now that he knows about at least one surviving god and about the immortal descendants of the others, our ancestors back home know that as well."

"Okay." Kalugal folded his arms over his chest. "What difference would it make if the Clan Mother confirms it or not? Are you going to relocate the clan? Find a better place to hide? There isn't really anything you can do. So why risk letting Annani anywhere near that monster?"

"Knowledge is power, nephew," Annani said. "And Kian is going to take every precaution possible so that Igor doesn't realize who I am or that I am anywhere near him at all. I do not even have to speak to him to get into his mind."

63

VANESSA

On the way back to the village, Vanessa sang along with the radio, which she hadn't done in years.

Not conducting any interviews during the weekend and spending the entirety of it with Mo-red had been one of her best ever ideas.

The Guardians had been great, letting them use the gym and the pool. Mo-red couldn't swim, and trying to teach him had been both frustrating and fun.

Like a typical male, he'd assumed he was ready to take the plunge within minutes of her demonstration and had jumped into the deep end. Naturally, he had sunk like a rock to the bottom and hadn't surfaced.

Thankfully, she was a strong swimmer, and she dove after him to pull him out. After that, they'd made out in the shallow end of the pool and finished back in their tiny suite.

When she got home, she found Lusha in the kitchen.

"I'm making breakfast. Do you want some?"

"Sure." Vanessa dropped her bag on the counter. "What are you making?"

"Eggs."

That was quite obvious since she was cracking one after the other into the pan. "Besides the eggs."

"Bagel with cream cheese. We don't have a lot of time. I scheduled our first meeting of the day for ten, and it's already a quarter after nine. You said you'd be here by eight-thirty."

"Traffic was bad." In Los Angeles, where traffic was always congested, it was a convenient excuse for almost any tardiness.

In Vanessa's case, though, traffic had been precisely as she'd expected, and the culprit for her late arrival had been a joint shower with Mo-red that had turned steamy.

"Who are we meeting?" Vanessa poured water into the coffeemaker.

"Borga, Pavel's mother."

Vanessa's good mood morphed into an anxious apprehension.

She'd avoided talking with Borga using the excuse that the female's English was not good enough, and she didn't want to bother Toven too often with translations. The truth, however, was that she was afraid to hear what the female had to say about Mo-red.

He was sure her attitude toward him was positive because he'd gotten her gifts and had treated her with respect, but even though Mo-red was incredibly insightful for a guy, he might be totally wrong about Borga's feelings toward him.

Vanessa had witnessed enough cases in which two people had very different reactions to the same event and made assumptions about the other that were completely wrong.

Popping a coffee pod into the machine, she put two mugs under the twin spouts and leaned against the counter. "Did you speak with her already?"

"Of course." Lusha divided the contents of the pan between two plates and brought them to the counter. "I had to make the appointment, and it took some convincing. She wasn't eager to talk to us. Especially you."

"Why? Was it because of my relationship with Mo-red?"

Lusha shrugged. "Borga said that language was a barrier, and she didn't want to talk through an interpreter who might give her words a spin and vice versa. I told her that she could trust me to translate every word as accurately as I could, and she said okay. But to tell you the truth, I don't think it was just about the language. It might be the Kra-ell's disdain for shrinks."

"Disdain is a strong word." Vanessa removed the two coffee mugs from under the spout and brought them over to the counter. "They don't appreciate the work I do, and they believe it to be useless, but they have no reason to hate me for trying to help."

"It's not as simple as that." Lusha brought a plate piled with bagels and sat down. "They equate mind manipulation with the gods, and as you know, they don't like the gods."

She hadn't considered that angle. Only the original settlers had any reason to dislike the gods, but they might have imparted their attitudes to their offspring.

"Aren't the purebloods immune to the gods' mind tricks?"

"They are not as susceptible as humans or even immortals, but as evidenced by what Igor and Tom did, it's not only possible but has been done to them successfully. You can't blame them for being suspicious of an immortal whose profession is mind manipulation."

"That's not what I do."

"I know." Lusha scooped a hefty portion of eggs onto her fork. "And most of them know that as well, but there is a difference between knowing and believing."

"Yeah. I guess you are right." Vanessa reached for a bagel. "Did Borga say anything to that effect?"

Lusha scrunched her nose. "She was quite rude, so I'd rather not repeat it."

"I need to know what she said," Vanessa insisted. "I'm not thin-skinned, and I'm not easy to insult."

Taking a breath, Lusha put the fork down. "She said that she didn't want to talk to the horny immortal bitch who wanted to mess with her head."

64

GILBERT

Gilbert was in bed, not because it was the weekend and he could laze around as much as he pleased, and not because he was tired or sick, although he wished he was.

That would mean that his transition was starting.

Three days had passed since his induction, which didn't seem like a lot, but given that his brother had also been induced by the god and had started transitioning the next day, three days were worrisome.

Other male Dormants had transitioned within forty-eight hours of their induction or not at all, and then had to get induced again. But he'd gotten the crème de la crème on his first round, so there was nowhere to go from there. If a god couldn't induce him, no one could.

What if he was too old to transition?

Everyone talked about how dangerous it was for older Dormants, but had anyone considered that an old body would know not to start transitioning when it couldn't take the strain?

Prior to the induction, Bridget had done all the tests on him and had determined that he was perfectly healthy for his age and that the symptoms he was complaining about were all stress related.

Well, duh.

He was always stressed despite the jovial persona he fronted, and now he was more stressed than ever.

Damn, his stomach was cramping.

Maybe he should get up and give the throne another go?

He'd had coffee with Karen before she left for work, so maybe that had helped move things along in his digestive tract.

She'd wanted to stay and watch him, but since the twins' daycare was at the university and Idina's preschool not far from there, it would have meant all three staying home, which would have made Karen too busy taking care of the kids to pay attention to him.

He'd convinced her to go by promising that he would call Eric to come over.

Eric was the clan's fourth pilot, which meant that he had plenty of free time on his hands. They could spend the day watching reruns of games, eating pizza, and drinking beer.

Gilbert's head liked the idea, but his stomach didn't, and the call of the throne became urgent. As he sat there naked and watching YouTube videos to relax, his brother called.

He answered, "What's up, Eric?

"Karen told me to check up on you, so I'm checking. What are you doing?"

"I'm on the throne, trying to relax."

Eric chuckled. "Am I stressing you?"

"No, I'm already stressed out of my mind. It's been three days and nothing. It took you what? Twelve hours from the induction to the start of the transition?"

"Yeah, that sounds about right. Listen, I think you should go to the clinic and have Bridget monitor you. I'm sure you will start to transition any minute now, and you are all alone in the house."

"Then come over."

"I am on my way. Finish your business and get showered and dressed. I'll take you to the clinic."

"I don't want to go." Gilbert pouted. "I'd rather stay in my own bed and watch stupid YouTube videos for hours to take my mind off everything that's stressing me."

"You can watch videos in the clinic too, and the bed is not bad. I still remember fondly how Darlene and I squeezed together on that narrow thing."

"That's because you are a masochist, and you like to suffer. I don't have even one masochistic bone in my body."

"Yeah, yeah. Get ready. I'll be there in twenty minutes."

Half an hour later, the two of them were out of the house, heading toward the clinic with Eric carrying an overnight bag for Gilbert.

"You are really taking this assuming-the-win to the next level. I don't feel hot, sweaty, or fatigued, and here you are taking me to the clinic with an overnight bag."

"Tonight is the night." Eric clapped him on the back. "Take my word for it."

The thing was, Eric had always been intuitive. His only blind spot had been his psychotic cheating ex.

When they reached the clinic and Eric opened the door, Gilbert swayed on his feet, and when he forced himself to step inside, his legs gave out, and he collapsed.

The last thing he heard was, "I told you it was happening today."

Eric had said that it was happening tonight, but Gilbert couldn't open his mouth to correct him.

65

VANESSA

Lusha hadn't been kidding. Borga was hostile.

Vanessa had hoped that Pavel would be there to soften up his mother, but he was at the keep on guard duty, so there was that.

At least Toven wasn't there on translation duty, so she was saved from that embarrassment. For some reason, having Lusha as the intermediary was less awkward.

Well, the reasons were obvious—Lusha wasn't a god, and she wasn't a male.

"Mo-red wasn't as bad as the others," Lusha translated for Borga. "But he also acted as if the females were his property to do with as he pleased. So he brought small gifts, so what? I didn't need his trinkets. What I needed was the option to refuse."

The words were like a slap in Vanessa's face. Mo-red had assured her that he had never pressured any of the females to accept his invitation. On the other hand, none had ever refused him, and that was suspicious. He had told her that he'd felt guilty, thinking that they couldn't refuse because Igor had compelled them to accept any invitation, but then his cellmate had admitted to having been rejected plenty of times and Mo-red no longer felt that.

But what if he'd been intimidating?

What if the females had believed that he would retaliate if they rejected him?

They had been well aware that even one complaint to Igor could make their lives in the compound intolerable. Igor could have compelled them to do a thousand humiliating things so no one would dare to refuse a male again.

She had to get to the bottom of the issue with all of its ugly nuances.

Looking Borga in the eyes, she said, "Mo-red told me that he rarely invited pureblooded females to his bed and that when he did, they came willingly."

Borga snorted. "Of course, he would think that. What choice did we have? To become celibate? It wasn't as if there were any other males to choose from, and we had a duty to perform. Kra-ell females are charged with preserving our species by producing the next generation. If we had abstained and produced no more children, our kind would have died out when we did."

Vanessa was relieved.

Borga hadn't claimed to have felt intimidated or pressured by Mo-red or the others to have sex with them. She had done it out of obligation to her people or perhaps to the Mother of All Life. Her resentment was over not having a choice of partners, which was understandable. It also explained why she had done nothing to speak on Mo-red's behalf, although given that they had a son together, she should have done that for her son's sake.

Especially since Pavel had asked her to do it.

"Pavel likes his father. He wouldn't if Mo-red was a monster." Vanessa waited for Lusha to translate.

"I am a good mother, and I knew it would hurt Pavel to think that he was sired by a monster. Not that I think that of Mo-red. He's not a monster like Igor, but he is tainted by association. I raised a good male by making Pavel believe that he had good genes in him from both his parents. I never turned Pavel against Mo-red like the other females secretly did with their children."

"Do you hate Mo-red?" Vanessa asked point blank.

Borga shook her head. "I don't hate him. He gave me Pavel, and he protected the boy the best he could. For that, I am grateful."

Good. That was a good start.

"Would you testify on his behalf in front of the judge and jury?"

The female grimaced. "I don't want to talk about those things in front of everyone. It was bad enough that I had to live through that ordeal. I don't need to relive it by talking about it." She waved a hand in the air. "All you shrinks do is talk and talk and talk. Do you ever do anything good for anyone?"

Vanessa didn't deign to answer that. Instead, she focused on the one thing that seemed to matter to Borga. "We need as many people as possible to testify on behalf of Mo-red and the others and highlight the good things they have done. If you say nothing and the jury sentences Mo-red to death, Pavel will never forgive you."

Borga shrugged. "Pavel is an adult. He makes his own decisions, and I make mine, and we don't get in each other's business."

"It doesn't work like that, and you know it." Vanessa called her out on her bullshit. "I also have a grown son, and his opinion matters a great deal to me."

Borga's lips twisted in a sardonic smile. "Does he approve of you sleeping with a murderer?"

"No, he does not."

"And yet you spend every night with Mo-red at his dungeon cell. So, your son's opinion doesn't matter all that much to you, now, does it?"

"It does. I hope he will change his mind once he gets to know Mo-red." Vanessa smiled. "Mo-red is a wonderful male. I'm sure Jackson will be as taken with him as I was from our very first meeting."

Borga tilted her head, her nearly black hair cascading down one side. "Mo-red knows how to be charming when he wants to, but he can be cold and cruel too. You just haven't seen that side of him yet."

66

MARCEL

Sofia smoothed a hand over her wavy hair. "Can you please hand me the mirror? It's in my bag under the clothes."

"Of course, my love." He reached into the overnight duffle bag she'd packed and searched for the item she'd requested.

Finding the large mirror at the very bottom, he pulled it out and frowned. "Is this your magic mirror?"

It was the one Sofia had jokingly claimed showed a person's true nature in the reflection. She must have repeated at least a hundred times that it wasn't a real talent and that she'd made it up in order to get accepted into the paranormal retreat, but he had suspected that, on some level, she believed in it and was embarrassed to admit it.

Was that why she had brought it with her to the clinic? To see if the transition affected her personality as well as her body?

"So, despite telling me over and over again that it's only a party trick and that there's nothing to it, you actually believe that you can see your true self in the reflection?"

"It was my grandmother's, and it's precious to me." She

smoothed a loving hand over its tarnished back. "Besides, I do believe in it just a little. You know, it's similar to how people wear their lucky socks to a game or avoid the thirteenth floor and all that nonsense. Thinking that we have some control over the outcomes of things that are important to us gives us comfort, and it doesn't matter that it's totally made up."

Sofia lifted the mirror to her face and raked her fingers through the hair she'd worked so hard on styling just right. It was beautiful when she wore it in the big bun on the top of her head, but it was breathtaking when she let it fall in loose curls down her front and back.

"You are beautiful," he murmured.

She moved the handheld mirror aside and smiled. "Thank you. I feel beautiful, on the outside as well as on the inside."

He sat next to her on the bed. "Did you really need the mirror to tell you that?"

She put it face down on her blanket-covered thighs. "I needed reassurance, especially in preparation for the test."

There was no need for the test, and Marcel didn't want Sofia to go through it. She was long-lived, not immortal, and the cut would take her much longer to heal than it would a newly-transitioned Dormant. Why suffer through the discomfort?

"Are you sure you want to go through it? There is no doubt that you transitioned. You grew an inch and a half in the span of four days, and you are growing venom glands and fangs. That's all the confirmation you could ask for."

"I know." She lifted her hand and cupped his cheek. "But those things don't lend themselves to a transition ceremony, and I want my family and friends to be here with me when Bridget welcomes me to immortality. Well, in my case, just to a very long life. I heard that she does it for everyone who transitions in her clinic, and I want that too. It will be a memory that will stay with us for a long time and that we can tell our children about." When she noticed his pained expression, she smiled. "Don't look so sad. A thousand years is a very long time, and by then, humans will develop genetic knowledge to rival the gods' and will be able to extend life indefinitely." She leaned toward him and kissed the tip of his nose. "I don't intend to leave your side even in a thousand years."

Regardless of how many times Sofia had repeated her hope for the future of genetic research solving the problem of her shorter lifespan, Marcel couldn't dispel the dread of one day losing her. That day was far off, but life had a way of sneaking up on you, and that dreaded day might come much sooner than a millennium implied.

Shaking his head, he resolved to shove those depressing thoughts away and not dampen Sofia's exuberant mood. "Shall I call everyone in?"

"Yes." She handed him the mirror. "Can you put it back in the bag first? I don't want Helmi to turn this into a viewing party."

"Right." He put it under the clothing items it had been hidden by before and pushed the duffel bag under the bed. "That should do it."

Sofia took a deep breath. "I'm ready. You can open the door now."

67

SOFIA

Sofia's patient room was bursting at the seams, with her family and friends crowding around the bed. Some even had to stay on the other side of the doorway.

Perhaps she should have gone home first and invited everyone to a transition ceremony there. After all, she didn't need the doctor to make the cut. She could have done it herself or asked Helmi to do it.

Marcel would have surely refused because he couldn't bring himself to hurt her even if she asked him to. Heck, he'd tried to dissuade her from having it done by the doctor. But all the other transitioning Dormants had gone through the test in the clinic and had Bridget welcome them to immortality.

Doing it any other way might jinx it.

"I'm so happy for you." Helmi wiped tears from her eyes. "You are going to live forever."

"Not forever. I'm not immortal, only long-lived."

"Whatever." Helmi waved a dismissive hand. "Can you even imagine what living a thousand years is like? Think about the people who lived a thousand years ago. They wouldn't recognize today's world." She snorted. "Did they even know that

Earth was round back then? They probably still thought that they were living on a plate supported by four giant elephants."

"Don't underestimate your ancestors," Toven said. "The Sumerians knew that Earth was round and that it orbited the sun because they learned it from the gods."

Helmi gaped at him. "Really? So, what happened to that knowledge? I thought that Galileo was the first one to realize that the sun was in the center of this planetary system and not Earth."

The god sighed. "A lot of what the gods imparted to the humans was lost, some of it deliberately and some just because there was no one to teach it again after all the records had been destroyed by one war or another. It has taken humanity five thousand years to climb out of the darkness and reach the societal and humanitarian level of the ancient Sumerians."

"Make room, people!" Bridget's voice rose above the chatter. "I can't come in and perform the test with you blocking my way."

Somehow, the crowd parted to let her through, people pressing against each other to make room.

Sofia's throat was suddenly dry, even though she wasn't afraid in the slightest. She was transitioning, there was no doubt about that, and the pain of the incision was nothing to get overly excited about. She'd suffered through much worse without making a fuss.

Bridget put her metal tray on the side table, lifted a square of gauze, and wiped Sofia's palm with it. Turning around, she scanned the room until she found Tomos, who was the tallest person there. "Do you have a phone, Tomos?"

"I do." He lifted it over everyone's heads so she could see it.

"Do you know how to film with it?" Bridget asked.

"Of course."

"Then please start recording."

"Yes, ma'am."

"Here we go." The doctor smiled and moved so fast that the cut was made before Sofia could even suck in a breath.

The pain was minimal, and as her blood welled over the cut, she was glad that there were no purebloods in the room. The hybrids were much better at controlling themselves, even if they liked sucking on blood and were thirsty.

"It's not closing," Toven said.

Bridget turned to look at him. "I didn't expect it to. It will take at least five minutes until it starts to mend, and the line will stay on Sofia's hand for a couple of days before it fully disappears."

Toven nodded. "That's significantly slower healing than the immortals enjoy."

Did he have to state the obvious?

Everyone knew that the Kra-ell didn't heal as fast as the immortals, but it was still a hundred times better than what human bodies could do, and Sofia was grateful beyond words to the Mother of All Life and to the Fates that Marcel believed in for the miracle they had bestowed on her.

Still, as the seconds ticked off and her blood started to coagulate and crust the same way it would have done if she were still human, she started to worry.

What if her transition was only half successful? What if she got the extra height, the fangs, and the venom but not the longer lifespan?

Marcel would be devastated.

"Don't look so crestfallen," Bridget said. "Kaia turned immortal, but her healing time was terrible. It wasn't any faster than yours. For some, it takes longer than others to transition, and you've only just started the journey. Your healing speed will improve with time."

As Sofia nodded, her mother pushed through the crowd to

get nearer. "I heal just as slow." She gave her a tight smile. "You are one-quarter Kra-ell hybrid. You shouldn't expect more."

Joanna was doing her best to be supportive and messing it up, but it was the intent that mattered, and Sofia was glad that her mother tried to show her she cared.

Marcel just kept looking at her hand with an intense glare as if he was mentally willing the injury to mend faster.

When the wound finally closed, and Bridget wiped away the excess blood, there was a collective sigh of relief in the room, and the loudest one came from Marcel.

Putting away the bloodied gauze, Bridget lifted Sofia's hand high in the air. "Welcome to your immortality, Sofia. The transition might only give you a thousand or so years, but I'm positive that science will get you all the way to forever."

"Amen to that," Marcel said.

As the affirmation was repeated by others, Sofia took Marcel's hand and added her own, "Amen."

68

ANNANI

"These pants are surprisingly comfortable." Annani smoothed a hand over her thigh, reassuring herself that she was actually wearing pants.

The legging-type garment was like a second skin, soft and stretchy like pantyhose but opaque and thicker. Syssi had said that everyone was wearing them these days and that no one thought they were immodest.

Given that every curve of her body was clearly outlined, Annani begged to differ.

She missed the feel of her silk gown flowing around her legs as she walked—the sensuous material making her feel like the goddess she was.

Regal. Ethereal. Eternal.

It was not vanity, or at least she did not think it was. It was the way she liked to feel about herself and the way she wanted others to regard her. She had worked hard for her status, and she deserved it.

That being said, there was a time and place for playtime, and the stretchy jeans and loose T-shirt made her feel like a schoolgirl, which at her age was not a bad thing.

Except, Syssi was correct, and her silly outfit was not going to fool anyone into believing that she was just another visiting immortal. Hopefully, Eva's theatrical makeup would do the trick.

Kian looked her over for the third time since he had first seen her this afternoon. "Forgive me for saying this, Mother, but that outfit looks ridiculous on you."

"It is just a game." She patted his cheek. "Is Eva coming over anytime soon?"

"Yes," Syssi said. "She called me a few minutes ago to say that she's on her way."

"Is she bringing Ethan with her?" Annani asked.

"He is in preschool." Syssi rose to her feet. "Would you like a cappuccino while we wait?"

"I would love one," Alena said.

"I would like some as well." Annani sat on the couch, her hand reaching for the folds of the gown she was not wearing. "This is so strange." She folded her legs and looked down at her soft silk slippers. "I do not have the appropriate footwear for this outfit."

Syssi winced. "I'm sorry, but my shoes are not going to fit you."

"No, of course not. My feet are so small that I could probably borrow Phoenix or Idina's shoes." Annani turned to Kian. "Which reminds me, is there any news on Gilbert?"

He had been admitted to the clinic early that morning, and given his age, Annani expected that he would need Toven's special assistance. But if Toven, for some reason, could not offer his blessing, Annani would gladly offer hers.

Fortunately, Sofia had not needed her help and had transitioned successfully on her own.

"It has only been a few hours," Kian said. "There won't be any news yet."

"Did he lose consciousness?" Alena asked.

"I didn't get an update." Kian lifted his phone off the coffee table. "By the way, the ship should be ready by next Friday. If we somehow manage to wrap things up with Igor within the next few days and nothing else comes up, we might be able to actually sail in a couple of weeks."

Alena looked doubtful. "The trial is not going to be over by then, and you can't leave the Kra-ell alone in the village and the keep."

"I know. Some of the Guardians will have to stay behind. If we wait for everything to be perfectly quiet and orderly, we will never get to do it. Compromises will have to be made. The Guardians can hold a lottery to determine who stays behind."

"What about Kalugal's men?" Syssi asked from her cappuccino station. "Some of them might volunteer to stay and guard the prisoners in the keep and the Kra-ell in the village. After all, we need the Guardians on the ship to protect us."

Alena let out a breath. "The cruise was a nice idea, but it is just not going to happen, and I'm fine with that. We can have a beautiful wedding in the village."

As Syssi served the cappuccinos and Okidu served his freshly baked orange cake, Annani leaned back and tried to think the problem through. The best option was to load everyone on the ship, including the Kra-ell and Kalugal's men, and leave all three locations vacant. The village could be locked down tight, and the same was true for her sanctuary. The castle in Scotland was a little trickier to defend in the absence of its occupants, but the bridge leading to it was rigged with explosives and could be triggered remotely if anyone dared to trespass.

It was not an optimal solution, but it was the best she could come up with. The only other option was to cancel the cruise, and that was like accepting defeat, which went against her nature.

"Is there enough room on the ship for everyone?" Annani asked. "And by everyone, I mean every member of the clan, Kalugal and his people, and the Kra-ell, including the prisoners."

Kian shook his head. "There are not enough cabins. We could possibly fit everyone if we put the Kra-ell in the crew quarters, but that would mean no service staff, and given their history with the gods, it would also be a really bad move."

Annani could not argue with that. "What if we have a lottery for the accommodations?"

Alena chuckled. "Not one of your better ideas, Mother. What if the couples about to be married end up getting the service quarters? Talk about a bummer."

69

KIAN

"How many cabins does the ship have?" Syssi asked.

Kian put down his cappuccino. "Three hundred and sixty guest double cabins and one hundred and eighty crew. The guest cabins have two small bedrooms each and a living room between them. On each of the main six decks, there are two larger cabins, which I planned to allocate to the couples getting married on the cruise."

"That sounds like plenty," Syssi said. "Seven hundred and twenty bedrooms just in the guest cabins should be enough if some don't mind sharing a bedroom. Are the beds singles that are combined into a king or just regular kings?"

"Regular king beds."

"What about the living room?" Alena asked. "Is there a sofa someone can sleep on?"

He nodded. "It's a pullout bed type of couch."

"Then we should be good." Syssi pulled out her phone, launched the calculator app and started typing. "We have five hundred and ninety-two clan members in total, including their human relatives, Kalugal and his people are an additional fifty, and the Kra-ell, together with the few humans who chose the village, are two hundred and two. That's a total of eight hundred and forty-two. Since the Kra-ell are used to more modest accommodations, I'm sure they wouldn't mind having one cabin for three people, especially since some of them are kids, and the prisoners can be all in one cabin like they were before. That means that they need a total of sixty-five cabins. That leaves two hundred ninety-five for the remaining six hundred and forty-two. Since we have eight children that can stay with their parents, that also reduces the number of cabins we need. Gilbert and Karen, and their four younger children can all fit in one cabin. So, if we only count the adults, that's six hundred and thirty-three who need to fit in two hundred ninety-five cabins." She grimaced. "That still leaves us a little short. Forty-three adults will have to sleep on the couch in the living room or stay in the service quarters."

"What about Valstar?" Annani asked. "I assume that Igor will be in stasis by then, but we can't put Valstar in stasis."

"We can put him with the other prisoners," Kian said. "Given Edna and Vanessa's assessment, he's no more or less guilty than the others. Jade disagrees, and I suspect many of the Kra-ell feel the same way as she does, but as far as we are concerned, we will treat him the same way as the others."

Why the hell were they discussing the damn cruise when they were getting ready for the riskiest endeavor he'd ever agreed to?

Annani was about to get into Igor's head, and instead of going over their plan, they were discussing the ill-conceived wedding cruise.

What had possessed him to purchase the ship in the first place?

Had it been the Fates' work?

Perhaps the cruise fit in with their matchmaking plans.

"It's such a complicated issue." Syssi let out a breath. "On the one hand, these males were forced to do those terrible things by Igor, but on the other hand, they enjoyed the fruits of those deeds. Then again, what options did they have? If they refused to have sex with the females, Igor would have compelled them to do so because he wanted to create the next generation of Kra-ell." She shivered. "I'm glad that I don't have to sit on that jury. I wouldn't know how to vote."

Kian wrapped his arm around her shoulders. "We have to leave it up to the Kra-ell, so there is no point in tormenting ourselves over these questions."

"Yeah," Alena said. "That's what everyone is talking about, and I'm tired of hearing it. Let's get back to the issue of the cruise. Do we really want to load everyone on the ship?"

"Why not?" their mother asked. "I think that it is safer than leaving people behind, and it is also a great bonding opportunity." She smiled. "Who knows? Maybe some of Sari's people will find love with Kalugal's men or with the Kra-ell. In the short time that our people have had together, we already have two love matches between immortals and Kra-ell. I think it is a wonderful sign for the future."

Kian wasn't sure about that, but the Fates weren't asking for his opinion. They were busy matchmaking whether he approved or not.

What he had to decide was whether the idea of taking everyone in their combined communities on the cruise made sense. Perhaps he should talk it over with Turner because right now, his gut was telling him to agree with his mother, and that put his sanity in question.

"What about the humans in Safe Haven?" Alena asked. "We

can take them along as well. They can be our service crew, and then we won't have to worry about thralling them. They are already under Toven's compulsion."

Kian groaned. "Let's invite Eleanor's paranormals as well, shall we? And while we are at it, we can invite Mia's friends too."

His mother pursed her lips. "That is not as absurd as you make it sound."

"Trust me. It is." He leaned back and crossed his arms over his chest. "What's keeping Eva?"

As if on cue the doorbell rang, and Okidu rushed out of the kitchen to open the door.

"Good afternoon." Eva walked in with Okidu carrying her trunk of disguises behind her. "Apologies for keeping you waiting, Clan Mother." She dipped her head. "The trunk slipped from my grip, burst open, and my makeup got thrown all over the place."

"Why didn't you call us?" Syssi rose to her feet. "I would have sent Okidu to help you carry the trunk. In fact, I should have thought of it when you called earlier. This thing is huge."

"It is." Eva chuckled. "But I'm strong, and I didn't expect the accident to happen." She smiled and motioned Okidu to put the trunk down. "I'll work fast to make up for lost time."

Annani chuckled. "I am about to meet the famous Jade, but instead of an impressive goddess, she is going to meet an ugly version of me, wearing jeans and a T-shirt."

Smiling, Eva crouched next to her trunk and popped the lid open. "I'm a talented makeup artist, but I doubt anything I can do will make you ugly. The best I can achieve is to make you a little less perfect."

"You don't have to meet Jade today," Kian said. "I can tell her that I don't need her to accompany us to the keep and that you will see her later this evening. After all, we don't need her there while you do your thing."

Annani shook her head. "I am a vain female, but not that vain. It is important for Jade to be there in case we need to ask her something about Igor that will help me sift through his memories."

70

JADE

Jade looked herself over in the mirror and frowned. She didn't have anything appropriate to wear for her first meeting with the Clan Mother, and she couldn't borrow anything because then she would have to explain why she needed the outfit, and the goddess's presence in the village was supposed to remain a secret.

How was it even possible to hide her?

Everyone other than the Kra-ell knew the goddess and what she looked like, while the older Kra-ell would not have any trouble recognizing her for what she was. Her perfect features and her glow would give her away.

She could suppress the glow, but not her beauty.

Come to think of it, Toven didn't glow even when there was no reason for him to hide it, but that was probably an anomaly or a mutation.

Huh. There was a thought. What if the Eternal King had wanted to get rid of his heir not because he was afraid of his son dethroning him but because Ahn had been defective in some way?

The gods were intolerant of imperfections, even worse

than the Kra-ell, but since they had the knowledge and the technology to correct any defect, there was no reason to eliminate a less-than-perfect heir. If the Eternal King hadn't been pleased with his son, he could have changed whatever needed fixing.

Unless the abnormality had been discovered when the son was already an adult and Ahn had refused to get altered.

Then another thought followed on the heels of this one, making Jade's frown deepen.

What if the twins had inborn defects like everyone had suspected, and the Kra-ell Queen had made a bargain with the Eternal King to fix their abnormalities in exchange for something?

Oh, Mother of All Life.

What if the price was eliminating the entire rebel colony on Earth?

The twins' compulsion ability could probably rival or surpass Igor's. Perhaps their job was to assist Igor? Or maybe it was the other way around, and Igor's job had been to assist the royals, which was why he'd been told about them?

That made so much more sense.

Igor had never said who the other assassins were, and no one had thought to ask him whether the twins were assassins as well. There had been no need to send an army of assassins to kill just Ahn and his two siblings. The plan must have been to kill all the gods on Earth, take over the gold-mining operation and subjugate the human population like the gods had done before them.

That was why Igor had been told about the twins.

The puzzle pieces fit so well together that Jade couldn't believe none of them had put the picture together until now.

The problem was that it made sense from a Kra-ell point of view, but not from the gods'.

Why destroy all the gods on Earth and hand the planet over to the Kra-ell?

"The treaty." In the mirror, Jade saw her fangs elongating and her eyes blazing red. "Damn liars, one and all."

That was the real bargain the Eternal King and the Kra-ell queen had struck.

In exchange for peace, the Eternal King offered Earth to the queen. It was a fertile planet with a large humanoid population for the Kra-ell to use as they pleased—the same way the gods had used them before.

Getting rid of the rebels, where there were no witnesses to report what had really happened to them, had just been a bonus.

Earth was supposed to belong to the Kra-ell, not the gods, and if not for the settler ship's malfunction, human history would have been very different.

Jade wished she could share her newfound realizations with someone, but she couldn't even tell Kagra. Kian could never find out about it, or he would do everything he could to find the twins and kill them.

Damn, she was about to meet Kian's mother, and the goddess was supposed to test her thralling ability on her before heading out to the keep to do the same to Igor. The Clan Mother would pluck those very recent memories out of her head.

Could she bring in a substitute at the last moment?

She could, but then Kian would become suspicious.

Unless she faked a PTSD episode.

Kian would buy it because he believed the therapist's assessment, and if Kian bought it, everyone else would too.

The problem was that Jade couldn't bring anyone with her because no one from her people was supposed to know who the Clan Mother was.

The other problem was Igor and what was stored in his head. If he was aware of the plot, the goddess could get it from his memories even if Jade managed somehow to avoid being her test subject.

The solution to both problems was simple, provided that Jade managed to pull it off.

She would perform her best acting ever, claiming an episode of PTSD and refusing to be the goddess's test subject. Since no other Kra-ell was supposed to know that the goddess was in the village, Annani wouldn't have anyone to test her thralling on, and Kian wouldn't allow her near Igor without first conducting a test.

Then another thought struck Jade. Did she really owe loyalty to a queen who had lied to her people? Or did she owe it to the clan of immortals who had saved them from slavery, accepted them as equals, and given them a home?

So yeah, she had given her vow to the queen, but the queen was dead, and she hadn't deserved Jade's vow in the first place.

The queen hadn't acted with honor. The Kra-ell did not conspire to assassinate unsuspecting people. They fought their enemies face to face.

Except, vows did not expire with the recipient's death, and breaking a vow meant that Jade's soul would end up in the Valley of the Shamed, and after a lifetime of following the Mother's way, she deserved a place in the fields of the brave.

It didn't seem right, though.

The Mother's way was all about honor, and the honorable thing to do was to protect Kian and his clan. Hiding what she believed was the Eternal King's master plan was dishonorable and would surely earn her a ticket to the Valley of the Shamed.

71

ANNANI

"Do you want to take a look?" Eva handed Annani the mirror. "The transformation could have worked better with a wig, but you have too much hair to hide. Your head would have looked misshapen."

Annani looked at her reflection and marveled at Eva's fantastic work. There were dark circles under her eyes, freckles covering her entire face, and wrinkles fanned out in the corners of her eyes, making her look like someone who smiled a lot.

She liked it.

"What do you think about the freckles?" Eva asked. "Most human natural redheads have them, so I thought you would look more authentic with them."

"I love it." Annani lifted her finger to touch the painted-on wrinkles but stopped when Eva hissed. "My apologies. They just look so real that I was compelled to touch them."

"Please, don't. If you smear them, the shadowing effect will be destroyed, and with it, the illusion of wrinkles.

"Yes. I understand." She handed Eva the mirror. "You are very talented."

"Thank you." Eva dipped her head. "To take it off, just use whatever you normally use to remove makeup."

Alena chuckled. "My mother does not use makeup. I'm surprised that she hasn't complained yet about how terrible these products feel on her face."

Annani cut her a look. "I do not need paint to enhance my beauty. This was done for a good cause." She smiled. "Well, it was mostly done for my own amusement."

Her clan members had been notified via group text that her presence in the village needed to be a secret, and since she would no doubt travel from Kian's home to the pavilion in that covered golf cart, the chances of any of the Kra-ell seeing her passing by were slim.

"As long as it meets with your approval, I'm happy." Eva returned the tools of her craft to her trunk and closed the lid.

"Would you like another cappuccino?" Syssi asked her.

"No, thank you." Eva hefted the wooden trunk and put it under her arm. "I should head back."

"Thank you," Annani said. "And give hugs and kisses to Ethan."

Eva's face brightened. "I will." She dipped her head. "Good day, Clan Mother, and good luck with Igor."

"Thank you."

After Eva left, Alena rose to her feet and came closer to admire the female's work. "Finally, you look my age and not like my much younger sister."

"Were the other goddesses as youthful looking as you?" Syssi asked.

"No. I look particularly young because I am so petite." A sore point. "Most goddesses looked like what you would expect a twenty-two- or twenty-three-year-old human woman to look like."

When the doorbell rang, Okidu rushed once more to open it.

"Mistress Jade. Please, come in."

Annani lifted her cappuccino cup to her lips and didn't move from her spot. If the disguise was successful, Jade might assume that Alena was the goddess.

As the female walked into the room, she looked just as Annani had imagined she would. Very tall, very slim, and beautiful. Her confidence was as palpable as Kian's, and she seemed just as troubled.

The mantle of leadership was not light, and this majestic female carried it with pride.

Jade cast a quick look at Alena, dipped her head in greeting, and then turned to Annani and bowed. "Good afternoon, Clan Mother."

"How did you know it was I?" Annani asked.

Jade smiled. "You radiate power, Clan Mother. You could not hide it no matter what disguise you wear."

Kian chuckled. "That's what I said."

"Oh, well." Annani let out a breath. "I guess I can let my glow flare as well."

"Please, take a seat." Syssi motioned for Jade to sit in the armchair. "Would you like a cappuccino?"

"Thank you, but I can't tolerate any kind of milk."

"An espresso, then?"

"I would love some, thank you." Jade turned to Kian. "Where is Julian?"

"At the keep."

She arched a brow. "Shouldn't he be here to administer the drugs?"

Kian looked at her with puzzlement in his eyes. "Why would we drug you again?"

"I was under the impression that the Clan Mother would experiment by thralling me before thralling Igor."

That was almost insulting.

Annani looked at the female down her nose. "I do not need your mind to be compromised for me to be able to thrall you. Toven has already proven that your mind is penetrable when weakened by drugs, but I am curious to see if I can penetrate it without them." She smiled. "In fact, I am quite confident that I can."

72

JADE

Jade swallowed.

Without the drugs, her post-traumatic stress disorder excuse wouldn't work.

It was good then that she had decided her loyalty to the clan superseded her loyalty to the lying, dead queen.

Furthermore, if the goddess plucked it out of her head or out of Igor's, it wouldn't be considered vow-breaking. After all, she wasn't volunteering the information.

Jade nodded. "Let's do it. Where and how do you want me, Clan Mother?"

"I need a quiet space." The goddess looked at her son. "Can we use your home office?"

"Of course."

As Kian rose to his feet, Jade did the same, and a moment later, the goddess joined them.

It was shocking how tiny the Clan Mother was. The goddess barely reached Jade's chest, but her diminutive stature was misleading. Jade had a feeling that Annani was more powerful than Toven in order of magnitude. She wasn't sure how she knew that, though.

Perhaps it was instinctive.

Feeling awkward about towering over the goddess, Jade dipped her head and slumped her shoulders.

Annani smiled and then stunned Jade by reaching for her hand.

The surprise move left Jade speechless, and as soon as the goddess's tiny fingers closed around her hand, it was like getting connected to a power outlet.

"There is no need to bow to me," the goddess said. "And you can call me Annani when we do not have an audience. In public, everyone addresses me as Clan Mother."

"As you wish." Jade struggled to leave her hand in Annani's light grip.

The goddess noticed and let go. "Forgive me. I was told that the Kra-ell do not enjoy public displays of affection, but I assumed it referred only to amorous displays. I did not know that you do not like to be touched."

"It's just not something I'm used to," Jade murmured. "Casual touching is not part of our culture. In that regard, we are a lot like the Japanese. We keep physical distance."

Annani laughed. "Then you and your people will have to adjust. My family and I are all big huggers. We believe in the power of hugs. They are therapeutic, uplifting, and generally good for the soul."

Chuckling, Kian opened the door to his home office and motioned for his mother to step in. "Consider it a compliment, Jade. My mother only holds the hands of people she likes."

"I'm a complete stranger to her." She followed the goddess into the sprawling office. "The Clan Mother has no reason to like or dislike me."

"I am a very good judge of character." The goddess sat on the couch and patted the spot next to her. "Come, sit with me, Jade."

When Kian walked around his desk and sat down, his mother lifted a brow. "Are you going to stay?"

"Yes. I will be very quiet. Pretend that I'm not here."

Evidently, Kian didn't trust her enough to leave her with his mother, which was funny and sweet at the same time. Unless he had a gun on his desk, he couldn't protect Annani from her.

Besides, Jade had a strong feeling that Annani did not need her son's protection.

The goddess could take control of Jade's mind and freeze her in place without saying a word.

How did she know that, though?

More instinct?

The goddess radiated power, and once she allowed herself to glow, the luminescence was so intense that it was like having the sun shine directly on her. But that didn't translate into Annani having incredible mind control powers.

Except it did.

"Please try to ignore my overprotective son." The goddess took both of Jade's hands in hers. "Close your eyes and try to relax."

Jade did as the goddess commanded in regard to the eye closing, but there was no way she was going to relax unless someone fed her a bunch of Motrins.

That was actually not a bad idea.

She should have thought of that sooner and asked Kian or Syssi if they had any in their house.

As the goddess chuckled softly, the sound of her laughter raised goosebumps on Jade's arms. Had Annani chuckled because Jade had thought about the effect Motrin had on Kra-ell?

The gentle squeeze was the goddess's way of confirming that without saying a thing, and it also confirmed that Annani was inside her head.

As it felt like hours were passing as they sat together with the Clan Mother holding her hands, Jade let her mind roam aimlessly, shifting from one subject to another, the fragments of thoughts swirling in her head. She wasn't doing it on purpose to confuse the goddess.

On the contrary, it was the best way she could relax enough to let Annani inside her head without her natural barriers slamming into place.

Jade only hoped Annani could make sense of what she was seeing because she wanted Kian to know what she'd figured out without having to say it.

73

KIAN

Kian watched his mother holding Jade's hands with an amused expression on her face and wondered what she was seeing.

Hopefully, it wasn't a review of Jade and Phinas's intimate moments, but knowing his mother, he wouldn't put it past her.

What he found surprising was the ease with which she was doing it. Edna had worked hard to probe Jade, and after she was done, she had to take the rest of the day off to rest.

Thankfully, that wasn't what he was observing with his mother.

But what if she wasn't seeing anything, and her amused expression was about something unrelated?

Finally, his mother let go of Jade's hands, opened her eyes, and smiled. "You have a very interesting imagination, Jade. You see conspiracies in every corner." She shifted her gaze to Kian. "No wonder the two of you get along so well. You are kindred spirits."

"First of all, it's a relief that you were able to thrall Jade without the help of drugs and with what looked like relative ease."

"Well." Annani straightened and reached for the skirt she wasn't wearing. Frowning, she let out a sigh. "I would not describe the experience as easy. Jade has a very active mind, and chasing her thought process felt like I was on a rollercoaster." She lifted a hand to her temple. "There was so much going on in there that I am still trying to make sense of it."

"Sorry," Jade murmured. "I was trying to relax, and the only way I could do that was to let my mind wander aimlessly."

"What did you see?" Kian asked.

Looking uncomfortable, Jade shifted away from Annani but didn't say a thing.

His mother nodded. "Normally, I would have let Jade tell you, but she prefers for me to do it. It has to do with what she suspects about the royal twins."

Kian arched a brow. "Didn't we cover that subject already?"

"Jade has a new theory. She suspects that the twins were born with defects, as everyone suspected, and she thinks that the Kra-ell queen made a bargain with the Eternal King to fix their abnormalities."

Kian leveled his gaze at Jade. "What could she offer him?"

Jade shook her head. "I can't say it without breaking my vow."

Now he understood his mother's comment about Jade preferring her to tell him what she'd seen.

"Jade thinks that the twins were supposed to kill Ahn, his siblings, and all the other rebels. Igor and the other assassins were sent to assist them. Ahn was a formidable opponent who was a powerful compeller, so to overcome him they needed someone stronger or several compellers that could combine their powers. The queen was a powerful compeller, and her children were rumored to have similar abilities. That they were sent with an army of assassins at their disposal indicates that they didn't plan to stop with just the Eternal King's children.

Their plan was to wrest control out of the hands of the earthly gods, probably by killing them all, become the new rulers of this planet, take over the gold-mining operation, and subjugate the human population like the gods had done before them."

That didn't make any sense.

"Why would the Eternal King hand over Earth to the Kra-ell?"

"Jade asked herself the same question just before coming over. She thinks it was part of the treaty and that the two rulers kept the details secret from both their peoples. Perhaps the Kra-ell were closer to winning that war than anyone had suspected, and the Eternal King had to offer the queen something very valuable in exchange for the peace treaty."

Kian frowned. "That's an angle I didn't consider. Earth was a valuable resource, with an existing population that was easy to control. The king ceded control of Earth to the Kra-ell, but he still needed its gold for all the things we know gold is necessary for. The mining operation on Earth was done by humans, who were not nearly as strong or fast as the Kra-ell. The treaty could have included a provision for the continuation of the mining and for the Kra-ell to sell the gold to the gods." He let out a breath. "The king must have been desperate to make a deal like that. Perhaps the Kra-ell queen had uncovered some dirt on him, and he was willing to do anything to guarantee her silence."

Jade nodded. "The Eternal King was very concerned about bad publicity. If he could, he would have arranged an unfortunate accident for her, but the queen was smart. After the peace treaty was signed, she had a bunch of journalists follow her everywhere."

"Smart." Raking his fingers through his hair, Kian groaned. "I'm afraid that even Igor will not have the answers we seek. We won't know the truth until we find the twins."

"Perhaps not even then," Annani said. "They might not have been privy to the whole story either."

74

VANESSA

Lusha put the two coffees they had gotten from the vending machines on the table and sat down. "Do you want to cancel the last two interviews of the day? You seem distracted."

The interview with Borga had deeply bothered Vanessa. What the female had said about Mo-red kept playing on repeat in her head.

Mo-red knows how to be charming when he wants to, but he can be cold and cruel too. You just haven't seen that side of him yet.

Was that true? Or was Borga just being jealous and spiteful?

Vanessa couldn't imagine Mo-red ever being cruel without Igor's compulsion making him do that, and she couldn't wait to get back to the keep and confront him about it.

Would he even know what Borga had referred to?

Vanessa took the paper cup and removed the lid. "I can't. We don't have the luxury of taking our time."

Lusha nodded. "Borga was in a bad mood. I don't think she meant to sound so critical of Mo-red. He's not a bad guy."

The girl had known him all of her life, and she seemed sincere, but Vanessa doubted Borga had lied.

Her impression of the Kra-ell was that they didn't lie if they could help it. They were straightforward to the point of being rude, and they didn't care about hurting people's feelings.

"What is your impression of him?" she asked. "And I want the truth, not the sugarcoated version of it."

Averting her eyes, Lusha lifted the cup to her lips and took a sip. "I don't know him well. The purebloods didn't interact with humans except to have sex with some of the females. I wasn't one of them." She smiled. "They like tall and lean, not short and plump."

"You are very pretty, Lusha. Don't sell yourself short."

"I know that I'm not ugly." Lusha pushed her glasses up her nose. "It's just a fact that I'm not attractive to the purebloods, and I'm glad of it. I wasn't interested in them."

Vanessa let out a breath. "I know you are trying to dodge the subject, but I need to know. What is it about Mo-red that you are trying to hide?"

"Nothing." The girl put the cup down. "He wasn't the smiley type, but then none of them were except for Kagra. She always looked like she was plotting a prank, and she liked to get a rise out of people, especially the pureblooded males. I sometimes wondered if she had a death wish."

"That's fascinating, but I'm not interested in hearing about Kagra. I want to know what you are hiding from me about Mo-red."

Lusha rolled her eyes. "I told you. I don't know him that well. I had a few Kra-ell lovers or rather hookups, and they were all hybrids. They liked to say bad things about the pure-blooded males to make themselves look better. They also complained about not having access to the pureblooded females because Igor's lackeys were monopolizing their fertile cycles. Mo-red's name came up a few times."

That didn't sound too bad, but Vanessa had a feeling that there was more to it than Lusha was admitting.

"Perhaps I should talk with Kagra."

Given Lusha's description of the female, Kagra might be less reserved and tell her what she needed to know.

Lusha's eyes widened. "I thought that you'd already made her assessment."

"I did Jade's, but not Kagra's. Both of them stated that they didn't care what happened to the prisoners because they didn't kill their males. They only want Valstar dead."

"So, what do you want to talk to her about?"

"Perhaps she has a better insight and can tell me what Borga meant when she said that Mo-red had a cold and cruel side to him."

Lusha looked relieved that the pressure was no longer on her. "I know where she is right now. She's in the training complex underground."

"I know." Vanessa pulled out her phone. "But since all the Kra-ell have phones now, I can just text her and ask her to meet me here when she's free."

Lusha snorted out a laugh. "You'd better tell her that you want to talk about Mo-red, or she will never find the time to talk to you."

"Why is that?"

"The assessment. She doesn't want you to assess her."

"That's silly. I have to assess everyone, and eventually, I'll get to her as well."

Lusha shrugged. "People will do anything to avoid pain. Logic has very little to do with it."

Vanessa was taken aback. "What pain? I'm very courteous, and my questions are not intrusive. What is there to fear?"

"As I said, it's not logical. The Kra-ell, especially the pure-bloods, hate the idea of anyone getting inside their heads. They are grateful to Tom for freeing them from Igor's compulsion, but at the same time, they resent him for asserting his will over them."

"I can understand that, but they have to realize that it's necessary." Leaning back, Vanessa crossed her arms over her chest. "Tom is not compelling them to kill anyone. His compulsion is all about keeping everyone safe."

Lusha lifted her cup and took a sip. "As a therapist, you should know that logic has very little to do with how people feel."

"That's true." Vanessa uncrossed her arms. "Thanks for reminding me."

Lusha winced. "I'm sorry. Did I offend you?"

"Not at all. I'm too close to the subject to think objectively. That's why Borga's words had such an impact on me. If I weren't involved with Mo-red, it would have occurred to me that she might harbor resentments that are not specific to him or the things he did or didn't do. She also might resent me for capturing his heart while she didn't." Vanessa sighed. "Until I came along, Borga might have never thought of having anything more with Mo-red. They have a son together, which is as connected as the purebloods get to be. Suddenly a descendant of the hated gods arrived and stole him from her. That must have rankled."

"Yeah, that was what I thought too. She's just jealous." Lusha smiled. "In their culture, jealousy is a sin. They feel it just like we do, but they will never admit it. It was much easier for Borga to throw accusations at Mo-red than admit to something that would have reflected badly on her."

"You're a smart young lady, Lusha."

"Thank you." The girl grinned.

Vanessa felt the tension drain away.

She hadn't been wrong about Mo-red. He wasn't a monster

in a charming disguise. He was a good male, and he had captured her heart just as much as she had captured his.

"What are you smiling about?" Lusha asked.

"I can't wait to see Mo-red tonight and tell him how I feel about him."

The girl smiled. "Oh yeah? And what is that?"

"I love him."

75

KIAN

On the way to the keep, Kian mulled over Jade's conspiracy theory while his mother shared the details with the brothers.

The more they talked about it, the less logical it seemed to him that the Eternal King would conspire to kill his own people so the Kra-ell could rule Earth.

What could the queen possibly hold over him to make him do that?

Everyone knew that he had countless concubines with whom he had numerous children, and some of those children were probably powerful compellers like their father. If he wanted to eliminate his one legitimate son, he could have sent any one of Ahn's half-siblings to assassinate him.

Human history was full of rulers who had ordered their heirs' deaths, either because of treason, of which Ahn had been guilty, or because they had done bad things that had shamed their fathers.

But if Jade's theory was true, then the Eternal King had wanted the entire colony dead. Since all the exiled gods had been rebels, that wasn't such a far-fetched notion either. The one piece of the puzzle that didn't fit was gifting Earth to the Kra-ell.

Was it possible that the Eternal King had become unhinged?

Power was corrupting, and since the god had been holding on to it for hundreds of thousands of years, he was probably corrupt to the core.

Then again, the king might have engineered a plot within a plot to ensure that his benevolent reputation remained untarnished, and he hadn't been in a rush to execute those plots. Given his lifespan, he must have developed endless patience.

For appearances' sake he'd sent the rebels to Earth, not as punishment, but to mine for gold, which was, for some reason, needed on the home planet. That was also a part that Kian found doubtful. A civilization advanced enough to engage in interplanetary travel and genetic manipulation that gave them immortality must have discovered how to make gold or other synthetics with similar properties instead of mining for it on a faraway planet. Still, it was possible that, at the time, they hadn't figured that out yet, or maybe it was cheaper to mine for gold than to produce its manufactured equivalent.

The operation had continued for a couple of hundred years, which wasn't long from their perspective, and then communications with the colony had been accidentally lost. In the meantime, the settler ship had left, and it was supposed to arrive shortly after communications had been severed.

The Kra-ell were supposed to eliminate the rebels, and if any visitors from Anumati made it to Earth, they would have assumed that the ungrateful Kra-ell had murdered all the gods.

The king's hands would have remained clean.

The problem with this scenario was that it made the Kra-ell look bad, and the plan demanded cooperation between the Eternal King and the Kra-ell queen, who wouldn't have agreed to it. But it was also possible that the queen didn't care about the Kra-ell reputation, and getting Earth into the bargain had been worth the loss of face to her.

Her children would get to rule the entire planet, and she could excuse her actions in some way. Maybe she could claim that the gods tried to subjugate her people, and they had no choice but to rebel, but that would have been a weak argument since those gods had rebelled against their own king to help the Kra-ell's resistance and had fought alongside them for their equal rights.

Also, to betray them like that went against everything the Kra-ell believed in.

No wonder Jade was pissed at her former queen and was even willing to stretch the boundaries on the vow she'd given her to their utmost limits.

"What are you thinking about so hard?" his mother asked.

He hadn't noticed the lull in the conversation between her and the brothers. "The Kra-ell queen and her part in all of this." He turned to Jade. "The puzzle pieces don't fit."

She arched a brow. "Really? Because I thought that they did."

"How likely is it that your queen betrayed the very people who had helped her cause?"

"Not very likely," Jade admitted. "But what do I know? Perhaps she was just as manipulative and dishonest as the Eternal King, and I was too naive to see it." She smiled, but it didn't reach her eyes. "Evidently, monarchs are not bound by the same rules as the common people. The elite get to do whatever they please while asking us to make sacrifices for the greater good."

"I do not do that," his mother said. "Well, to be fair, I allow myself some liberties. Not many, though."

"Yeah." Kian glared at her. "You demand that two bodyguards accompany me whenever I leave the village while you and Alena used to travel with just your Odus as guards. How is that fair?"

His mother sighed. "I do not like to boast, my son, but I can defend myself better than you can."

Kian opened his mouth to argue and then closed it.

She was right, of course. While he could seize the minds of humans, his mother could seize the minds of immortals as well. The only two people on the planet who posed any possible threat to her were Toven and Igor, and probably not even them.

76

ANNANI

Annani waited outside Igor's cell while Kian verified that the prisoner was drugged, properly bound, and blindfolded.

In preparation for her visit, all the other cell doors were locked, and the two young Kra-ell who had been assisting the Guardians had been told to take the day off.

Next to her, Jade was one big knot of tension.

"Be at ease, child," she whispered. "Neither you nor I have anything to fear from Igor."

"Forgive me," Jade whispered. "But Kian was very clear in his instructions about you talking in the vicinity of the prisoner."

They were outside the cell, the prisoner was drugged, and Annani had spoken in a whisper that did not carry the unique vibrations of her voice. But everyone was so stressed that she did not want to add to their anxiety.

Nodding, she put her hand on Jade's arm.

The female gave her a tight smile. "If he dares anything, I'll smother him myself."

Annani had no doubt that Jade would do that. But there

would be no need. The prisoner was bound in heavy chains that even someone as strong as him could not break free from.

When Kian walked out, she smiled and arched a brow instead of asking whether Igor was ready for her.

"You can go in," Kian said quietly. "Do you have to touch him to do what you need?"

It was not necessary, but since the prisoner was blindfolded, and she could not look into his eyes or speak to him, it would be helpful. If his mind provided more resistance than Jade's, she would have to touch him.

When Annani nodded, Kian let out a breath. "I don't like it, but do what you have to, and I'll do what I must."

Kian did not carry a weapon, but Anandur had his gun out and Brundar his dagger. Their instructions were to kill Igor if she was in any danger.

Annani nodded again and took a step forward, but Kian stopped her.

"Let me check your earpieces one more time. I want to make sure that they fit properly." He leaned down and lightly tapped each earpiece. "Looks good."

She wanted to answer but then remembered that she was not supposed to talk near the prisoner.

It was really annoying.

Annani did not like being silent.

Uttering a huff, she lifted her chin and walked into the cell, with Kian and Jade following her inside.

As she sat down in the chair that had been provided for her comfort, Kian and Jade took positions next to her.

"Who is this?" Igor slurred.

"It's me," Kian said.

"Liar. Who did you bring with you?"

"The doctor."

"It's not the doctor." Igor took in a deep breath. "It's a female."

"You're smelling me," Jade said.

"I know what you smell like. It's a different female."

"She is our other doctor," Kian said.

Julian was outside, waiting to be called in if needed.

"Why do you answer for her?" Igor asked. "Is she mute?"

"She doesn't want to talk to murderers. She's here to observe you."

A smile lifted Igor's lips. "Do you like what you see?"

"She doesn't," Kian said. "She's repulsed by you."

A frown creased the male's forehead, and his lips tightened into a thin line.

He was tall, at least six and a half feet, slim, and his hair was jet black and long. He was handsome and not as alien-looking as Annani had expected. In fact, there was something familiar about his features that she could not put her finger on.

Strange.

Was it his prominent cheekbones? The shape of his nose? Or maybe the cut of his stubborn jaw?

Yes, that was it. The jaw. It reminded her of Kian. Stubborn, unyielding.

Since she could not look into Igor's eyes, Annani closed hers and put her hand on his exposed forearm.

Igor twitched as if he had been touched by a live wire. "What the hell? Who are you?"

"It doesn't matter," Kian said. "What do you know about the royal twins?"

"Not much."

Focusing, Annani reached into the male's head. His mental shields were formidable, but she knew how to navigate around them instead of throwing her mental powers against them.

When she saw a vague outline of two veiled figures, she

pushed closer, but the image did not sharpen. Igor had not seen the twins in person. The image he was thinking about was a picture of them that had been taken from above, probably from a drone or a satellite.

Turning to Kian, she projected what she had seen into his mind.

He nodded, indicating that he got it. "Were the twins supposed to conquer Earth from the gods and take over?"

"What nonsense is that?" Igor said, but his mind was showing her a picture of the same two veiled figures sitting side by side on two thrones.

It was not a conclusive answer, and his memories were nonverbal, but since the twins had not been supposed to inherit their mother's throne, which thrones were they sitting on?

Annani turned to Kian and inserted the image into his mind.

He nodded. "Were you supposed to help them wrest control from the gods?"

Again, Igor did not respond verbally, but his mind showed her in pictures what he was thinking. He was standing behind the two thrones, looking regal in a fancy outfit.

So that was what he had expected in exchange for his assistance—to be the twins' advisor or some other position of importance.

With a sigh, she sent the image to Kian.

Leaning against the wall behind him, Kian crossed his arms over his chest. "Since the gods were gone when you got here, what was your next move?"

"You know what my next move was."

Indeed, Igor's mind showed her what he had been attempting to do throughout the years since his arrival, which had been building a colony of Kra-ell, who bowed to him as their supreme ruler. He had also been amassing a fortune to finance future expansion.

The Earth Igor had found was very different than the one he had expected.

The gods were gone, the human population was too large and too advanced for a small group of Kra-ell to control, and the grand plans of conquering the entire planet were changed to creating a thriving colony and growing it the way he wanted to.

As another image flitted through his head, Annani stifled a gasp.

It was thousands of years into the future, the Kra-ell were as numerous as humans, and Igor was the ruler of the entire planet. The shocking revelation was not his long-term conquer-the-Earth plans. It was that he was still around.

Igor was immortal.

Had he been given immortality by the gods? Or had he been born with the gene? And if it was the latter, how did he look so entirely Kra-ell?

"Are you immortal?" Kian asked.

Igor's lips lifted in a smile. "You know the answer to that."

77

KIAN

"Bastard," Jade said. "How is that possible?"

That was what Kian wanted to know.

"Were you born immortal or given immortality by the gods?"

"I told you that I was created. Who knows what they put inside of me?"

Despite the mega dose Julian had given him, Igor seemed only minimally affected by the drug. As with the tranquilizers, his body was learning to neutralize the agents. Soon, they wouldn't work on him at all, but Kian had a feeling that his mother didn't need Igor to be drugged to enter his mind. She was doing it as effortlessly as she had done with Jade.

He should have known not to underestimate her.

The granddaughter of the Eternal King was most likely as powerful as her grandfather but without his megalomaniac tendencies. Perhaps the queen, whose name he still didn't know, had contributed the genes of love and generosity to her son and granddaughter. Ahn had not been nearly as benevolent as Annani, but he was a much better male than his father.

"How do you know that you are immortal?" Jade asked.

"The other doctor, the weird one, found out how fast I heal. I wasn't sure before, but he confirmed it for me."

Kian had assumed that Igor was a half-breed, but when the male told them about his enhancements, he'd assumed that the gods had given him fast healing, but he hadn't extrapolated that they had given him immortality as well.

He should have.

The fast healing was probably the key indicator of immortality.

Igor had most likely lied about not knowing for sure that he was immortal before Merlin had tested his healing speed, but just in case Annani could not access Igor's mind without him being drugged, it was time to ask the other questions Kian needed answers for, while the guy was still under their influence.

"Why did you bite me?"

Igor chuckled. "That again? I told you why. My fangs were the only weapons available to me. What else could I have used to threaten your people into releasing me?"

"That wasn't the only reason. Why did you suck my blood?"

Kian waited for his mother to project into his mind what she saw in Igor's, but this time, the answer didn't arrive as fast.

As long minutes passed in silence, Annani's forehead creased in a frown as if she was having a hard time inside Igor's mind or was worried about what she was seeing.

Kian was about to ask her what was going on when she rose to her feet, motioned for him to follow, and walked out of the cell.

She kept walking until they were almost near the elevators.

"What happened?" Kian asked when his mother stopped and turned to him.

"He drank your blood to analyze and compare it."

Kian's blood chilled in his veins. "Can he communicate the information to someone on Anumati?"

His mother shook her head. "No."

That was a huge relief. "Are you sure?"

She shrugged. "I did not see anything about him transmitting information, and if he could, it would have been prominently displayed in his mind."

"I don't understand. If he has no way of communicating with anyone back on Anumati, what did he need to analyze my blood for?"

"It was what he was programmed to do. His job was to find and eliminate all of the Eternal King's descendants." She turned to Jade. "As well as the royal twins, just as you suspected."

Jade sucked in a breath. "I knew it."

Kian lifted his hand. "I don't think this is a conversation that should take place in the hallway. Let's move it to my office."

When they got there, he pulled out a chair for his mother, and as he sat next to her, Jade pulled out a chair on her other side.

Anandur walked up to the refrigerator. "Who wants what?"

"I'll take a beer," Jade said.

"Just water for me," Annani murmured.

Kian had never seen his mother so disturbed, not even when Amanda had been kidnapped by Dalhu.

When Anandur handed her the bottle of water, she unscrewed the cap and took a few long sips.

"Before I continue, I want you to know that what I saw in Igor's mind was a movie without sound. He stores his memories as visual content, so all I saw were images. What it means is that I could have misinterpreted some of the content."

"I know," Kian said. "That's the limitation of thralling."

"Not always," his mother said. "It depends on whether the person is more visual or auditory. Igor is entirely visual, which is surprising given his personality. He is very methodical, and that usually goes together well with auditory recall."

Kian had a feeling that his mother was stalling, which was also atypical of her.

"What did you see that has shaken you so?"

She turned to look at him. "Igor's job was to eliminate the king's children and secure the planet for the twins, but not because the Eternal King wanted them to rule it. That was only the ploy to get Igor close enough to them to kill them, provided that they posed a risk to the king's rule. If they were a threat, it also meant that they were too powerful for even an assassin like Igor to kill. He had to gain their trust to be able to catch them unguarded."

Jade gasped. "I knew it. Igor lied when he said that his only task had been to eliminate the Eternal King's children."

"He did not lie. He just did not tell the entire truth." Annani closed her eyes briefly. "The twins' power did not come just from their mother." She opened her eyes and leveled her gaze at Kian. "They also got it from their father, which made them potentially stronger than the Eternal King."

"Who was their father?" Kian asked, even though he already suspected the answer.

"The king had reason to believe that it was Ahn."

Coming up next in the
CHILDREN OF THE GODS SERIES
Book 73
DARK HEALING BLIND CURVE

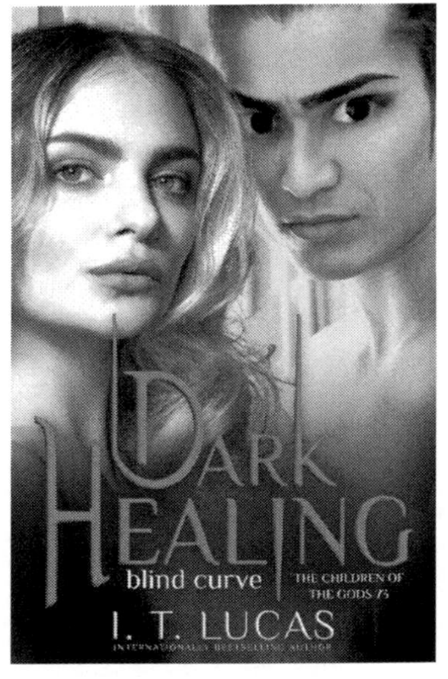

To read the first 3 chapters JOIN the VIP club at ITLUCAS.COM *—To find out what's included in your free membership, flip to the last page.*

Kian is still reeling from the shocking revelations about the twins when a new threat manifests, eclipsing everything he had to deal with until now. In light of the new developments, Igor, the other Kra-ell prisoners, and the pending trial are no longer at the forefront of his mind, but the opposite is true for Vanessa. As her relationship with Mo-red solidifies, she is determined to save the male she loves, even if it means breaking him free and living on the run.

Coming up next in the
PERFECT MATCH SERIES
The Dragon King

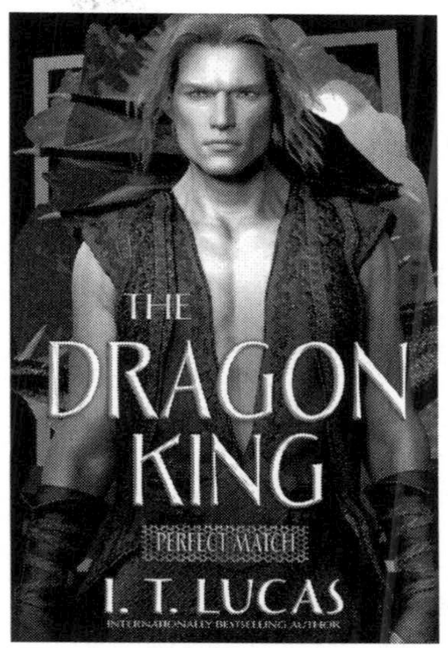

To read the first 3 chapters JOIN the VIP club at ITLUCAS.COM *—To find out what's included in your free membership, flip to the last page.*

To save his beloved kingdom from a devastating war, the Crown Prince of Trieste makes a deal with a witch that costs him half of his humanity and dooms him to an eternity of loneliness.

Now king, he's a fearsome cobalt-winged dragon by day and a short-tempered monarch by night. Not many are brave enough to serve in the palace of the brooding and volatile ruler, but Charlotte ignores the rumors and accepts a scribe position in court.

As the young scribe reawakens Bruce's frozen heart, all that stands in the way of their happiness is the witch's bargain. Outsmarting the evil hag will take cunning and courage, and Charlotte is just the right woman for the job.

Dear reader,

Thank you for reading the Children of the Gods.

As an independent author, I rely on your support to spread the word. So if you enjoyed the story, please share your experience with others, and if it isn't too much trouble, I would greatly appreciate a brief review on Amazon.

Love & happy reading,

FOR EXCLUSIVE PEEKS AT UPCOMING RELEASES & A FREE COMPANION BOOK

JOIN MY *VIP CLUB* AND GAIN ACCESS TO THE VIP PORTAL AT ITLUCAS.COM
http://eepurl.com/blMTpD

INCLUDED IN YOUR FREE MEMBERSHIP:

YOUR VIP PORTAL

- READ PREVIEW CHAPTERS OF UPCOMING RELEASES.
- LISTEN TO GODDESS'S CHOICE NARRATION BY CHARLES LAWRENCE
- EXCLUSIVE CONTENT OFFERED ONLY TO MY VIPS.

FREE I.T. LUCAS COMPANION INCLUDES:

- GODDESS'S CHOICE PART 1
- PERFECT MATCH: VAMPIRE'S CONSORT (A STANDALONE NOVELLA)
- INTERVIEW Q & A
- CHARACTER CHARTS

IF YOU'RE ALREADY A SUBSCRIBER, YOU'LL RECEIVE A DOWNLOAD LINK FOR MY NEXT BOOK'S PREVIEW CHAPTERS IN THE NEW RELEASE ANNOUNCEMENT EMAIL. IF YOU ARE NOT GETTING MY EMAILS, YOUR PROVIDER IS SENDING THEM TO YOUR JUNK FOLDER, AND YOU ARE MISSING OUT ON **IMPORTANT UPDATES, SIDE CHARACTERS' PORTRAITS, ADDITIONAL CONTENT, AND OTHER GOODIES.** TO FIX THAT, ADD isabell@itlucas.com TO YOUR EMAIL CONTACTS OR YOUR EMAIL VIP LIST.

Also by I. T. Lucas

THE CHILDREN OF THE GODS ORIGINS

1: Goddess's Choice

2: Goddess's Hope

THE CHILDREN OF THE GODS

Dark Stranger

1: Dark Stranger The Dream

2: Dark Stranger Revealed

3: Dark Stranger Immortal

Dark Enemy

4: Dark Enemy Taken

5: Dark Enemy Captive

6: Dark Enemy Redeemed

Kri & Michael's Story

6.5: My Dark Amazon

Dark Warrior

7: Dark Warrior Mine

8: Dark Warrior's Promise

9: Dark Warrior's Destiny

10: Dark Warrior's Legacy

Dark Guardian

11: Dark Guardian Found

12: Dark Guardian Craved

13: Dark Guardian's Mate

Dark Angel

14: Dark Angel's Obsession

15: Dark Angel's Seduction

16: Dark Angel's Surrender

Dark Operative

17: Dark Operative: A Shadow of Death

18: Dark Operative: A Glimmer of Hope

ALSO BY I. T. LUCAS

68: Dark Alliance Kindred Souls
69: Dark Alliance Turbulent Waters
70: Dark Alliance Perfect Storm
Dark Healing
71: Dark Healing Blind Justice
72: Dark Healing Blind Trust
73: Dark healing Blind Curve

PERFECT MATCH

Vampire's Consort
King's Chosen
Captain's Conquest
The Thief Who Loved Me
My Merman Prince
The Dragon King

The Children of the Gods Series Sets

Books 1-3: Dark Stranger trilogy—Includes a bonus short story: **The Fates take a Vacation**

Books 4-6: Dark Enemy Trilogy —Includes a bonus short story—**The Fates' Post-Wedding Celebration**

Books 7-10: Dark Warrior Tetralogy
Books 11-13: Dark Guardian Trilogy
Books 14-16: Dark Angel Trilogy
Books 17-19: Dark Operative Trilogy
Books 20-22: Dark Survivor Trilogy
Books 23-25: Dark Widow Trilogy
Books 26-28: Dark Dream Trilogy

Books 29-31: Dark Prince Trilogy
Books 32-34: Dark Queen Trilogy
Books 35-37: Dark Spy Trilogy
Books 38-40: Dark Overlord Trilogy
Books 41-43: Dark Choices Trilogy
Books 44-46: Dark Secrets Trilogy
Books 47-49: Dark Haven Trilogy
Books 50-52: Dark Power Trilogy
Books 53-55: Dark Memories Trilogy
Books 56-58: Dark Hunter Trilogy
Books 59-61: Dark God Trilogy
Books 62-64: Dark Whispers Trilogy
Books 65-67: Dark Gambit Trilogy

MEGA SETS

INCLUDE CHARACTER LISTS

The Children of the Gods: Books 1-6
The Children of the Gods: Books 6.5-10

TRY THE CHILDREN OF THE GODS SERIES ON AUDIBLE

2 FREE audiobooks with your new Audible subscription!

Published by Evening Star Press

EveningStarPress.com

ISBN: 978-1-957139-73-9

Made in the USA
Las Vegas, NV
18 May 2023